The Gorge

ALSO BY MATT BROLLY

Detective Louise Blackwell series:

The Crossing
The Descent

Lynch and Rose series:

The Controller

DCI Lambert series:

Dead Eyed
Dead Lucky
Dead Embers
Dead Time
Dead Water

Standalone novels:

Zero

The Gorge

MATT BROLLY

This is a work of fiction. Names, characters, organizations, places, events, and incidents are either products of the author's imagination or are used fictitiously. Any resemblance to actual persons, living or dead, or actual events is purely coincidental.

Text copyright © 2021 by Matt Brolly
All rights reserved.

No part of this book may be reproduced, or stored in a retrieval system, or transmitted in any form or by any means, electronic, mechanical, photocopying, recording, or otherwise, without express written permission of the publisher.

Published by Thomas & Mercer, APub UK

www.apub.com

Amazon, the Amazon logo, and Thomas & Mercer are trademarks of Amazon.com, Inc., or its affiliates.

ISBN-13: 9781542005357
ISBN-10: 1542005353

Cover design by Tom Sanderson

Printed in the United States of America

For Chris Conolly

Prologue

He remembered him.

Like the hundreds of times he'd stood on the cliffside before, the view was different. The gorge that cut through the village of Cheddar was an ever-changing kaleidoscope of shifting colour and shape. It was early evening. A blanket of shadow coated the cliff sides, the ghostly effect intensified by the haze of mist rising into the sky. He could have stood there for hours without getting bored of the sight, were it not for the cold air that stung his aching lungs.

Peering over the cliff edge was like glimpsing the past. The angle made the road invisible, taking him to a time before humanity had made its indelible mark on the area's natural beauty.

Behind him, a small flock of wild sheep grazed, oblivious to his presence. The land hadn't forgotten him. It remembered the boy; the strong brave boy who'd spent his days trailing the Mendips for miles on end across wild hills and through dense woodlands, over cliff edges and through the caves, the secret places he still kept with him.

And although that boy was gone, he still remembered him. He saw him now and again, peering out from the trees, on the lip of the cliffside, on the horizon calling him but fading away as he approached.

Sometimes he called that boy by his own name, sometimes by another.

He dwelled on that for a second, fighting an onslaught of memories: him, standing outside his parents' house, his hair a crude short back and sides; the boy, smaller, his features squashed together on a rounder face; him, older, driving; the boy, smiling, looking at him. Pleading.

The last memory lingered. It began to fill his vision – the cliff edge shimmering out of view, replaced by a rudimentary road, a car, his car . . .

He blinked away the memory, remembering why he was here on the cliff walk. Why he'd been here since first light.

He'd been searching for something.

Something for her. Something for him. Something for them.

But he'd failed again and that disappointment stung more than ever and he was unable to control his anger. His hand shook as he withdrew the hunting knife, a high whistling sound leaving his lips. The flock eyed him as he approached but he was used to dealing with their kind.

Chapter One

Louise Blackwell was pleased to be out of Weston. She'd spent the last few nights in the small bungalow she rented in Worle, on the fringes of the seaside town, but it was beginning to feel like a prison.

Greg Farrell had offered to meet her in town. She'd taken this as a chance to escape her enforced confinement. Farrell had hesitated when she'd suggested meeting at the Avon and Somerset headquarters in Portishead where he was currently a detective sergeant. Louise understood his reluctance. This time last year he'd been working under Louise in Weston. Now Farrell was a rising star in MIT – the Major Investigation Team – and was involved in the investigation of the brutal murder of Louise's brother, Paul.

Fog had descended over the M5. Louise joined the lines of vehicles creeping along the motorway. Visibility was reduced to metres. She'd received the all-clear from her psych evaluation and was due to return to work tomorrow. She'd expected the news to alleviate the emptiness she'd been carrying in the pit of her stomach for the last five months, but as the day of her return approached, nothing had changed.

During her psych evaluation, she'd studiously avoided telling the young woman who'd interviewed her about the fires haunting her recurring nightmares. It had been easy to fool the woman, but even now, as Louise drove up the inside lane of the motorway, she could smell the black smoke from that evening on the old pier.

Her omission was the reason she had been allowed to return to work. Though many people in the force had considered her actions foolhardy and dangerous, Louise had managed to save the lives of two women from a deadly fire on the old pier while capturing a deluded serial killer. Had it not been for this success, and the subsequent publicity, the consequences of Paul's murder could have had a much wider impact for her. Professional standards had declared her free of misconduct but she'd known Paul had absconded with her niece before he'd died, and she hadn't officially reported it. The heroics on the pier had kept her in a job, despite the best efforts of many in the constabulary to use it as a means to get rid of her.

The fog cleared as she headed on to the Portway and stopped at The Mariner, a small bar where Farrell had agreed to meet. Three men stood outside. Each smoking, they lowered their eyes as Louise walked past them through the entrance. The smell of disinfectant hit Louise as she entered the main bar area. Music blared through the bar's speakers, too loud for the early hour and empty space. She ordered a sparkling water from the barman and asked him to turn the music down.

Some hero, she thought, as she took a seat at the far corner of the seating area. Her brother had been stabbed seventeen times, possibly in front of Louise's six-year-old niece, Emily, and she'd done nothing to save him. Her parents argued to the contrary, but the disappointment in their faces was evident every time she saw them, and the burden of her brother's death was one of the many reasons she was still undecided about whether she would make the trip back to the office tomorrow morning.

Thankfully, Farrell was alone. She noticed the pronounced swagger as he entered the bar as if he owned the place, waving as he spotted her. On the way over, he lost a little of his composure as if contemplating the best way to greet her. 'Ma'am,' he said.

Louise remained sitting. 'Greg,' she said. 'Do you want something to drink?'

Farrell shook his head as if he didn't have the time for such pleasantries. 'I'm fine, ma'am.'

'That's twice you've called me ma'am now, Greg. Something bothering you?'

'Sorry, Louise,' he said, elongating her name as if testing the sound of the word.

Although Farrell was a strong officer, she'd had her doubts about him being attached to her brother's case. The SIO was a detective from Devon and Cornwall, where Paul's body had been discovered, but as Paul had lived in Bristol, Farrell's role was pivotal. Louise had raised her concerns with her boss, DCI Robertson, who'd told her in no uncertain terms that the decision was not hers to make.

'So what do you have for me?' she asked.

'Not that much, I'm afraid. We've exhausted every one of the Mannings family. They even consented to DNA testing. Nothing.'

Over the last five months, Louise had discovered things about her brother she wished had remained secret. She'd known about the drinking and subsequent gambling but it appeared his life had descended into something murkier. He'd owed money to the Mannings family – a two-bit crime organisation in the city – but it had become apparent they were not the only people Paul had borrowed from. He'd left a trail of debt all over Bristol and Louise understood now more than ever why he'd left for Cornwall. 'So what's next?'

Farrell sighed and she glimpsed a hint of his occasional arrogance. She wanted to grab his tailored suit and shake the information from him. 'You're not shelving the case, Greg.'

'No one's saying that, Louise, but . . .'

'Don't try and palm me off, Greg,' she interrupted, a little louder than intended.

'We're not giving up but you know as well as I do how this works. It's been five months. We can link your brother to a number of people but unless they speak, we're at a standstill.'

Louise had reached the same stage in investigations many times before but it was difficult to separate experience from personal interest. Paul's attack was not typical. The majority of homicide investigations were domestic in nature. Predominantly, the victim would know the killer, who was more often than not a friend or family member.

Although this couldn't be ruled out for Paul, his ties with various factions increased the scope of potential suspects. They had a potential motive – Paul's debts and links to numerous drug dealers – but little else. No murder weapon had been discovered and no one of interest had been found in the area when Paul died.

Louise took a sip of the tasteless fizzy water, a hint of bleach from the floors tickling her throat. 'Be straight with me, Greg.'

Farrell lowered his eyes. 'We've been given three weeks before the case gets shelved.'

Louise sucked in a breath. Shelved was an unofficial term but effectively it meant the case would be closed. It would still be looked at on an occasional basis but no one would be investigating full time. In normal circumstances she would have understood the decision; it was the natural order of things. Investigations could only last so long, and new cases arrived daily. And while she conceded her obvious personal interest, shelving the case now still felt premature. 'How the hell can that happen, Greg? There's still so much we don't know.'

Farrell played with his fingers, failing to meet her eye.

'This is Finch's doing,' said Louise.

DCI Tim Finch was the reason she now worked in Weston instead of MIT. Her last investigation for MIT had been the Max Walton case. Walton was a known serial killer. As they were among the few officers to have received firearms training – a failed initiative in the area – Louise and Finch had been issued handguns due to the potential threat posed by Walton. After locating their suspect in a deserted farmhouse, Finch had instructed Louise to shoot Walton, who she subsequently discovered had been unarmed.

In the aftermath, Finch had lied, both to save his own skin and to secure a promotion. He'd wanted her off the force ever since as she was the only one who knew the truth about what had happened. Louise understood more than anyone that mentioning his name made her sound weak and paranoid but she was sure that he was involved in burying the investigation into her brother's death.

Farrell looked embarrassed. Finch was now Farrell's direct superior but Louise believed the young officer still had a sense of loyalty to her. It was tough on him being in this position but for now she had bigger things to worry about. 'How do you plan spending the next three weeks, Greg?'

'I won't let this go, I promise,' said Farrell.

Although she believed his good intentions, Louise understood that the decision about her returning to work the next day had now been made for her. She wasn't allowed to directly investigate her brother's murder but she could help. She needed to fully assess what was happening. She'd kept an eye on things over the last few months but only by returning to work could she ensure everything was being done to find Paul's killer, especially with the looming deadline. 'I know you won't, Greg,' she said.

'How's Emily?' asked Farrell. For the first time since arriving, he smiled. He'd come to know Emily during the investigation, and Louise had been touched by the way he'd interacted with her niece. He'd been kind and patient. Emily still talked about him.

'She seems to be doing well. I'm seeing her after school today.'

'Say hello for me.' Farrell paused, the smile fading. 'You're back at the station tomorrow?' he asked.

'Nothing gets past you, Greg,' said Louise, offering her own smile as a way to break the tension.

'Tracey mentioned it.'

DI Tracey Pugh was Louise's closest friend from her time at MIT. Along with DS Thomas Ireland from Weston, she'd driven Louise to Cornwall on the night of Paul's murder. 'She's not worried about me, is she?'

'No, of course not. She wanted to be here today but Finch has her working over in Yate.'

Farrell squirmed after mentioning Finch but Louise didn't react. She'd long ago stopped being threatened by the thought of the man. Despite his best intentions, she was still in a job. In Finch's world, he would see that as a defeat. Louise got to her feet. 'Thanks for coming over to see me, Greg. I'm sure we'll see each other once I'm back at work.'

'Good luck with it, boss.'

Louise appreciated the endearment. 'Don't you worry about me, Greg. You realise the second I'm back at work I'll be on at you even more.'

Farrell smirked. She'd once been annoyed by the mannerism but now accepted it as part of his character. 'It had crossed my mind,' he said.

As she drove to her parents' house, Louise understood that there had never really been any question about her returning to work. Her mother called it an iron-clad strength, others called it a wilful stubbornness, but Louise wasn't the type of person to act one way just because it was expected of her. She hadn't done so when Finch had tried to force her out of her job three years ago, and she wasn't about to do so now.

Finch and his golf buddy, Assistant Chief Constable Morely, would love nothing more than for her to call and say she'd decided not to return after all. It would make their lives so much simpler, and would give them the victory they'd sought for the last three years. But her decision was nothing to do with them. If, one day, she did decide to leave, their input would be irrelevant. No, she was staying because it suited her. She'd given her life to the police, had achieved things most officers only dreamed of, and wasn't ready to give it all up. Not that she really had a decision to make. If the investigation into Paul's murder was going to be shelved in three weeks, that meant the investigation was already winding down and she had to make sure it was still at the front of everyone's mind.

The sun had pierced through the fog, the sky a pale spring blue by the time she reached her parents' house. Emily wasn't due to be home for another two hours so Louise was surprised to see her niece as she opened the front door. Emily must have registered her surprise. Her face drained of colour and she ran upstairs without saying hello.

'In here,' called her father from the kitchen.

Her parents were sitting at the kitchen table, their faces as pale as Emily's. Louise noticed the bottle of wine on the side counter and couldn't stop herself from checking if it was open. Her mother's drinking had been getting out of hand ever since Paul's death and it wouldn't be the first time she'd started drinking so early in the day. 'What's happened?' said Louise, pleased to see the screw top still in place.

Her mother had noticed Louise check the bottle and there was a coldness in her eyes when she answered. 'Emily was sent home from school.'

Louise looked around to check Emily wasn't eavesdropping. 'Why?' she asked, controlling the mixture of concern and frustration at her parents' silence that was overtaking her.

'She bit someone,' said her father.

'Is this some sort of a joke?'

'No. She bit one of her classmates on the arm,' said her mother.

Louise pinched her nose and closed her eyes. It sounded so ludicrous that she wanted to laugh; she would have done if it weren't so tragic. Emily had been seeing a child psychologist, Dr Morris, ever since Paul's death. They were still unsure whether or not Emily had witnessed Paul's murder. Dr Morris had told them the sessions were progressing well but this wasn't Emily's first outburst. Two weeks ago she'd thrown a bowl of cereal at Louise's father when he'd told her to eat quicker. It was so out of character; at least out of the character she'd once had.

Louise hated the fact she had to even think in those terms about her niece. The girl was six, yet she'd suffered so much. Her mother had died when she was four, from a virulent form of cancer, and now this. It was a wonder her rages were so limited. If only it was possible, Louise would have gladly absorbed all the pain from the little girl. As it was, she felt more helpless than at any other time in her life. She could accept what was happening to her at work – was able to fight against Finch and his efforts to sabotage her career – but with Emily she was impotent. And this was all before she'd considered the effect it was having on her parents. Her father was trying to remain strong but it was as if her mother had already given up. Something was bound to break, and Emily being sent home could become the thing that broke everything.

'What did the school say?'

'It's a suspension in all but name. They've suggested Emily stay home for the rest of the week pending a meeting with Dr Morris and the boy's parents,' said her father.

'What has Emily said?'

'She won't speak. It's as if she's blaming everyone but herself,' said Louise's mother, who was reaching for the wine bottle.

'You can't be serious,' said Louise, blocking her mother's path to the wine.

Her mother frowned. 'What?'

'*What?* It's the middle of the day.'

'Don't make this about me, Louise.'

Louise glanced at her father who rolled his eyes as if his opinion was of no consequence. 'This probably isn't the best time to discuss this, Mum, but don't you think your drinking is getting out of hand?' Her mother clearly either couldn't see, or was in denial, about what was happening to her. Paul had been a big drinker in his youth, but marrying Dianne, and the birth of Emily, had steadied him for a time. It had been no surprise that he'd returned to his old ways after Dianne's death.

Louise had to wonder if alcoholism was something of a family curse. In the past, she'd caught herself having one too many late night drinks. She'd managed to contain her behaviour before it became a problem, but it was something she had been able to monitor as she understood how easy it could be to let things get out of hand.

'You're right, Louise, it isn't,' said her mother, her eyes clouding.

'Can we just talk about Emily for a second?' said Louise, fearing the conversation was slipping away.

'We're struggling to cope, Louise,' said her father. 'And with you going back to work tomorrow . . .'

Her father wasn't blaming her for the situation but the words still stung. Her suspension had meant she'd spent much of her recent time at the family home. She wasn't sure the present arrangement was sustainable but at the moment she couldn't offer a suitable alternative. They'd discussed the possibility of Emily moving in with her but that didn't seem feasible with her unpredictable work patterns and the extra care Emily needed. 'Dr Morris has been notified?'

'I just spoke to her. We're going with Emily to see her tomorrow morning.'

'I guess you won't be available,' said her mother.

'That's not fair, Sandra,' said her father.

Louise sighed but didn't engage with her mother. 'Let me speak to her,' she said, leaving the room.

Emily was sitting upright on her bed. She had a book held out in front of her but was gazing beyond it.

'Can I come in?' asked Louise.

Emily frowned, her bottom lip protruding. It would have been funny if it wasn't for the hint of tears welling in the girl's eyes. Louise wasn't a parent and didn't know the best way to deal with the situation. Emily had done something wrong but the last thing she wanted to do was punish her. She sat on Emily's bed and placed her arm around her niece, surprised by the rigidity of the girl's body. 'No one is angry with you, darling, you know that, don't you?'

Emily sighed and there was so much angst in the act that Louise had to look away. She was failing her niece and didn't know how to change things. She wasn't used to being so powerless. Guiltily, she cursed her dead brother as Emily spoke. 'Is Billy okay?'

'He'll be fine. I'm more worried about you at the moment.'

'Do Grandma and Grandad hate me?' said Emily, tears falling from her eyes as she turned to Louise.

Louise grabbed the girl and pulled her close. 'You can't possibly think that, Emily,' she said, her words muffled by her niece's hair. She let the girl cry for a few minutes until she was ready to let go. 'Grandma and Grandad love you. You never need to doubt that.'

'They must be angry with me.'

'Nobody is angry with you, Emily. You shouldn't have done what you did,' she added, remembering why they were there, 'but we're not angry. We just want to make you feel better. Did Billy say something to you? About your dad maybe?'

Emily blinked. Louise noticed the hint of defiance and strength in the gesture and it gave her some encouragement. 'He's always talking but I shouldn't have . . .'

Louise never ceased to be amazed by her niece's maturity. As Emily jumped from the bed and headed towards the kitchen to see her grandparents, Louise thought, not for the first time, how tragic it was that Emily's father had not shared his daughter's ability to learn from her mistakes.

Chapter Two

Louise arrived at Weston police station at six the next morning. She'd returned a few times in the last five months for various meetings but it was still surreal being back. Fortunately there was only a couple of uniformed officers in, and she escaped any questions about her well-being as she made her way upstairs to the CID department.

The open plan office was deserted. The faint hum of the air conditioner filled the space. The office had been cleaned during the night, and the air was heavy with polish and pot-pourri. DS Thomas Ireland had taken over Louise's role during her leave of absence but Louise's work area remained untouched. She logged into her computer with no difficulty and for a second it was as if she'd never been away, and she wasn't sure how that made her feel.

Checking the first of hundreds of waiting emails, she was startled by the sound of her name being called from the other side of the floor. She glanced over at the darkened office of her superior, DCI Robertson, and wondered if he'd been sleeping in his room. In the kitchen area, she poured two coffees and barged through Robertson's door.

'Ah, Louise, it was you,' said Robertson, his desk lit by a small lamp.

'You been here all morning, Iain?'

'Early worm and all that shit, Louise. How are you?' The question was borderline rhetorical. Robertson wasn't the most emotional of leaders and was trying to downplay her return. Louise was pleased there was no fanfare or motivational pep talk, just a simple enquiry as to her well-being.

'I'm fine. Ready to get back at it.'

'Good. Well, as you're the first in you can deal with this,' said Robertson, handing her an email printout. 'Just had a local councillor from Cheddar give me an earful for the last five minutes about it.'

Louise looked down at the paper and began to laugh. 'Sheep?'

Robertson narrowed his eyebrows. 'Not any old sheep, Louise.'

'Come on, this is a wind-up. You didn't even try something this stupid on me on my first day.'

'I kid you not, Louise. I considered sending over uniform on this but the councillor sent me some images. Here,' he said, tilting his screen around.

Louise half-expected some cartoon image sheep with a welcome back message underneath. Instead, Robertson scrolled through three images of dead sheep, each with its throat ripped out.

'Members, or former members, of one of the last flocks of wild sheep in the UK,' said Robertson. 'It appears they were slaughtered last night.'

Robertson was hard to read. Despite years of living in the West Country, he had a thick Glaswegian accent and Louise still wasn't sure if this was all part of the wind-up. 'Wild sheep,' she said, frowning. 'Even so, Iain, is this really something for CID?'

'Maybe, maybe not. No one from Cheddar is available so this rests with us for now. Thought it might do you some good to get back out there.'

'Fantastic. First day back and I have to start tracking foxes.'

The sound that came from Robertson's mouth could best be described as a chuckle. It came and went in a flash, his face returning to its usual granite impassiveness. 'Not according to the councillor. She has had one of the local farmers look over the carcasses and he is adamant the wounds inflicted are not from any animal. The throats have been sliced open with some sort of blade.'

'A sheep serial killer?' said Louise. 'Come on, Iain, you can do better than that!'

Robertson held his arms open. 'Welcome back.'

If it was a prank, it was an elaborate one. The office manager and a couple of the other ancillary staff had arrived by the time Louise left Robertson's office. They said hello and welcomed her back before returning to their desks. They acted as if she'd been away on holiday, rather than five months of enforced leave. No doubt they would have been talking about her, about what had happened to Paul, but she couldn't focus on that.

She took the printout and headed downstairs in time to see Thomas arriving.

'Leaving us again so soon?' he said.

'Have to catch a fox,' she said. 'Cheddar Gorge. Something's been killing the sheep.'

Thomas frowned. 'You sure someone isn't pulling your leg?'

'Not totally, but I've seen the pictures and it's not pretty. Fancy a trip to the country?'

'How could I say no to that?'

Cheddar was a small village thirty minutes inland from Weston. As well as being known for the cheese originating in the area, Cheddar was also famous for the gorge that lay on the south of the Mendips.

Sheer vertical cliffs loomed over them as Louise drove along the cliff road.

They drove past a row of quaint, olde worlde shops selling woollens, cheese and other tourist miscellany before the shops thinned out and they were surrounded by the cliff faces.

'I think you've gone too far,' said Thomas.

Louise swung the car round, noticing the sprawled graffiti painted impossibly high on the grey cliff face:

> SAVE OUR VILLAGE
> NO TO THE DEVELOPMENT

The car-park was situated at the other end of the village, where they were greeted by the local councillor, Annette Harling, who'd been giving Robertson a hard time on the phone.

Annette was a short, stocky woman, in her mid-fifties, with an overgrown grey fringe falling over her eyes. The councillor led Louise and Thomas past the pay kiosk and through the tourist entrance of the pathway known as Jacob's Ladder. 'Two hundred and seventy-four steps,' she said, taking a purposeful stride on to the first concrete step. 'There are some people already on the cliff walk.'

It was a steep climb, made harder by the fierce breeze that bit into Louise's skin. By the time they reached the top of the steps, Louise's hands were numb. It wasn't what she'd expected for her first day back and she was disappointed when Annette told them they had further to go. The councillor led them up one climb after another. Behind them, to the west, the village of Cheddar began revealing itself and as they climbed further the perfect circle of the man-made Cheddar reservoir was visible; its surface alien-like in its perfection.

'A bit further along here,' said Annette. The councillor appeared not to be hampered by what must have been her second walk along the path that morning. 'It's absolutely horrific, let me warn you,' she said, as they pushed up the trail, the cold wind behind them, a figure of a man coming into sight.

Two men were bent over the corpse of a sheep. One of the pair stood on seeing Louise and Thomas; he was a good four inches taller than Thomas who was at least six foot tall. He was a similar age to Annette. Behind his thick, grey beard, Louise noticed the redness of his eyes that suggested he'd been crying.

'DI Louise Blackwell,' said Louise, offering her hand. 'This is my colleague DS Ireland.'

The man struggled to maintain eye contact. 'Sandy Osman. I'm with the National Trust. We maintain this area. This is Ted Padfield, one of our helpers.'

Louise bent down next to the other man, who like Osman appeared to be close to tears. He looked at Louise before standing up to cough.

Louise tried to ignore the sheep's eyes as she studied the zigzag gash that ran across the width of its throat, its chocolate-coloured coat matted with blood. Louise was no expert but the wound didn't look like something another animal would make.

'We've counted three so far,' said Osman. 'These two are ewes. The ram is over there.'

'These are wild animals?' asked Louise.

'Yes. Soay sheep, one of the few feral flocks left in the UK,' said Padfield, between coughs.

'We conduct an annual census on the animals,' said Osman. 'Obviously, numbers fluctuate every year but I have never seen anything like this.'

Louise had read about the flock in a newspaper article some time ago. 'You get quite a lot of tourists to see these sheep, don't you?'

'That's correct,' said Annette.

Since arriving, Louise had noticed Annette and Osman exchange the occasional look that suggested they were close. Neither wore a wedding ring and Louise wondered if they were in a relationship.

'Can you show me the others?'

'Not easily,' said Osman. 'They come and go as they please. We leave the water for them,' he said, pointing to metallic troughs attached to a wooden fence. In the distance, a flock of sheep glared over at their dead relatives, keeping their distance as if the deadly wounds were contagious.

'They get to roam completely wild?' asked Louise, moving to the fallen ram, his spiral horns dotted with blood.

'They're completely feral. We estimate there are one hundred to one hundred and fifty at last count. Apart from the census, there is no human interference. The sheep go where they please. They even make their way down into the village on occasions.'

Louise studied the spatter pattern on the ram's horns further. This was a new situation for her, but if a human was responsible for killing the sheep, then it was a serious crime. Furthermore, the link between animal abuse and further serious crimes on humans was well documented. That the vast majority of serial killers began by torturing animals as children wasn't something she was going to dismiss out of hand.

With Thomas, she walked over towards the edge of the cliff face. Somewhere below them was the main road that bisected the gorge, but from their view all they could see was the tops of trees.

'I'll call the SOCOs,' said Thomas, out of the earshot of the three civilians who were still tending to the animals.

'I don't think an animal did this,' she said, as he reached for his phone.

'Could be something like the Beast of Bodmin.'

'Something tells me you're not taking this seriously, Thomas.' Louise recalled the grainy images of a large cat-like creature who'd been blamed for the death of a number of sheep on Bodmin Moor in the seventies and eighties.

'Sorry. It's just a weird one.'

'What did you notice about the wounds?'

'Ragged but precise.'

'I agree. Looks like a hunting knife to me.'

'Why would someone want to do that?'

Louise shook her head. She'd long ago stopped trying to quantify people's motives.

'Mr Osman,' she said, walking over to the National Trust worker who still appeared grief-stricken. 'Have you ever seen anything like this before?'

'No. We see the odd corpse naturally, but there aren't any real predators here.'

'Has anything happened of late that we should be aware of, Annette? In the community? Disgruntled landowners, or shopkeepers, that sort of thing?'

'You think a person did this?' said Annette.

'The scene of crime officers will help us determine what happened, but if there was any potential conflict you could tell us about?'

'Nothing that would warrant this. This will only reflect poorly on the village. I can't imagine what twisted type of human would do such a thing. Certainly not in my community.'

Thomas raised his eyebrows at the last comment but didn't speak.

The SOCOs arrived. They photographed and recorded everything, placing the mutilated sheep into body bags for further examination.

The National Trust man, Osman, looked on the verge of tears as the sheep were carried off. Louise noticed the way he moved towards Annette, as if hoping for comfort. The councillor tensed as he moved towards her, as if she had been made self-conscious by Osman's public show of affection. Osman's reaction to the death of an animal seemed extreme, and as Louise glanced over at Osman's assistant, Padfield, she saw a hint of contempt in his eyes.

Annette left Osman and Padfield with the SOCOs, and accompanied Louise and Thomas to the village. The pathway was pitted with rocks, the varying descents making it hard to keep balance. By the time they reached the foot of the climb, a local news team had arrived and were setting up cameras.

'I guess any chance of keeping this quiet has been blown,' said Annette, as a camera pointed at them.

'No such thing as bad publicity,' said Thomas, as they drove back to Weston.

'You think the National Trust did it?' said Louise.

'Merciless bunch,' said Thomas, with a grin. 'I think the councillor and the National Trust guy have a thing going on,' he said, confirming her earlier suspicions. 'You realise we're going to get stick for this when we return?'

'*Ewe* can't be serious,' said Louise, cringing at her bad pun; pleased she felt comfortable enough to embarrass herself in front of Thomas.

Thomas shook his head. 'Glad to be back then?'

'If this is the shape of things to come, then no. Much animal murder when I was away?'

'A few donkeys on the beach, the odd seagull, nothing out of the ordinary.'

Louise was grateful Thomas hadn't questioned her about Paul. He'd been with her on the pier when she'd rescued the women from the fire. She wanted to ask him if the same type of dreams plagued him, if he could still smell the smoke from that night, but at the moment it felt like too much of a personal question.

Thomas had also been with her in Cornwall where she'd broken down at the sight of her murdered brother. He'd seen her at her weakest and she wondered if that had shifted their relationship in some undefined way.

Thomas's prediction about the mickey-taking was proved correct the second they entered the station, the duty sergeant making a bleating noise before buzzing them through; a sound that was repeated three times before Louise had taken her seat.

Louise welcomed the humour. She hadn't been sure how her return would pan out. She'd worked hard over the last three years to become more accepted by the team, realising eventually that it was a two-way thing. She'd spent her formative months at the station feeling aggrieved by her transfer from MIT in Portishead and had slowly turned her approach around after working on a high profile case.

Although it had definitely been a secondary concern over the last few months, she'd worried that all that hard work would prove to be for nothing following Paul's death. She'd been concerned she would be treated with suspicion within the small station. Paul had been involved with some dubious people, and it was possible she would be implicated by her relationship to him. Yet, so far she'd been treated as if nothing had changed, and she was grateful for the fact.

Despite this, her thoughts returned, as they often did, to the night of Paul's death. She'd rushed to Cornwall after being hospitalised following the fire on the pier. Paul had taken Emily away without telling anyone. She guiltily recalled that most of her concern that evening had been centred on finding her niece. Even when she'd viewed the mutilated corpse of her brother she'd felt disassociated, her immediate concern at the time being Emily. The grief had come over the following weeks, with Emily safe and sound, but she both regretted and had been confused by her initial reaction to seeing Paul's body.

Blinking away the memory, she took out a small file from her bag. She glanced around the office before opening it. She wasn't able to access Paul's case on file but she'd managed to accumulate some details from various sources in the police over the last few months. She lowered her eyes at the photographs of Paul's corpse, clenching her fists at the sight of his dead eyes, the wounds dotting his body. She was still angry with her brother for letting it get as far as it did, and for the horrendous mess he'd left behind. She worried that anger would stay with her forever, especially with what was happening with Emily.

She spent longer than she should have rereading her case notes, still reeling from the thought of the case being shelved. As Farrell had suggested, much of the investigation had centred on the Mannings family, the small-time gang Paul had owed money to. Naturally, they denied having any dealings with her brother. They'd been involved in violence before but nothing like this.

Louise returned to the images of Paul's corpse. It was still hard to believe he was gone. She studied the images of his wounds, trying to remain dispassionate, but in the end it became too much and she closed the file and began the arduous task of checking the emails that had collected into an unmanageable number in her absence.

Chapter Three

'Dempsey is pissed off with us,' said Thomas.

Louise had spent the last few hours flitting between emails and her file on Paul, and had all but forgotten about the attack on the feral sheep. Dempsey was the county pathologist and would be responsible for examining the sheep.

Thomas stood at the end of her desk and Louise wondered how long he'd been there, such was her attention on the screen. 'Says he'll never eat lamb again,' said Thomas.

'Sounds like him.'

'He must like you,' said Thomas, the regret evident in his eyes as he realised what he'd said. It was common knowledge in the office that Louise had slept with Dempsey when she'd first started in Weston. 'He's already examined one of the sheep,' he added, hurriedly. 'He agrees the marks to the throat are consistent with a knife attack.'

Louise took the printed report from Thomas. The ram had been killed with a partially serrated knife. Dempsey estimated the blade used was between three to four inches long. It wasn't the sort of case CID would usually handle but the revelation about the knife brought an intriguing dimension to the case. 'I can't believe I am saying this, but we need to find some sort of motive,' she said.

'Why would you kill three feral sheep?' said Thomas.

'And in such a manner?'

'I don't like to get ahead of myself, but the killer could be practising. Wouldn't be the first psycho to start their handiwork on animals before escalating things.'

'I think that's a bit of a stretch, don't you?' Louise thought again about the proven link between cruelty in animals in childhood to violent behaviour later in life but didn't think this had been committed by a child. It was too public and too extreme. Louise thought about what Thomas had said earlier. *No such thing as bad publicity.* Could anyone truly gain by this incident? Although there had been some press activity, there were much easier ways to garner publicity.

'I've been doing a bit of research on the area. There's been talk for years about regenerating the place. Remember when they were going to build that cable car?' said Thomas, after Louise had shared her thoughts.

'Faintly, yes.' Louise recalled a plan to build a cable car across the gorge a few years back. There had been some complaints about it destroying the natural beauty of the area, and there had been little traction for the idea since.

'Well, there's a new guy in town. Stephen Walsh, some international property developer. No cable car this time, but he has some plans for regenerating the area. Some flash newbuild apartments overlooking the gorge, that sort of thing. Article in *The Mercury* last year suggested he was still looking for extra investors. Though, I'm not sure how killing some sheep would help stimulate investment in the area.'

'Could be the opposite,' said Louise. 'Someone trying to dissuade potential investors. See if you can set up something with this Walsh character. Who wrote *The Mercury* article?'

'Your friend and mine.'

'Tania Elliot?'

Thomas nodded. Tania was a local freelancer who'd courted much success reporting on two of Louise's recent investigations. Louise had clashed with her during her last investigation and had ignored all her requests to speak about Paul's murder.

'Just perfect,' said Louise, with heavy sarcasm. 'Let me know when you get a meeting arranged with Walsh. I suppose I'll have to give Tania a call.'

The Kalimera restaurant in Weston had been Louise's refuge when she'd first moved to the town. Tania had agreed to meet the second Louise had called, and was already waiting at the bar when Louise arrived.

'Inspector Blackwell,' said Tania, standing and holding out her manicured hand.

'Tania,' said Louise, noticing the engagement ring on the journalist's left hand.

They took a window seat, with a view of the seafront. The tide was a distant shadow, the beach an endless stretch of brown. It was early April, a quiet time for the town, and only a handful of people were willing to face the cold breeze that swirled across the promenade.

'Thanks for taking the time to see me,' said Louise.

'Actually I was glad you called,' said Tania, taking off her tailored jacket. 'There are a few things you may be able to help me with.'

Louise's meetings with the journalist rarely ended well. Their relationship had become fractured following articles Tania had published during Louise's first major investigation in Weston. Tania had found some nationwide fame turning the articles into a true crime book, though Louise thought 'true' was stretching the point.

She'd hated reading the account, and Tania's use of artistic licence had soured their relationship further. She was currently writing a second book about Louise's last case that had ended with the fire on Birnbeck Pier. Louise knew she should be less sensitive about the journalist's involvement, but she'd refused every offer from Tania to speak about that night and now feared her bargaining position would be weakened should she need any information from the woman.

'First things first,' said Louise, pleased that a young waitress had chosen that moment to walk over.

'Just a green tea for me,' said Tania.

'Coffee, please,' said Louise.

Tania was smiling intently at her, her left hand extended across the table with an admirable lack of subtlety.

Louise glanced at the diamond on her ring finger but didn't comment. 'You would have heard about the incident in Cheddar this morning?'

'Naturally. In fact I saw a fleeting glimpse of you on the local news at lunchtime. Strange business. Social media is rife. More than one sighting of big cats. Looks like they could have their own Beast of Bodmin. Is that why you wanted to speak to me?'

'In part. I read your article about Stephen Walsh in *The Mercury* last year.'

'You think Walsh killed those sheep?' said Tania, with a false laugh, as the waitress returned with the drinks.

'He's not answering my calls so who knows.'

'It was someone though, wasn't it?' said Tania.

Louise sipped the fresh cup of coffee, burning her tongue on the oily liquid. 'Someone?'

'Rather than some*thing*. Who killed those sheep? I've seen the images.'

Louise squinted her eyes. She wanted to know how Tania had seen any of the images so soon. 'I can't confirm that at the moment.'

Tania glanced at the ceiling, her face an open book as she ran questions through her head. 'So you're wondering if someone would have something to gain by all this media attention on Cheddar. Is that correct?'

'Or something to lose.'

'Feasible I suppose but a strange way to go about it. I guess no one gets hurt and the hope is people begin to remember that Cheddar is a tourist attraction.'

'The sheep would disagree with you.'

'Well, yes,' said Tania, sipping her tea. 'So you think Walsh is involved?'

'No one is saying that at all, Tania. Your article suggested he was looking into developing the area and I wanted to get your take on things.'

Tania appeared amused as she took another drink of the tea. Strange to think she was the same woman Louise had met when she'd first moved to Weston. She'd been a cub reporter then. She'd had an air of confidence at the time, but the arrogance she'd developed following her book's success had yet to fully form. Now she talked to Louise as if she was above her. Louise wondered if this was what she'd always been like, or if her success had turned her this way. 'I met with Stephen recently actually. He was after some PR advice.'

'I presume you didn't tell him to kill wild sheep?'

Tania's lip curled into something resembling a smile. 'I can't say much, but he is still very much involved in his Cheddar project. Have you seen the development plans online?'

Louise nodded. She had glanced over the proposals before heading to the restaurant. To her untrained eyes they appeared to be quite ambitious. Cheddar was a beautiful area but she wasn't sure people would be willing to pay some of the suggested prices for the apartments Walsh wanted to build, however spectacular the views. 'When will the developments be taking place?'

'I believe he is close to securing the necessary investments. From what I can gather his main hurdle has been the council. They seem to be divided by those willing to change and a faction who want to keep the village and surrounding area the way it is.'

'So he hired you to change the opinions of the second group?'

'No comment on that, Inspector, but killing some sheep is not Stephen's thing. Anyway, it would be a very risky strategy. As likely to put investors off the area as to attract them.'

'And the protestors?'

'Protestors?'

'I don't think it could be any clearer. The fifty-foot-high graffiti on the cliff walls.'

'Environmentalists. You always get these sort of things when change is occurring,' said Tania, with an air of dismissiveness Louise didn't find convincing. 'If you want my opinion?'

Louise lifted her head for Tania to continue.

'Either kids playing games or some demented farmhand with a thing against the wild sheep.'

'Thanks for your insights, Tania. I'll keep them in mind,' said Louise, regretting once again her decision to meet the journalist.

'Let me know if you need any more help. I can give Stephen a call and set up a meet if that helps?'

'No, that won't be necessary, Tania,' said Louise. The journalist was being suspiciously helpful. It was only a matter of time before she got to the point so Louise decided to do it for her. 'So what would you like to talk to me about?'

Tania touched the side of her face with her hand, her engagement ring catching a ray of sunshine from the window. 'I'm closing into the end of my book about the Birnbeck Pier case,' she said.

'You work quick, I'll give you that.'

Tania hesitated, Louise catching a glimpse of the less confident person she'd once been. 'There is still an untold story, Louise.'

'You're talking about Paul.'

'I know it's difficult, Louise . . .'

'It's not difficult, Tania,' said Louise, interrupting. 'I'm just not going to talk about it.'

'I realise it's still an on-going case but—'

'That's irrelevant, and you know that. I'm sorry if you need the lowdown on my brother's death for your next bestseller but you're not going to get anything from me.'

Louise looked away, disappointed in herself. Tania had an uncanny ability to get under people's skin, and it helped no one if Louise allowed herself to get worked up. It was hard to admit, but they were similar. In many ways, Tania was a better detective than some of Louise's colleagues and she'd thought before that the journalist could have made a decent career in the force.

'I do understand,' said Tania. 'I just wanted to hear your side of things. At the moment I only have the other side of the story.'

'The other side?'

At least Tania had the good grace to look embarrassed. 'The drinking, the loan sharks, the drugs, the gambling. Need I go on? I know he loved Emily, but putting her in danger like that . . .'

Louise shook her head and raised her hand. 'Don't,' she said.

'I'm sorry,' said Tania. 'I truly am. I'm just doing my job.'

'What do you really want from me, Tania? You want me to say Paul was a great guy, a great brother, a great dad. Of course I think that. He went through some horrendous things and he made huge mistakes as a consequence. Would that even get a footnote in your book?'

'I've heard some rumours they are shutting the investigation down.'

Louise bit her lip. She'd only received the information yesterday from Farrell and she wondered if the journalist had known before her. 'And that would make an unsatisfactory ending to your book?' she said, wondering how much the journalist knew.

'I think there's something they're missing.'

'I presume you've shared your theory with DS Farrell?'

'I'm sure he knows about it.'

'Just tell me, Tania.'

'It's a rumour, but I've heard it more than once. About why Paul really left Bristol.'

'What's that rumour, Tania?'

'Apparently Paul was seeing someone. Someone he shouldn't have been seeing.'

Chapter Four

Richard Hoxton stopped and tried to listen. He thought he'd heard a familiar sound but it was hard to hear anything over the braying of the other men in the cave. It was strange being here so late. Not that the hour should have made any difference. Time was an abstract concept inside the cave – there was no light aside from the garish spotlights along the path, and it was always the same exact temperature – but being here when it was dark outside was a surreal experience; made all the more so by the amount of alcohol he'd consumed that night.

They were less than a hundred metres through the opening of Cox's Cave in Cheddar Gorge, but Hoxton wanted to return outside. His mind wandered, time and memory playing tricks on him. At one moment he was recalling the beginning of the night – meeting the men who were currently following him, for the first time – the next he was staring down at the limestone path, wondering how the hell he'd come to be there.

Light and shadow danced off the cave walls, each man fitted with a helmet torch. 'We should probably head back now,' said Hoxton, hearing the doubt in his words.

His words were met with a chorus of jeers. 'No way,' said Rolf Jennings. 'You promised to show us the imp.'

'The imp, the imp,' shouted the others, in drunken comradeship.

Jennings was one of their main targets. Hoxton's boss, Stephen Walsh, had given him specific instructions to do whatever Jennings wanted. Whether that extended to illegally breaking into the caves and embarking on a foolhardy journey to see the Cox's Cave imp was now a moot point.

Hoxton sighed and moved on, doing everything in his power to focus. He hated the way alcohol did this to him now. Once, he would have been carefree and laughing like the other men. Now, what had started out as a good idea filled him with dread and anxiety. Hoxton's working life was based on his ability to socialise. Even in such enlightened times that often meant being able to drink until the early hours; and although he was physically able, his mind was beginning to crack.

It gave Hoxton little comfort to think that, of the six men currently in the cave, he was probably the most sober. The others were laughing and joking, tripping over each other as they stumbled onwards following Hoxton as if he was the Pied Piper. Hoxton reminded himself that he was walking through a tourist attraction – hundreds of people passed through these caves every day – but even that rational thought wasn't enough to ease his mounting dread.

Walsh should have been there that night, pushing for the investments needed to secure his development, but the commotion with the sheep slaying earlier that day had thrown everything out of sync. Walsh was back in London at that moment, so it had been left up to Hoxton to keep Jennings and the others happy. It had worked so far but leaving the cave now would destroy all his hard work.

'Spooky as shit,' said Jennings, his fetid breath making Hoxton wince. 'How long to go now? I've a lovely bottle of Macallan Rare waiting for us back at the hotel.'

The thought of drinking anything more at this stage made Hoxton's guts twist. But his greater concern was getting everyone out of the cave in one piece. He stopped walking and switched on a high beam hand torch he'd apparently acquired at some point. He couldn't remember exactly where he'd been between 9 and 11 p.m., let alone the last time he'd been in the cave. His last visit had probably been in his early twenties, showing Becky the local tourist sights before she saw sense and left him. He shone the torch over the cave walls, hoping for a clue from the stalactites that fell from the ceiling like daggers.

'Through here, I think,' he said, pointing to the entrance of a small tunnel.

The sound of cans being opened echoed in the space as Hoxton led the mob through the gap, unreality hitting him again as he momentarily forgot what was happening. Two of the men were now ahead of him, and he couldn't recall them passing him. The word 'stop' formed in his mind, but he continued walking, lighting the men's way with his torch until they were there, standing in front of the imp.

'Spooky,' said one of the group, comically tilting his headlamp up and down so he could shine some illumination on to the sculpture hanging from the cave wall.

Seeing the sculpture by simple torchlight gave it an eerie quality. Although it didn't survive close inspection, the alien-figure, with its elongated limbs and stretched eyes, looked life-like, especially in his current inebriated state. The model was fixed to the cave wall, but it was all too easy for Hoxton to imagine the figure coming to life when the lights were switched off; easier still to imagine the deep caves were formed of such creatures.

'Let's get back to that Macallan,' said Jennings. He sounded amused but Hoxton noticed an underlying tone of unease in his suggestion; an unease that was amplified by the sound of rustling and breathing deeper in the cave.

At first Hoxton thought he was hearing things. The group of men fell silent one by one, and he knew they could also hear the rasping noise. The lights from their torch helmets pointed towards the imp as if to ensure it hadn't broke free of its shackles.

'Is this a joke, Hoxton?' asked Jennings.

Hoxton shook his head, startled by his sudden soberness. The sound was growing, a rapid breathing that belonged to no animal Hoxton had ever heard. The group of men looked at each other, perhaps hoping someone would explain what was happening. It had never been more apparent to Hoxton that they were somewhere they shouldn't be. He felt the narrowness of his surroundings and noticed the panic spread through the group like a virus until Jennings cracked.

'Well, what the hell are we waiting for?' screamed Jennings, grabbing the torch from him and stumbling back through the cave.

Hoxton scrambled after the man, slipping as he overtook him. The panic overtaking the group was laced with an excited humour as they rushed back through the cave, as if the strangled sound they'd heard couldn't possibly be real. By the time they reached the cave's entrance, they were in hysterics – a combination of excitement, relief and the alcohol that swirled in their bloodstreams. Two of the men threw up as Jennings slapped Hoxton on the back.

'That was one hell of a show. What the hell was it?' asked Jennings.

Hoxton could only shrug as the cold night air whipped his dry skin, and when Jennings suggested they return to the hotel to start the whisky he didn't argue.

Hoxton wanted to be drunk again.

He'd heard that sound before and knew it didn't belong to an animal.

Chapter Five

Louise was surprised how smoothly she'd transitioned back into working life. True, she'd only been away for five months, but buzzing back into the building for the second day, it was like she hadn't been away at all. In many ways, the tragedy that had befallen her had helped cement her place within the team. She'd been on duty when Paul had died, risking her life on the pier, and she knew the other officers respected that even if they may have questioned her decision-making.

The CID department was all but empty.

The sheep slaughter was the main case at the moment, and Louise wasn't sure what she felt about that. In a previous life she'd worked in MIT at headquarters. The thought of that team even looking at such a case was laughable, and here she was with it as her major investigation. She tried Stephen Walsh's office again only to be told he was out and that he had received her messages. It could wait, she decided, opening her case file on Paul.

Tania's revelation sounded like school playground gossip. According to her sources Paul had been seeing one of the women who drank in his local pub, The Two Swans. Jodi Marshall was married to a corporal in the army, Nathan Marshall. The rumour circulating the pub was that Nathan, who'd been on deployment in Nigeria, had got wind of the affair. He'd been due to return a few days after Paul had left for Cornwall but had been back in the country on the day Paul was murdered.

Louise only had piecemeal information. As it wasn't her case, accessing the investigation on HOLMES without permission was a sackable offence. And, due to her personal connection, that permission was never going to be granted. She skimmed through the notes and reports she'd acquired but there was no mention of Jodi and Nathan Marshall. Tania had acted as if the information was priceless but Louise trusted Farrell. Paul's case was the first high profile case he'd been lead investigator on, albeit with the SIO from Devon and Cornwall. He'd always been a thorough investigator and although not impossible, she thought it unlikely he'd overlook something of this significance.

So why had Tania made such a show of the relationship? Louise had sensed that things were not going quite to plan for Tania during their meeting, and it was possible Tania was trying to spark Louise's interest in Paul's investigation to give her something to write about.

At any other time, Louise would have contacted Jodi Marshall to get her side of the story but she hesitated. It wasn't her case and she was personally involved. It would be unprofessional to interfere, and it wasn't something she should risk on her second day back in the job, but Farrell's warning that the case would be shelved by the end of the month convinced her she had to act. Although she trusted Farrell, she couldn't say the same for Finch. She located the woman's address and wrote it on a scrap piece of paper just as her phone rang.

'Ma'am, we have a Richard Hoxton here to see you. Says he works for Walsh Investments?'

'Send him to one of the interview rooms. I'll be down in five,' she said.

◆ ◆ ◆

Richard Hoxton stood as she buzzed the door to interview room five a few minutes later. He was a tall muscular man, a beaming smile hidden behind an unkempt beard. 'Richard Hoxton. Apologies for just turning up. Stephen told me you've been trying to contact him and I happened to be in Weston today so thought I'd try my luck.'

'DI Blackwell, please take a seat. Mr Walsh too busy to come himself?'

'He's away in Europe at the moment. Making the most of our relationships while we're still in the union. He does send his apologies if that's of any use?' He raised his eyebrows, smiling. 'I'm guessing not. Sorry, he can be a bit obtuse and difficult to get hold of.'

'You're here now,' said Louise.

'I guess I'll just have to do. So how may I help?'

'We could have done this over the phone. With what happened yesterday at Cheddar, we're contacting local businesses and Walsh Investments came up on our list.'

'Understandable. Very strange business with those sheep. Do you have any idea what happened?'

'We're making progress.'

Hoxton tilted his head, a mischievous glint in his eye. 'Mum's the word,' he said, touching his nose.

Louise suppressed a laugh. 'I'm really just trying to get a feel of the local community. When something like this happens, it's usually innocuous. However, as you've seen, the incident made the news. National news last night I believe. It's possible some people stand to benefit from such publicity.'

'Sales of Border collies have gone through the roof I hear,' said Hoxton, tilting his head to test the joke. 'Sorry, poor taste,' he said, when Louise didn't answer. 'No, I completely understand. I guess an incident like this can bring a bounce in tourist activity though I could think of easier ways.'

Hoxton was a charmer. Louise was used to charming men. A few months back she'd sat in this very room opposite another charming man who'd proven to be a deluded killer. She'd seen right through him, but Hoxton was different. She wasn't one to reach conclusions about anyone, especially so quickly, but Hoxton seemed genuine. Yes, he had a way about him – a confidence and easy humour that probably helped him in the business world – but Louise thought he was authentic. 'What can you tell me about your company's interest in Cheddar?' she said.

Hoxton regurgitated the plans she'd read about on the internet. He sounded passionate about the project, espousing the environmental qualities of the planned build. Louise could tell he was a practised salesman but unusually she wasn't put off by his presentation.

'There have been some objections to your plans in the local community?' she said.

'There always is, and I quite understand it. It's such a beautiful area. Obviously, I'd be disingenuous if I said we weren't trying to make money. Of course we are. We're setting up multi-million pound deals just to get the project off the ground but I can assure you that Stephen is the real deal. We've won awards for our environmental activism and I can say hand on heart that I wouldn't want anyone else developing that area. That said, some people don't want any development. The council are torn on the issue and we have pressures from the National Trust and the other landowners. It's not an easy job, Inspector Blackwell.'

'Has anyone been significantly vociferous in their objections?'
'You've seen the graffiti, I presume?'
'Hard to miss.'

'It's understandable and I get it. It's such a lovely area but I truly believe we are adding value. It's hard for people to see that at the moment.'

'And what is your specific role?'

'I'm the smiley face of the organisation,' said Hoxton, flashing his grin once more. 'I work with the investors and try to smooth out relationships. I show people that we're not just a merciless and faceless corporation.'

'And how does that work out for you?'

'I'm so, so tired,' said Hoxton, holding her gaze, the smile still on his lips.

'So tell me. Who would want those sheep dead?'

Hoxton went to speak then stopped, as though thinking better of making another joke. 'I'm not buying the publicity thing. I don't think having mutilated sheep benefits anyone or anything. Certainly, no one I deal with – and I do meet the odd crazy – would be so stupid as to try something like this. But who the hell knows? People surprise me all the time.'

Louise stood. 'Thank you for your time,' she said, extending her hand.

'Pleasure was all mine,' said Hoxton. 'Listen, I'm sure this is wildly inappropriate but I'd kick myself later if I didn't say something.'

'You know who killed the sheep?' said Louise, with a smile.

'No, but I'd be happy to discuss a list of potential suspects over dinner.'

It wasn't the first time Louise had been asked out during an interview, but it was the first time she'd been tempted. She saw a hint of vulnerability in his eyes. At another time, in different circumstances, she may have taken him up on the offer. And still she hesitated before replying. 'That's very kind of you, but if you think of anything please call the station,' she said, handing him her card.

'Of course, of course. I hope you didn't mind me asking. I'm devastated, naturally, but . . .'

'It's fine,' said Louise.

'Then you'll take this?' said Hoxton, handing her his business card.

Louise returned his smile. 'How could I refuse?' she said. She took in a deep breath as Hoxton left. She'd been surprised by her reaction to Hoxton handing her his business card. She'd felt heat on her skin and hoped she hadn't given herself away. It wasn't a time to be distracted, but as she placed Hoxton's card in her pocket she thought that, when the case was over, it might be time to take a chance on something new.

Chapter Six

He remembered her.

She'd been different then, the happiest he'd ever known her. He smiled at the memory now and she berated him for it.

'What are you smiling for?' she said. 'You need to be organised. I shouldn't have to come here and do this any more.' She was tidying the kitchen, working through a pile of dishes that didn't appear to be getting any smaller.

'Just remembering,' he said.

'Have you remembered to take your pills, more to the point?'

From his pocket, he took out the plastic container with its seven sections – SU, M, T, W, TH, F, SA. The container rattled – the sound reminiscent of his chest – and he pretended to empty one of the sections and to dry swallow its contents as she watched him like a wary parent.

'I'm not going to keep doing this,' she said later, as she put on her coat.

'Where are you going?' he asked, an unexpected wave of loss washing over him.

'You know I don't live here,' she said. At first he was pleased to see the sternness vanish from her features, as she hesitated by the front door. Then he saw the pity as if his confusion was painted clearly on his face. He went to touch her, realising a second too late that it wasn't allowed.

'I'm sorry,' she said, flinching from his hand before walking away.

◆ ◆ ◆

He walked to the house. His house. Their house.

It had always been too big for them and he wondered how she coped with the extra space now he was gone. Her car was parked outside but it was easy enough to walk around unnoticed.

The door to the converted barn was open and he crept in. The barn had been his halfway home and she hadn't decorated since his departure. The air was fetid as if something had died within. He tasted the dryness of the dust in the air and stifled a cough, his lungs feeling as if they had acid running through them.

He stood to the side of the window with its dank brown net curtain as a car he'd never seen before parked outside. His chest stung, the sound of his breathing reverberating in the hollow room as the man left the car and opened the front door as if it was his house.

He couldn't hold back the cough. It burst from his lungs, a terrible hacking sound rumbling through his body sending mini-convulsions through his muscles. For a time, it took up all his concentration. He spat out the red-yellow phlegm on to the ground, forgetting where he was before lying down on the wooden floor.

He closed his eyes, the heavy sound of the fluids in his lungs matching the increased beat of his heart. He recalled the caves and the stupid men he'd scared away the other night, the vision fading to the sight of the hills where he was a boy again, potholing with his dad; and then, too quickly, he was the dad, driving his own child along a wet road; and then he was in a hospital bed, his wife telling him with accusing eyes what had happened.

If he screamed, the sound was absorbed by the other noises emanating from his body. Above him, spiderwebs hung from the wooden beams and he studied the grey tangles as he tried to remember where he was and how he'd got there.

The air was thin down on the floor and he dragged his aching body to a standing position and stumbled outside, the fresh air reinvigorating him. He edged towards the main building, stopping short at the sight of the silhouetted figures within, holding each other.

Retreating back towards the village, to the calming embrace of the cliff faces, he fought the images plaguing his mind. It was a blip, a momentary betrayal to punish him for what he'd done. He'd destroyed their family but he was sure there was a way to make amends. The hills held so many secrets and there was a reason they kept calling him back.

The solution was there.

He could win her back.

Somehow, Jack was coming back. All he had to do was find his boy and they could be a family again.

Chapter Seven

When Louise arrived at her parents' house that evening, she found Emily sitting on a lone chair in the middle of the kitchen. 'Now, why are you sitting there all alone?' asked Louise, receiving a scornful look in return.

'Don't speak to her,' said Louise's mother. 'She's on time out.'

'Is that still a thing?'

'It is when a young madam has been writing on her bedroom walls.'

Emily's scowl intensified, her head lowering on to her shoulders at her grandmother's words.

'Ah,' said Louise, feeling guilty as she furtively glanced around the kitchen for evidence that her mother had been drinking again.

Her mother caught her looking but didn't say anything. 'So how's work? Good to be back?'

'Bit surreal really,' said Louise, proceeding to tell her mother about the sheep in Cheddar.

'I'm surprised they've got you looking at that,' said her mother, with a hint of disapproval.

'I go where the work takes me,' said Louise, thinking again how laughable such a case would have been back at MIT. 'So, apart from the illustrating, how's she been?'

'I think she's going a bit stir crazy. The school have said she can go back but that it would be best to leave it until after the Easter break. We're thinking of taking her away somewhere. Dad's been looking at some bed and breakfasts in Tenby.'

'That sounds lovely, doesn't it Emily? Oh, sorry, Mum.'

'It's about time she was getting down anyway. What would you like to say?'

'Sorry, Grandma,' said Emily, wrapping her arms around Louise's mother.

Her sullenness eradicated, Emily ran over to Louise and jumped into her arms. 'Aunty Louise,' she said, eyes wide.

'Hello you.'

'Will you come and play?'

'Just a second. I need to speak to Grandma and Grandad.'

'Sounds ominous,' said Louise's mother, retrieving a bottle of white wine from the fridge. 'Want some?'

Louise sighed. 'No thanks. So what was she writing on the walls?'

Her mother shook her head as if she could shake away the memory. 'Just her name. Multiple times. Thankfully it was in pencil so we've got most of it but it will need a new coat of paint.'

'I've been summoned,' said Louise's father, entering the kitchen and distracting Louise before she could fixate on the significance of Emily's graffiti.

'Hi, Dad.'

'Hi, sweetheart. So what's this all about?'

They sat around the kitchen table, Louise checking the door was shut before speaking. 'Look, this might be hard to discuss,' she said, as her mother downed half of her drink in one gulp. Louise couldn't help but be distracted. Sometimes, she was convinced her mother was deliberately trying to provoke her with her drinking. Her father noticed she was distracted and shook his head, dissuading her from commenting. 'Do you know if Paul was seeing anyone?' she said.

Her mother's brow creased as if the thought had never crossed her mind. 'Seeing someone? I suppose anything's possible, but you know how secretive he was. He wouldn't tell me something like that.'

'Dad?'

Her father had never been great at hiding anything. He looked frozen in position, as if he was trying to hold the words in place.

'Danny?' said her mother.

Her father lowered his eyes. 'Remember that time I found him at the flat, after he didn't pick Emily up?'

Which time? thought Louise, disappointed that her memory of her brother was always clouded with such negativity.

'I may have seen some . . . underwear. That didn't belong to him. At least, I hope not.'

'Dad,' said Louise, with a warning look.

'Why didn't you say something?' said Louise's mother.

'I don't know. I didn't think it was any of our business, and I was more concerned about everything else at the time. In truth, I was a little pleased. I thought it meant he might be getting things together. I was wrong about that though, wasn't I?'

Louise placed her arm around her father, his eyes reddening. 'Did you ever speak to him about it?'

'There was never any time. It was only a few days before he left for Cornwall.'

'What's this about, Louise?' said her mother, reaching for more wine.

'Nothing probably.'

'You've been looking at this case. Have they been missing something?' said her mother, her voice rising.

'Don't you think you should ease back on that, Mum?' It was the second time in as many days she'd dared speak to her mother about her drinking. She could recall hundreds of similar conversations with Paul, many during the days leading up to him disappearing to Cornwall with Emily.

'Don't tell me what to do, Louise.'

'I'm not. It's just . . .'

'What?'

The tension in her mother's face suggested the conversation was at an end. As if to prove the point, she took another gulp of wine. Louise wondered if her mother had even considered the irony that she was drinking so much after her son had all but drunk himself to death. Like Paul, it was almost pointless discussing the matter with her. She didn't think she had a problem, and Louise worried about what would need to happen for her to change her mind.

'You could ask Emily,' said her father.

'I'd like to talk to Dr Morris before I do that, really.'

'She'd have a better idea than we would. Do you think it has something to do with his . . . ?'

Her father could never come to say the word *murder*. 'No, not really. I'm sorry but I can't talk about it beyond asking questions.'

'Are you allowed to work on his case?' said her father.

'Dad,' said Louise, her tone putting the conversation to rest.

Emily was waiting in the living room. She sat cross-legged on an armchair, reading.

'What you got there?' asked Louise.

Emily looked up from the paperback. '*The Sleeping Bug*. It's about a girl who can enter the world of any book she reads,' she said, lifting the book cover so Louise could see.

'Sounds great,' said Louise, understanding all too well why such a story would be of interest to her niece. She hoped Emily could take some comfort from escaping into the fantasy world of the book.

Emily smiled and continued reading. Louise enjoyed the peace of sitting there in silence watching the tiny shifts of Emily's features as she read her book. For the briefest of times, all thoughts about Paul's murder case, work and Emily's suspension faded and it was just her and Emily in a perfect moment.

The low hum of her mobile ushered her back into the present. 'Thomas?' she said, clicking on the screen.

'Hi boss, sorry to call but thought you'd want to know. There's been an attack in Cheddar.'

'More sheep?'

'Unfortunately not. This time it was a human.'

Chapter Eight

Richard Hoxton sat in his car, outside the hotel in Cheddar that had been his on-and-off home for the last six months, and waited for the wave of pain to leave his head. With the heater on, the car was like a mini-sauna. What the hell had he been thinking? The last person he'd asked out, in fact the only person he could ever recall asking out, had been Becky and that was some twenty years ago. As for asking out a policewoman, and during a police interview?

He put it down to the Dutch courage that was surely still in his bloodstream. He wouldn't have dared otherwise. Not that DI Blackwell was without her charms. She had an easy way about her. He'd noted her keen intelligence in the subtle way she'd questioned him, and her dry sense of humour was evident during the interview. She'd even laughed at his lame jokes, which was a good, if rare, sign. But still he couldn't fathom how he could have been so bloody foolish as to ask her to dinner. Fortunately, she'd eased his embarrassment and accepted his business card, so at least he'd managed to leave with a sliver of pride intact.

The truth was, the whole of the day had been passed in a daze. He'd been trying to piece together the previous evening ever since his eyes had opened to the blurred sight of his hotel room that morning. He had no recollection of getting back to the hotel, or of what time he'd left. His last real memory, and that was foggy, was being in one of the local bars around closing time. He'd heard of having twenty per cent amnesia, but recently he'd been losing over half his nights. The curve of his stomach, currently bisected by his seat belt, gave an indication of why. When he was sober enough to consider it, he knew Becky had left him because of his drinking. Maybe now was the time to stop. The men he'd been out with last night were pivotal to the Cheddar investment, and he still couldn't recall what had happened with them even though he was sure the night hadn't ended at last orders.

Walsh called as he was about to leave the car.

'Stephen,' said Hoxton, forcing enthusiasm into his voice.

'Rich, how are you? I heard from Jennings that you had one hell of a night last night?'

Hoxton felt the gorge rising. 'You could say that.'

'Jennings said he woke up next to an empty bottle of Macallan. Great work.'

At the mention of the whisky, Hoxton felt a burning sensation at the back of his throat. A dim memory of being in Jennings' hotel suite returned to him, as did distorted images of the other men grinning and out of breath. 'Thanks,' he said, thinking there was something wrong in being credited for losing his memory.

'You manage to speak to that policewoman? She keeps leaving messages.'

'Yes. Nothing to worry about. She just wanted to get a handle on what was happening locally. She thinks the sheep thing could have been a publicity stunt,' said Hoxton, as a memory from last night fought to return.

'Does she now? Make sure you keep her on side. Don't need any more hassle before we get this over the line. Jennings is on board now. Once I finish up my work here, we should have everything in place for the council meeting next week.'

'Don't worry about things here, Stephen.'

Hoxton collapsed back in his seat once Walsh hung up. Last night's whisky swirled in his stomach. He could smell his own body odour, the dankness of his breath, and it was taking all his will-power to keep his stomach contents in place. Now that Walsh had reminded him about Jennings, snippets of memory teased him just out of reach. Hoxton turned to his side, trying to force the memory to return.

He opened the car door just in time, the acrid vomit rising like a geyser and splattering on to the damp tarmac. It stung his eyes and throat, the smell of regurgitated whisky making him wince. As he coughed and spat up the remains, his stomach now a welcome hollowness, his mind snapped to a vision of standing outside a cave entrance with the men, a torch strapped to his head.

Hoxton shook his head as a young man walked past him . . . and continued walking at the sight of the congealing vomit. He'd taken them into the caves – if there was ever a signal that he should quit drinking, then this was it. Yet it wasn't just that foolhardiness that troubled him. Something had happened in the caves. It couldn't have been that disastrous or Jennings would have mentioned it, but it bothered Hoxton. He didn't want to add it to the growing number of missing memories, but without quizzing Jennings or the other men, he didn't know what to do.

In his room, he showered and changed. He was exhausted but it was too early to sleep. He would have returned to his apartment in Bristol but couldn't face the effort. It was an uneasy inevitability that guided him downstairs to the bar area. He scanned the area for any hint that he'd done something inappropriate the night before but the barman welcomed him with a beaming smile. 'Usual, Mr Hoxton?' he said, reaching for a pint glass.

Hoxton glanced behind the bar at a row of mineral waters. 'If you insist,' he said, taking his pint to a generously padded leather armchair in the corner of the room.

The first drink was a struggle but after that things started flowing. As he ate alone, he absently looked at his mobile phone on the extreme off chance that the policewoman had called. It was only then that he decided to look at his photo app, chiding himself for not doing so earlier. His heart sank at the string of poorly lit snapshots that told some of the story from the previous night. The last of these was the sly grin of the goblin sculpture on the cave wall.

He laughed, remembering how they'd run away like overexcited schoolboys. It was a wonder none of them were injured but Jennings would have informed Walsh if that had been the case.

It was such a relief, and called for a celebration. He'd been worrying about it all day when the evidence had been on his phone all along. To think, he'd been on edge all day because of a fibreglass monster.

'Another one, Mr Hoxton?'

'Why not,' said Hoxton. 'And get me a shot of Macallan Rare while you're there, please.'

Chapter Nine

The mist thickened as Louise drove further inland. She'd never really grown accustomed to driving in darkness through the country roads. Every time a car drove past, the glare from the headlights blinded her. She was distracted further by the smell of manure from the surrounding fields, her mind returning to a former case on a desolate farmyard where she'd tracked down and eventually shot the infamous serial killer Max Walton. It had been her last case at MIT, and was rarely far from her thoughts. She could still taste the decay in the abandoned shed, and hear the words of her former colleague, Finch, who had instructed her to shoot the unarmed suspect.

As she drove the road that bisected the gorge, the sight of flashing lights returned her to the present. They acted as a beacon, and five minutes later she pulled into the same car-park she'd visited yesterday. Thomas was already there, organising the uniformed officers from the local station.

'George Tabart,' said Thomas. 'He's being seen to by the paramedics. Looks like a close escape. Says he was attacked at knifepoint up on the cliff. I've sent two officers up there now but not holding out much hope.'

Louise was surprised by the sight of a small dog tied by its leash to the rear of the ambulance.

'Molly,' said Thomas, by way of explanation.

'Molly?'

'Mr Tabart's dog. He refused to let it out of his sight but the paramedics won't let it up into the ambulance.'

Louise bent and patted Molly, the dog going wild as if they were long-lost friends. It began to bark but was so excited that no noise left its mouth, the only sound the snap of its jaws opening and slamming shut.

'The dog whisperer,' said Thomas, receiving a frown from Louise.

'DI Blackwell. May I speak to Mr Tabart?' said Louise to the attending paramedic who was taping a band to Tabart's arm.

'Sure. Please don't be too long. I'd like to take him in as soon as possible,' said the paramedic, jumping down.

Louise took the paramedic's place, sitting next to Tabart who was lying on a stretcher. 'Hello, Mr Tabart. My name is DI Louise Blackwell. Do you mind if I ask you a few questions?'

Tabart lifted his head and gave her a weak smile. From what Thomas had told her, the man was sixty-two and had been walking his dog along the cliff walk when he'd been attacked. In his current state, the man looked a good ten years older. 'Will you promise to look after Molly?' he said, his voice a surprisingly rich baritone.

'Of course. We'll get someone to look after her.'

'No, I mean you. She likes you.'

'Ah, I don't have much experience with dogs I'm afraid, but I promise we'll do our best. I don't imagine you'll be in hospital for long.'

'Okay, thank you.'

'Can you tell me what happened, Mr Tabart? I realise you've spoken to my colleagues, but I'd like to get the full story from you if that's okay?'

'Of course, but I'm not sure what else I can add. I told your colleague that it was all probably my fault.'

'Your fault?'

'For being out so late. We like to go on long walks but I was feeling a little tired today so we left a bit later, and I was walking a bit slower than normal . . .'

'You mustn't blame yourself for being attacked, Mr Tabart, whatever time you were out,' said Louise, marvelling at the strange ability some people had to blame themselves for events out of their control.

'Well, okay, but we should have turned back much sooner. The darkness sort of crept up on us and with this mist, it took us by surprise. I was heading back towards Lynch Lane when Molly must have heard something. Initially I thought it was a stray sheep or goat, but then this figure sort of burst through the hedge.'

'Figure?'

'I didn't get much of a look I'm afraid. It was so dark. I'd say he was a man, approximately six two. From what I saw he was dressed all in black.'

'And he attacked you?'

'I can't honestly say for sure. I heard some loud, rapid breathing, and the sound of his arms moving. I instinctively put my arms up to shield my face – old army training kicking in – and received these as a consequence,' said Tabart, glancing down at his bandaged arms. 'Quite lucky he didn't nick something.'

'What happened next?'

'It was bloody painful, let me tell you. Molly was going crazy. I wanted to stay on my feet but I'm afraid some weakness overtook me and I fell to the ground. Worst thing you can do. I don't need to tell someone in your position that. I thought I was done for and prepared for the worst but he didn't attack again. After some time I got up and stumbled down those bloody steps.'

'He left you?'

'Not initially. I was curled up in a ball but I sensed him there. I could hear his breathing. That was the odd thing, really. It sounded strained. If I was one for exaggeration I would go as far as to say it was inhuman. A horribly deep rumbling sound like thunder.'

'Did you see his face?'

Tabart grimaced, clearly still in pain.

'We need to get going now,' called the paramedic.

'I did look up at him but he appeared to be looking away. Not sure if the pain was playing tricks on me but his silhouette looked wrong somehow.'

'Wrong? How?'

'I can't explain it. It was like he was, how to say it, misshapen. I'd been in Cox's Cave earlier and seen that bloody stupid goblin thing. I guess my mind was recreating that type of image.'

'Right,' said the paramedic, jumping up. 'I think that's enough for now. As a reminder, DI Blackwell, Mr Tabart has been given some morphine for the pain.'

Louise thanked Tabart and jumped down.

'You're going to have to look after that,' said the paramedic, pointing at the dog.

Louise unclipped the dog from the back of the ambulance.

'New friend?' said Thomas, walking over.

'Looks like it. Unless you . . . ?'

'Allergic,' said Thomas, before Louise had a chance to force the dog on him.

She walked Molly to the police van and ushered her into the gated area at the rear of the vehicle. Molly whined as Louise patted her. 'Just for a bit,' said Louise, the dog's ears flat as she stroked its head.

The two uniformed officers Thomas had sent to the top of the cliff had returned. Their blank faces confirmed they'd been unsuccessful in tracking the attacker.

'We couldn't see more than a few feet in front of us,' said one of them to Thomas, as if he was in charge.

'We'll try again when it gets light,' said Louise.

With eight hours until first light, Louise organised a skeleton crew to man the car-park until the morning. 'I'm heading back now,' she said to Thomas. 'Get some rest and meet me back here in the morning.'

'Do you want to car share?' said Thomas. 'No point both of us driving back to Worle.'

After his recent divorce, Thomas had rented a two-bedroom flat a few streets down from Louise's bungalow. It had happened during Louise's absence and they'd never discussed car sharing before. 'Okay, I'll drive,' she said.

'You not forgetting someone?' said one of the uniformed officers.

Louise's heart fell as she looked down to see Molly, tail wagging, on the end of the lead being carried by the officer. 'I was going to call animal control,' she said.

'I could take her back to the station and sort out kennels for her, but you've asked us to stay here,' said the officer. He didn't look at her as he spoke, the dog's lead reluctantly held out in front of him. There was no provision to look after animals in Weston and waiting for someone to take the dog now would mean at least another couple of hours outside in the cold.

Louise grabbed the lead, the officer darting away before she could change her mind. 'First sheep then dogs. Who says life in the CID isn't interesting? You still want a lift? With your allergies and everything?' she said to Thomas.

'I'll keep a window open,' said Thomas, with a grin.

◆ ◆ ◆

'You think it's the same perpetrator?' asked Thomas, as Louise headed out of Cheddar.

'It will be interesting to see the wounds on Mr Tabart. From his description of what happened it sounds like he spooked whoever did this to him. My hope is the attacker was just up there after more sheep. Of course he could be getting more adventurous.'

'After two days?' said Thomas.

'I can't imagine the sheep were the first animals he ever killed. It would have taken some strength and skill to make those kills. Could be Mr Tabart was in the wrong place at the wrong time. Could be that he was fortunate.'

'Did he tell you about the weird breathing and the distorted face?' asked Thomas.

'I was going to ask you about that. He mentioned a goblin in Cox's Cave? You know what he's talking about? The paramedic said he was high on his meds so I didn't pay it much attention.'

'You don't know about the Cheddar imp?' said Thomas, with mock incredulousness.

'Should I?'

'You're a West Country girl.'

'There's West Country and there's West Country.'

'So you've never been in the cave?'

'When I was a girl. Get to the point, Tom.'

'In Cox's Cave, there's an installation. I think it's fibreglass. A green goblin on the wall. It received a bit of notoriety a few years back when it was used as a fake news item about goblins being found in caves in Russia.'

Louise pulled up outside Thomas's flat. 'I feel like I need to pinch myself. I've only been back a couple of days and I'm dealing with dead feral sheep, and now goblins in caves. It's like I'm in an episode of *Scooby-Doo*.'

With purposeful exaggeration, Thomas slowly turned around to look at Molly who sat with ears pricked as if part of their conversation.

'Wake me up when I stop dreaming,' said Louise.

Thomas hesitated before leaving the car and for a second she thought he might ask her in. They'd grown close during the last few weeks before her enforced leave, but she'd already decided it would be way too messy to get involved with him. Recent divorce notwithstanding, the work environment at Weston was too small for such a relationship to work out.

'Pick you up at five,' she said.

'Five?'

Louise smiled. 'Just think what the Mystery Gang would do.'

Chapter Ten

Louise stopped off at the twenty-four-hour garage for dog provisions before returning to the bungalow. Molly instantly made herself at home, doing laps of the small patio garden before locating a spot to defecate. 'Oh great,' said Louise, finding a plastic bag from the kitchen. It was ludicrous that she'd found herself in this position. No doubt she was breaking some sort of regulation by taking the dog with her but she had to admit she was enjoying the dog's company. She shook her head, dismayed that her social life was so starved that looking after a dog had become a highlight.

Initially she locked the dog in the living room but Molly began whining and she had to move her into the hallway. As Louise began to fall to sleep she heard Molly inching herself closer to the bedroom and at some point during the night she must have managed to scramble on to the bed.

The alarm went off at 4.30 a.m.. Louise was initially confused by the weight on the bed next to her and the smell of smoke in her nostrils – the legacy of the fire on the pier. She shone her phone at the shape and was rewarded with Molly's half-guilty, half-ecstatic eyes staring back at her. 'You are something,' said Louise, forcing herself from the bed, the imagined smell of the fire fading.

She let Molly have a run out on the patio before setting off to collect Thomas. He emerged from his front door as she parked outside, a flask in his hand. 'See you still have the mutt,' he said, getting into the car.

Louise turned around to Molly who tilted her head as if she'd understood the insult. 'Hey, don't talk to my lady like that.'

Thomas puffed out his cheeks. 'Coffee?' he said, unscrewing the flask.

'Now you're talking.'

The drive to Cheddar was a different experience that time of the morning. With the sun rising, and the roads all but empty, the journey was twice as quick. The early morning light gave the gorge a different type of other worldliness, the earthy colours on the cliff sides glimmering in the sun. It was truly a beautiful part of the world and Louise wondered to herself why she hadn't spent more time there in the past.

A new team had been dispatched to the car-park area and Louise introduced herself and Thomas.

'Sergeant Clarke and PC Chambers,' said the uniformed sergeant.

'We also have a helper with us,' Louise added, pointing to Molly. 'The victim's dog,' she added, as Chambers went to speak.

'Right, let's go,' she said, heading across the main road back to Jacob's Ladder.

'What exactly are we looking for?' said Chambers, as they made their way through the shop to the entrance to the walk.

'A weapon would be good. Hunting knife is our best guess. An attacker would be ideal,' said Louise. 'Right Molly, show us where it happened.'

'Now I get it,' said Thomas, with laboured breathing as he walked the final steps of the incline. 'If nothing else, I'm going to get fit.'

Bringing Molly was a long shot, but Louise let her run ahead to see where she would lead them. Mr Tabart had said the incident had happened approximately three to four hundred yards from the lookout tower at the top of the steps. The area was covered in dense woodland with enough coverage for someone to easily hide, especially in the dark. As they walked further along the cliff walk, catching sight of their first feral sheep, Louise was reminded how improbable their task was. Without a huge increase in numbers, it just wasn't feasible to search the area. And with chances high that the attacker had long since absconded and taken their hunting knife with them, it didn't seem like a constructive course of action.

They let Molly run around for twenty minutes before heading back. Returning, they passed a small group of early morning ramblers. Louise didn't think the walkers were in any imminent danger and didn't want to start spooking the local community without any justification but felt duty bound to warn them to be vigilant.

A small welcome party greeted them as they returned, Louise shaking hands with the councillor, Annette Harling. There was no Osman this time, but his assistant was doing some maintenance work on the troughs. The councillor introduced her to the man standing next to her. 'Inspector, this is councilman Robert Andrews. You remember Mr Padfield?' she added, pointing over to the other man who raised his hand in greeting.

'Pleased to make your acquaintance,' said Robert. 'It's come to our attention that there was an attack here last night.'

'That is correct,' said Louise.

'Has it anything to do with the sheep attack?' said Annette.

'We can't be sure at the moment. The victim is at Weston General under observation.'

Annette placed her hand against her mouth, the resilience Louise had seen the other day faltering. 'Are they okay?' she asked.

'Fortunately, they are just defensive wounds,' said Louise, not mentioning how serious things could have been had Tabart not been so quick acting. As it were, they were potentially looking at an attempted murder case.

'This won't do,' said Andrews. He sounded as if he was speaking to himself but Louise caught a hint of accusation in his words.

'What Robert means is that we have the Easter holidays coming up. The schools break up for two weeks tomorrow. It's a very busy time for the village. If something like this gets out it could be very damaging,' said Annette.

'I understand,' said Louise. The impact on the local economy was of no interest but she refrained from telling the councillor that.

'We'll need you to patrol the area,' said Andrews.

'That will be a decision for someone else, but I'll mention it,' said Louise, humouring the man. The area was too vast and there simply weren't the resources to manage an effective patrol.

'Jacob's Ladder and the cliff walk are pivotal attractions. If people are too scared to walk up here . . .'

'Both attacks occurred at night and we won't be able to have officers patrolling the area in the dark.'

'Why not?' said Andrews.

Louise didn't have the time or inclination to explain operation strategy to the councillor. Her willingness was tempered further by the man's entitlement. 'As I said, Mr Andrews, I'll speak to my colleagues and see what we can do. For the time being, I'll ask the two uniformed officers over there to monitor the area.'

'Thank you,' said Annette, glaring at her colleague in rebuke.

◆ ◆ ◆

A sense of déjà vu came over Louise as she entered the entrance to Weston General Hospital. She'd last been here following the fire at the old pier and hours later had been in Cornwall, viewing the dead body of her brother. She'd been in a daze then and the clinical, antiseptic smell of the place gave her an unpleasant reminder of that time. It cloaked everything, as if tricking its inhabitants from underlying smells of death and decay; yet the smell of the burning pier accompanied her to the ward where Tabart was resting.

The man was sitting up in bed, his bandaged arms to his side. He smiled as Louise approached. The colour had returned to his skin and he looked much closer to his age than he had done last night. 'How's Molly?' he said, before Louise had said anything.

'She's fine. She spent the night at my place. I've had to leave her in the car but the window is open and I have a tatty old blanket for her to sleep on.'

'You are very kind.'

'How are you feeling?'

'I'm much better, thank you. I think I was in a bit of a shock last night. It was a bit surreal walking down those steps with my arms all cut up and the threat of being attacked looming over me.'

'You did amazingly well to make the walk at all. I just wanted to go over what you told me last night.'

'I imagined I sounded a bit garbled. It all feels so unreal now, except for these,' said Tabart, lifting up his arms with a grimace.

'You said your attacker was a large man.'

'About six two I think. I didn't see his face in all the panic but as I mentioned there seemed to be something off about his appearance, as if he was wearing a mask.'

'You mentioned visiting Cox's Cave earlier that day.'

Tabart blushed. 'Oh yes, I think my imagination was getting away with me. I put it down to blood loss, and possibly whatever they pumped into my veins in the ambulance. I can confirm it was definitely a human male who attacked me, not a goblin,' he added, with a grin.

'That's a relief.'

Adam Disch, a SOCO dispatched from headquarters, arrived five minutes later. Disch had a no-nonsense practical approach to his work, and barely said a word to Louise as he pulled the curtains across and carefully undid the man's bandages. After studying the wounds he took a set of photographs before wrapping Tabart's arms with a fresh set of bandages.

Louise accompanied him out of the ward. 'They're definitely knife wounds; that much I can confirm. The incision in the right arm is deeper than the left.' He held his arms up in front of him, placing the right arm over the left. 'He was rather fortunate. The wound to his arm was close to the radial artery. You would probably be looking at a murder case if that had been cut. He would have lost a lot of blood in a short amount of time, and being alone in the dark . . .'

Disch had been one of the SOCOs who'd examined the dead sheep the previous day. Louise was reluctant to link the cases just yet but had to ask the question. 'Was the knife used on Tabart the same as the one used on the sheep?'

'I'll need to get these images over to Dempsey so he can crossreference. If you want an educated guess then I would say it is highly probable. Certainly a similar, if not identical, knife has been used in both instances.'

Louise thanked Disch and headed back to the ward. By the time she returned, Tabart had already been discharged. 'Do you have someone to look after you?' she asked, helping Tabart to pack up his things.

'My sister's going to collect me. I'll stay with her and her family until I've healed up.'

'I best go and get Molly ready for you then,' she said, surprised by how deflated the thought made her.

Chapter Eleven

Louise walked Molly for the last time at the back of the hospital. As she watched the unbridled joy Molly took in the simple pleasure of exploring a new patch of grass, she was surprised by the melancholy washing over her. Beyond a budgerigar the family had bought when she'd been a child, she'd never had a pet. It wasn't feasible for her to have a dog with the type of hours she worked, yet she didn't relish the idea of giving Molly up.

Self-introspection had always been something she'd prided herself on and she found herself questioning her decision to return to work. She'd hoodwinked the psychologist but maybe that had been a mistake. Clearly she hadn't recovered from the fire at the pier, and the death of her brother. And here she was looking after a dog that wasn't hers, distracted by the investigation into Paul's murder which wasn't her case. She could convince herself that she needed to take an interest in the investigation, that it was her duty to make sure Farrell and the others gave it the attention it deserved before shelving it, but what if she wasn't thinking straight?

She saw her confusion mirrored in Molly's wrinkled brow as she handed the dog over to Mr Tabart's sister.

'Thank you for looking after her,' said the woman.

'My pleasure,' said Louise. She turned away as Molly began whining, thinking how readily she would have accepted Molly into her life if circumstances had been different.

The melancholy remained with her as she drove from the hospital but she decided she wasn't going to second-guess herself any more. She owed it to Paul and her family to make sure everything was done to find his killer. If that meant she had to break rules, then so be it.

She took the route along the seafront where the sea was at high tide. The transformation never ceased to amaze her, the usual covering of gold sand and dark mud transformed into a shimmering blanket of water. She cut back through town and along Locking Road towards the station, the musty smell from Molly's fur still in the air.

◆ ◆ ◆

DCI Robertson summoned her into his office the second she entered the CID department. 'I see this sheep thing has taken a new turn.'

'You could say that, Iain.'

'You met a Robert Andrews this morning?'

'Yes. Has he been on at you already?'

'In a roundabout way, yes. He wants us to set up a patrol on the cliff walk. Especially for the two-week school holiday,' said Robertson, with a hint of incredulity. 'Unfortunately, he happens to be golfing buddies with the chief constable.'

'We have two uniformed officers in the area as we speak but nothing in place officially yet. It's going to take a lot of manpower.'

Robertson grimaced. 'Tell me about it. This Mr Tabart, we're sure he was attacked by the same person who killed the sheep?'

Louise updated him on Disch's feedback. 'We'll hopefully hear from Dempsey, but sounds likely.'

'Bloody fantastic. So this is an attempted murder case now? That escalated quickly.'

'That's the concern, sir. Also, both these attacks occurred after dark so if we are to patrol the area, it would make sense that we do it during the night as well.'

Robertson scratched his head. 'You know how hard that is, logistically, in an area that big?'

'Sir.'

'You think he'll strike again. It is a "he"?'

'According to Tabart, the attacker was male,' said Louise, omitting the details about Tabart's visit to the cave earlier in the day. The mere suggestion of the word 'goblin' wasn't going to leave her lips.

'Set up an incident room. Let's hope the attacker's setback with Tabart has put him off the scent,' said Robertson.

Robertson knew as well as she did that that was unlikely. If the incidents were linked, the escalation to a human target suggested the attacker was only getting started; in Louise's experience, the botched attack on Tabart would act more as a motivator. If he was to attack again, their main hope had to be that he would choose the same location. It was feasible the area had a significance to him, and if it did, they had to exploit that knowledge.

'One more thing,' said Robertson, as Louise stood to get up.

Louise lowered her eyes and returned to her seat. 'Sir,' she said. Robertson's tone suggested a reprimand was headed her way.

'The investigation into your brother's murder.'

'What about it, Iain?'

Robertson murmured under his breath. 'You met with Farrell?'

'It is an on-going investigation, sir, and I am a family member.'

'That's correct, Louise. In this circumstance you are a family member and not an investigating officer.'

'No one has said anything about investigating. I'm naturally curious about how the case is progressing.'

Robertson lifted his hands up. 'You have an active case of your own now, Louise. One that is under increased scrutiny. I need to know that I can trust you with it.'

It was strange now to think that Louise attending the scene of the dead sheep had been a way of easing her back into work. 'Have I ever let you down before, Iain?'

'That's not the point, Louise. I am concerned that you're distracted. It's understandable and I have no problem with it, but if it's going to affect the way you approach this case then I should reassign it. I'm happy for you to take some more time off if you think that's necessary?'

'That's not necessary, sir. I will give this my full attention,' said Louise. *As long as Farrell and the others do their job properly.*

Robertson put his hands behind his head and leaned back. Their mutual trust was important to Louise and she didn't want to betray that, but to ensure Paul's investigation was handled properly she needed to be active at work. 'Okay, Louise. Let me know when we hear what Dempsey has to say about this butcher.'

Louise nodded and left the office, a cold blast of conditioned air bristling her skin as she entered the main area. She'd expected the conversation at some point but it still rankled that Farrell had let slip about their meeting. At her desk, she glanced around her as if daring anyone to comment. She gave instructions to the office manager to set up an incident room in the adjacent space, and updated her report on the database.

She tried to drag her attention away from Paul and back to the incidents in Cheddar. It was a strange combination of events, and she couldn't even be sure if they were definitely connected. She considered the significance of Jacob's Ladder, and the gorge in particular. If location was linked to motive, it suggested the attacker was local and had strong knowledge of the area, but aside from that she had no idea where to begin. Were they looking for someone who had a grudge against the National Trust, the owners of the various tourist attractions in the area or the small community in general? Maybe when the blood and DNA test results from the sheep and Mr Tabart came back, they would have a better idea of what they were looking at. Until then, she had to hope the attacker had been unnerved by what had happened with Tabart and would delay, or ideally forever put on hold, his next attack.

Dempsey called after she'd finished discussing the case with the team in the incident room. She'd arranged to liaise with the Cheddar station and, together with the surrounding smaller stations, they were in the process of setting up a rota ensuring a police presence in the area for the next two weeks.

'I decided to rush through the work on Tabart's defensive wounds for you as I'm off on a break tomorrow,' said Dempsey.

'Thank you, that's much appreciated. What do you have for me?' said Louise, ignoring the awkwardness she always felt speaking to the pathologist.

'Not sure if it's good or bad news but I can confirm the same knife, at least the same type of knife, was used both on the sheep and on Mr Tabart.'

'It's consistent at least,' said Louise, partly to herself.

'The attacker used a knife with a serrated blade approximately four inches in length. Unfortunately, these types of hunting knives are very common. I couldn't give you a specific brand I'm afraid. Definitely a serious piece of kit though.'

Louise updated Robertson with Dempsey's finding and was pleased when he agreed to upping the manpower searching the cliff walk. It was a long shot but from what Tabart had stated, the attacker had been ruffled during the attack. If there was an outside chance the attacker had dropped the weapon, and could subsequently be tracked from it, then it was worth a day of trekking through the Cheddar Gorge undergrowth.

The defence wounds on Tabart's arms made her think about Paul. He'd been stabbed seventeen times in a frantic attack, but the weapon had never been found. Louise returned to her desk and glanced through her case notes on Paul once more. She couldn't help herself, despite how upsetting the photographs of the crime scene were.

She tried her best to view the images dispassionately. The mottled corpse with its puncture wounds was no longer Paul, she told herself, but she could only view two of the images before placing the file back in her bag. She tried to remember Paul as he'd once been. As the older brother she'd idolised growing up, the grinning groom on his wedding day, and the proud father he'd become. However, try as she might, the other side of him pushed its way into her memories. Images of him lying on the sofa in his flat, black-out drunk, slowly replaced the positive memories, and she wondered if she would always remember him as she did now: a mixture of the argumentative and irresponsible father, and the bloated corpse with its multiple stab wounds.

Drumming her fingers against her desk, she recalled what Tania had said about Paul's supposed affair. She would have liked to speak to Farrell but couldn't risk it following her talk with Robertson.

Instead she called someone she'd last spoken to a few days before Paul's murder.

Chapter Twelve

Louise had a sense of time replaying itself. She'd met Paul's old friend, John Everett, in a bar in central Bristol when she'd been trying to locate her brother following his desertion to Cornwall. Now here she was, tracking Everett to another pub, this time in the less salubrious surroundings of Whitchurch in south Bristol.

The Vault was a pub located on a housing estate next to a supermarket complex. She'd been here a few times as a youngster but it had changed since then. Stepping inside, Louise got the impression that the local bar was trying to be something it wasn't. It had the decor of a sophisticated gastropub. Dining tables were arranged neatly in one corner but were empty; the pub's clientele congregated by the serving area and fruit machines. A group of burly men, each wearing the matching overalls of a local scaffolding firm, ran their eyes over Louise without breaking conversation as a heavily made-up barmaid asked her what she'd like to drink.

Louise ordered a mineral water, taking her drink into the adjoining lounge area where she found Everett talking to a bored-looking woman half his age. He spotted Louise immediately, his shoulders swivelling away from her as if he was about to run.

'Hi John, how are you?' said Louise, walking over.

The bored young woman became more animated as Louise approached, a frown forming on her smooth skin as Everett said, 'Hello, Louise', ignoring the quizzical look from his companion.

'Can we talk?'

Everett's companion sighed and walked away. Everett looked around him, scanning the bar as if embarrassed to be talking to Louise. 'Over here,' he said, leading her to a table in the corner.

The smell of stale beer rose from the carpet as Louise sat down. Everett had the glacial stare of a functioning alcoholic, his skin a deathly white punctuated with ruptures of broken capillaries. It was hard to believe he was the same age as Paul had been, was only a few years older than her.

'How are you, John?'

'I'm fine. Surprised to see you,' said Everett, his hand shaking as he sipped on the dark liquid in his pint glass.

She'd last seen Everett at Paul's funeral but they hadn't spoken. She'd been too furious with her brother at the time to talk to one of his enablers. Everett had looked over at her during the wake, a guilty, haunted look in his eyes as if he was pleading for her forgiveness, but she'd looked away without acknowledgement.

'I need to talk to you about Paul,' said Louise.

Everett squirmed, his neck lowering into his shoulders. She could tell he wanted to put Paul's death behind him but had yet to come to terms with what had happened to his friend. 'I told your colleagues everything I know,' said Everett. 'I told you, Louise. Remember? I told you about his money troubles with the Manningses.'

'I remember, John, and I appreciate it. It was good that Paul had someone to confide in at the end, but I think there was something you didn't tell me.'

Everett began shaking his head. Louise tried to picture the man as he'd been in his teens. Of all Paul's friends he'd been the kindest.

He'd treated her as an equal rather than the annoying younger sister, and it saddened her to see what had happened to him. 'Paul was seeing someone,' she said, not giving Everett a chance to deny it.

'No, I don't know anything about it.'

'You're just wasting time, John. I know all about it.'

'What do you need to know from me then?'

'For one, I need to know why you didn't mention it when I was looking for Paul last time, John. How's that for a starter?'

Everett spluttered as he took another drink, his eyebrows furrowed. 'What do you want to know?' he said, lowering his voice.

'Her name would be a good start.'

'I thought you knew all about it?' said Everett.

'John,' said Louise, her tone warning him he was running out of time.

'Jodi. Jodi Marshall. Okay?'

Louise hadn't read Everett's statement but if he'd mentioned anything about Paul seeing someone, she would have found out about it by now. 'You didn't mention anything about a Jodi Marshall in your police interview,' she said, her raised voice causing Everett to squirm in his seat.

'You've just reminded me,' said Everett, laden with sarcasm.

'How long were they seeing each other, John?' asked Louise, wondering why Everett would have withheld this information during the initial investigation.

'I don't know, four or five months I guess.'

Louise pushed her back against the chair, the wood creaking. 'Four or five months? So they were serious?'

John nodded with a caution that suggested he already feared he'd said too much. 'He swore me to secrecy. Jodi's bloke is in the army. He's not the friendliest.'

'Was Paul running from him?' asked Louise.

'I don't know. When I knew Paul had gone, I thought he'd run away with Jodi. He'd talked about it before.'

Louise rubbed her forehead. 'Did she know about Emily?' she asked, somehow angered by the idea.

'Of course.'

Emily had never mentioned any woman in Paul's life. Louise had never posed the question, but it was still odd that she'd never come up in conversation. 'What do you know about the husband?'

'Nathan Marshall? Enough to know I'm glad when he's away playing war games. Pure psycho. Hangs out with a bunch of guys who were a couple of years above me in school. Really nasty bunch. Live to get in fights and cause general misery.'

'You think Nathan could have killed Paul?' said Louise, under her breath.

'Not kill, no, but I thought it was just a matter of time, if I'm being honest, before he did something. I knew, the second he found out, that Paul would be in trouble.'

'Why the hell didn't you tell me, John?' said Louise, her raised voice leading to a few locals looking over.

'I told you, Paul swore me to secrecy.'

'That's withholding evidence, John. You could get yourself in a lot of trouble. And I'm pretty sure Paul wouldn't have minded you telling me about his murderer,' said Louise, trying to control her mounting anger.

'Yeah, but that's the thing isn't it? Fucking Nathan wasn't the murderer was he? I saw him on the day Paul was killed. He was in The Bricklayers with Jodi.'

Louise felt as if she'd been punched in the stomach. 'You sure it was that day?'

'Yes. I've gone over it a hundred times. He was there all day and night. Doesn't it show in your reports?'

Louise swore under her breath. 'And Jodi was definitely with him?'

'That I do know. It was hard to miss her. That bastard must have given her a good beating. She had a bruise the size of a fist on the left side of her face. I wished I'd said something, but then what could I have done?' said Everett, wiping tears from his eyes with an angry swipe of his hand.

Louise was taken aback by Everett's outburst. It gave her a glimpse of the sweet teenage boy he'd once been, the only one of Paul's friends who'd really spoken to her. She was conflicted. In other circumstances she would have hauled him into the station for a witness statement, but after Robertson's warning, that was impossible. 'Don't tell anyone about this conversation,' she told Everett, getting to her feet.

'I'm sorry,' said Everett as she walked away, every single set of eyes on her as she left the bar.

Chapter Thirteen

Louise watched her niece eat breakfast, wondering what other secrets the girl was hiding from them.

Louise had spent the night at her parents' after seeing Everett. Her first thought after seeing Paul's friend had been to confront Jodi and Nathan Marshall. If what Everett had said was true, Paul had been in a long-term relationship with the woman, albeit an adulterous one. Louise wondered what sort of woman would be willing to put up with Paul – at least, the inconsiderate, alcoholic version – before chiding herself for being unfair. Despite his inconsistent behaviour recently, Paul had been a caring and loving person. He'd been a good dad to Emily and his mistakes had stemmed, in the main, from the tragedy of his wife dying. He could be funny and charming and, on a good day, she could understand why the woman had been attracted to him; especially considering what Everett had told her about Nathan Marshall.

She couldn't believe that Emily would have kept Jodi secret from them. She wanted to ask her niece some details, but with the biting incident and school suspension still a fresh memory, Louise had to be careful how she approached the matter.

It was Saturday, and Louise's parents had agreed to go to Cheddar for the day. Emily had never been to the area, and although a little guilty that she was using the day out in part to do some work, Louise thought it would do all of them some good to get out of the house.

Despite Annette Harling's concerns, a steady stream of cars was making its way down through the gorge by the time they arrived just after 10 a.m.. It was a crisp early spring day, with still, cold air greeting them as they left the car.

They headed along the main street, the imposing cliff sides stretching into the clouds as they walked past the village shops and restaurants. Louise paid for tickets in the shop and, for what felt like the hundredth time that week, walked up the steps of Jacob's Ladder.

Louise tried to enjoy the experience, Emily skipping ahead and returning to urge her and her parents onwards, but she was still preoccupied with both the case and Everett's revelation about the Marshalls.

They paused when they reached the summit, Emily desperate to climb the metal steps of the lookout tower. 'More steps?' said Louise's dad.

'Oh come on, Grandad, it's only a few,' said Emily.

'Can't I wait here?'

'Nope,' said Emily, grabbing his hand and leading them all to the entrance.

It was a steeper climb, and by the time they reached the top Louise was out of breath. 'It's quite an amazing place, isn't it?' said her father, as they gazed out at the surrounding countryside. 'You know we brought you here as a child?'

Louise stared out at the Mendips and, to the south, the Somerset Levels. The view stirred a memory in Louise that she couldn't quite place. The sprawling landscape of pastel colours reminded her of childhood visits to the countryside. 'I don't really remember,' said Louise, feeling guilty again as she considered the seemingly endless areas where the attacker could shelter.

'You wouldn't, you were only a baby,' said her mother. 'Paul was so proud of you. He kept worrying we'd drop you. You should have seen his face.'

Louise's mother glanced down to Emily as she spoke. The girl was holding the iron bars of the lookout tower, staring out with an intensity that belied her age.

'It's a shame we didn't come here with Emily when he was alive. Never mind,' her mother added, grabbing Emily's hand and walking back down the stairs of the tower before Louise had a chance to answer.

It was the first time Louise could recall her mother speaking about Paul in such a way since he'd died. Usually, the mention of her son would be a short prelude to a bottle of wine being opened, and Louise hoped this was a progression of sorts.

After heading back down Jacob's Ladder, they walked along to Cox's Cave.

Emily was a bundle of energy as they moved through the entrance of the tourist attraction. Louise felt the tension buzzing through her niece's arm as they held hands and followed the tour guide. Emily looked up at her, her face a picture of wonderment as they were led through the cave.

Emily was fascinated by the stalagmites and stalactites, the bizarre rock formations and the dizzying colours of the crystals. She kept squeezing Louise's hand to ask questions. Louise had forgotten the joy of seeing things through the eyes of her niece. It brought a completely fresh perspective to things and for the next few minutes she was able to lose herself in the beauty of the cave.

The guide told them that it took hundreds of thousands of years for the long stalactites to form from the cave ceiling. Usually they would grow less than ten centimetres every thousand years. The thought put everything else into perspective and Louise was glad to have made the decision to visit the village, to spend some time with her family while she had the chance.

The guide made a bit of a show as she led them around the corner. Playing up to the children, she built up some tension before revealing the sculpture Louise had come to see. It was anticlimactic but enough to startle Emily who grabbed her hand once more. Louise had seen the image of the imp online. The green model was sinister looking enough with a malicious grin and soulless eyes, but she was surprised that it had spooked Tabart. Maybe if it had been as old as the caves it would have had a greater effect on her, but to Louise it was a piece of childish art. No doubt the meds Tabart was given had affected his recollection and led to his confusion about his attack.

But for now, the most important thing was that Emily was thrilled. She couldn't stop talking about it outside. 'It was scary, wasn't it, Aunty Louise?' she said, skipping along the path.

A fine drizzle fell from above, the grey sky and poor light masking the colours of the cliff sides. Louise was about to cross the road to the café where they planned to have lunch, when she caught a glimpse of someone she recognised looking over at her. 'You go ahead,' she said to her parents, waiting until they'd crossed the road before approaching the man.

'I promise, I'm not stalking you,' said Richard Hoxton, his grin spreading as Louise walked over.

Bumping into witnesses and people related to active cases was an occupational hazard. As Hoxton worked out of Cheddar, it wasn't that huge a coincidence. 'Just happened to be in the area, I suppose?' said Louise.

'I like to do touristy things during my day off. I'm off to Cox's Cave in a minute.'

'Well, keep out of trouble,' said Louise.

Hoxton lowered his head. 'Will do, ma'am. Oh, and Inspector,' he added, as she was heading away.

Louise lowered her eyes, a smile forming on her lips as she stopped and turned around. 'Yes?'

'That invitation still stands.'

Louise's smile grew. She admitted to herself that Hoxton had popped up in her thoughts once or twice since their first meeting, and with everything that was going on in her life, that probably meant something. It had been some time since anyone had made such an impression on her and she wanted to accept the invitation. But, aside from the unprofessional element, it was too much of a distraction for her to consider at the moment. 'Thank you, I'll keep it under consideration,' she said, pleased when Hoxton matched a smile. 'Have a nice afternoon, Mr Hoxton.'

Chapter Fourteen

He remembered, then.

He'd hated leaving the village but it had been a necessity. His wife's work had taken them away, and her work was what had kept them going. He recalled the night of Jack's birth with photographic precision. If he closed his eyes, he could smell the antiseptic of the maternity ward, could see the dark green of the midwife's uniform as he handed the boy to him, and the way the baby had held his gaze as if he could look straight through him.

He missed those times but not the place. They'd lived in a cramped terraced house on the outskirts of the city. He'd found no solace in the so-called garden – the muddy patch of land an insult to the hills he'd left behind – but they'd been happy.

He was back in the Mendips now, happy to be submerged in the dense undergrowth, the branches of multiple ash trees all but blanking out the sky. After seeing his ex-wife, he'd left immediately for the cliff walk. There was peace in the solitude but he'd hoped for more. He'd holed himself up in the bushes, waiting, as if the past could wind its way above the gorge.

He'd become a voyeur, watching people make their way across the cliff path. At times he forgot himself. He was a boy again, roaming the hills that were his entire world; hiding from the adults as if he was doing something wrong. As the day had progressed, so had his disillusion. He'd rushed to the hills to escape what he'd seen at his old house, his ex-wife and her new lover. But he'd also gone there with the hope that he would see his son, Jack, again, and as the darkness fell that hope started to feel absurd.

It hurt his head to remember. When he'd seen the man walking his dog, he'd become confused and angry. He'd seen himself in the man and that had scared him. The attack was a blur. He thought he'd been in danger, thought the man he'd attacked had somehow been a danger to Jack. He'd fled when the dog started barking, the man clutching his ragged arms as he'd tumbled away into the shadows.

He hadn't been home since. He'd spent Thursday and Friday night preparing, visiting his other homes. He'd spent Thursday in the Tryst, the cave complex in the midst of the hills deemed too unsafe for explorers. Last night, he crept back closer to home; another restricted site close to the side of the gorge.

He was ready. All he needed now was Jack. His son spoke to him in his dreams. He would be there tonight. All he had to do was wait.

Chapter Fifteen

Hoxton didn't believe in anything as ludicrous as fate. It had been a pleasurable coincidence bumping into the inspector outside the cave. Nothing more, nothing less. Not that it had stopped him putting his foot in his mouth once more. He'd reminded her of his invitation for dinner, speaking before he realised what he was saying. She'd shrugged it off with charm but he felt like a bit of a pest for mentioning it again.

It was clear to him he still wasn't thinking straight. Once again, he'd spent the night in the hotel bar. Although he hadn't reached quite the state he'd achieved in previous nights, he still carried the hangover in his bones. He felt hollowed out and made a vague promise to himself to get an early night that evening.

Prior to visiting the bar, he'd spent an uncomfortable thirty minutes face to face with Walsh on a conference call. The on-going saga in Cheddar was a headache no one wanted, and in Walsh's estimation it was somehow Hoxton's fault. While it was easy to overcome the death of some feral sheep, the attack on the dog walker was proving to be more of an issue. Jennings was starting to get squeamish and Hoxton had to contend with the imminent council decision. Walsh had been working on securing the necessary planning permits for the last eighteen months but now he was hearing some whispers that certain members of the council were digging in their heels. It appeared the vote might not go as smoothly as anticipated, and Walsh had instructed, more demanded, Hoxton sort the issues out before the final decision.

In truth, he should have been working on that now but when he'd woken that morning he'd felt the need to visit the cave. It was like a criminal returning to the scene of the crime, he thought, as he stepped through the main entrance.

Following the guide, Hoxton was immediately reminded how little he could recall about the other night. He still couldn't remember how they'd managed to enter the cave in the first place, and as he glanced at the torch on the guide's helmet he realised he had no idea where they'd found all the equipment.

But it wasn't the cave he'd come to see. Breaking off from the group, he made his way to the wall where the imp was situated. Fragments of memory – the smell of Jennings' breath, the crazy patterns on the walls from the headlamps – nagged him as he walked gingerly along the stone path, until he was in front of the underwhelming sculpture.

It was a wonder none of the group had tried attacking the fibreglass figure. Their response was laughable now. Hoxton recalled the giddy panic as they'd run away, each egged on by the group's mounting hysteria. If he needed another excuse to give up drinking, then surely being so drunk that he ran away from a child's figurine was reason enough.

But hadn't there been something else? He recalled Jennings claiming to have heard something. It was that which had sparked the exodus and was the reason he was back at the site now. Hoxton closed his eyes and tried to conjure the memory, but the whole evening was dotted with too many blank spaces.

Try as he might, the memory didn't return during the rest of the day. As it was Saturday, his work was limited. It wouldn't do to call Jennings or any of the other investors on the weekend without worthwhile reason and his body simply wouldn't accept the idea of another evening out.

He'd taken a seat outside a pub on the main road that bisected the gorge. He was pleased with himself when he ordered a coffee instead of a beer from the waitress, disappointed that he could view such a simple action as a success.

From his seat he could see part of the area that would be regenerated under Walsh's plans. Although he worked for Walsh, he understood both sides of the development argument. The village and the surrounding area was mostly unspoilt. There were some of the tourist trappings that were inevitable in a place like this, but there was a quaint tranquillity to the place, an olde worlde charm that risked being destroyed by Walsh's developments. In his boss's defence, the plans were of the highest quality. It was the reason why Hoxton had remained loyal to the man over the years. The builds were ecologically sound. Hoxton had spent so long studying the plans that he could picture some of them on the hillside now. Made in part from wood and granite, the goal was to make them blend into the surrounding area. He'd seen other places destroyed by monstrous supermarkets and newbuild apartments that destroyed the area's character. Walsh's plans were nothing like that and Hoxton was sure that was the reason they'd got so far along the planning route.

The milk in his coffee was sour and he gave up after two sips. He hated this restless feeling that was helped in no way by his growing hangover. He knew the cure, albeit a short-term and foolish remedy, was to start drinking again so he left the pub before he could succumb to such a distraction.

Maybe if he could work out what was really troubling him he could act, but all he had was a vague worry about the other night at the cave.

The light drizzle in the cold air was a comfort. He let it fall, enjoying the sensation of the water dropping on to his skin. He stopped at the foot of Jacob's Ladder. Despite the recent attacks, people were still climbing the stone steps. It was still light, and he might have considered making the journey too, if the very thought hadn't made him feel breathless.

He was making a mistake but he decided to cure the breathlessness by stopping in the local pub for a quick beer.

He took a seat by the window. As darkness fell, the quick beer soon turned into a succession of drinks, and later he barely registered the wail of sirens and the sight of the police cars rushing past the window.

Chapter Sixteen

Louise had come close to accepting Hoxton's repeated invitation to dinner. After recovering from the surprise of seeing him in Cheddar, and her initial unavoidable suspicion, she'd enjoyed the few minutes in his company. He had a charm and confidence about him that was just on the right side of arrogance. She'd also noticed a hint of vulnerability in his downward glance as he'd asked her out again. She liked to think she would have accepted the invitation if it weren't for the case – it had been so long since she'd been on a date of any sort – but she couldn't be sure. The events that had led to her effective dismissal from MIT had impacted her beyond the professional. She found it difficult to trust anyone, and if she was being truthful she doubted she would have agreed to dinner with the man even if he wasn't indirectly involved in her work. She realised it was an issue she would have to face up to at some point, but that was for another time.

Although she'd enjoyed spending time with Emily and her parents, she couldn't shake the feeling that she'd been neglecting her work. The usual procedures were in place to find the attacker but she could always be doing more, especially considering this was her first week back at work. But she was still distracted and after dropping Emily and her parents back home, she drove to the address she had for Jodi Marshall. As she made her way to Knowle in south Bristol, she told herself that she wasn't going to approach the woman yet. From what Everett had told her, Nathan Marshall was unpredictable, and she didn't want Jodi to pay for her curiosity.

The house was at the bottom of a steep cul-de-sac. Louise pulled up opposite the house and pretended to look at her phone as a group of teenagers walked past the car and glanced inside. Their curiosity sated, the teenagers walked up the hill leaving Louise with a perfect sightline of the house. A sky-blue hatchback was parked outside and there was a light on in the downstairs front room.

Louise didn't know if Nathan Marshall was on leave or if he was at home with Jodi. Not that it would do any good approaching Jodi without speaking to Farrell first. Robertson had already warned her not to get involved. She knew that speaking to Paul's ex-lover now could lead to a reprimand, yet she couldn't drag herself away. Twice she went to leave the car, a restless energy spreading through her body. She had no idea what Jodi Marshall looked like, and despite her anger with Paul, she missed him and wanted to see for herself the person he'd made this secret connection with.

In the end she forced herself to drive away, fearing she would approach the house if she lingered any longer.

◆ ◆ ◆

Back at the bungalow, Louise took photocopies from her files and created two crime boards on opposite walls. Behind the sofa, she tacked the official police photograph of Paul and linked it to photos of the Mannings family. To the other side of him she pinned a piece of A4 paper where she had written the names Nathan and Jodi Marshall.

On the opposite wall, she pinned up pictures of the Cheddar case: close-ups of the wounds inflicted on the sheep next to Tabart's defensive injuries.

Standing in the middle of the living room, she conceded that the new additions were not healthy – her home should be a haven not an extension of her workplace. But it was the only way for her to control the myriad thoughts constantly swirling in her mind. Having the images laid out in sight gave her the opportunity to think straight, and again she thought about making a face-to-face visit with Jodi Marshall.

She was about to call Farrell and make a subtle enquiry when her phone rang. 'Iain?' she said, answering the call from Robertson.

'Good, you're not busy,' said Robertson, reaching his conclusion before she had chance to argue. 'I need you over in Cheddar immediately. I'll meet you there.'

'What's happened?'

'We've just had a report of an eleven-year-old girl who's been missing for the last two hours.'

Louise closed her eyes. 'I guess I don't need to ask where she'd last been sighted?' Already Louise's mind was in a whirl, trying to understand how the sheep, Tabart and a missing child could be linked.

'Afraid not. How soon can you get to Jacob's Ladder?'

Try as she might to stay professional and detached, Louise was worried about the missing girl. With the death of the sheep and the attack on Tabart, it was difficult not to imagine something sinister happening to her. She swallowed hard as an image of Emily formed in her mind, as lifeless as the dead sheep she'd seen earlier that week. 'I'll be there within thirty minutes,' she said, hanging up.

Chapter Seventeen

Louise switched on her siren and lights as soon as she got into her car. She didn't want to waste a second getting to the scene. Although she hoped it was all an innocent mistake, and the missing girl was at her friend's house playing video games oblivious to the concern of her parents, if she was missing, the first few hours were of critical importance. As she sped along the A371, she tried to ignore the other thought playing around her head. The plausible suggestion that they would find the girl somewhere on the cliff walk in a similar way to how they'd found the sheep.

The cliff road was cordoned off. Louise parked up and ran to the foot of the steps of Jacob's Ladder. It felt incongruous that she'd been there hours earlier with Emily and her parents. The presence of the emergency services – in particular the ambulance – cast a shadow over the area. Louise saw it in the worried faces of the pedestrians, concerned but curious, who stood on the other side of the barrier tape.

'DI Blackwell,' she said, showing her warrant card to one of the uniformed officers, as she bent under the tape towards Robertson who was standing at the foot of the steps.

'Sir.'

'Louise. The parents are over there,' he said, pointing to two slumped figures sitting on a stone wall talking to a third person. 'They're talking to Alison, the acting family liaison officer.'

Louise tried not to stare at the grieving couple, locked in each other's arms. 'What do we have?' she asked Robertson.

'Neil and Claire Pemberton. Their eleven-year-old girl, Madison, was out walking with two friends. They'd been in town together, looking at the shops. From what the two girls said, Madison wanted to take a walk up Jacob's Ladder and walk home that way. Down through Lynch Lane into the village. She has a season pass so can use the steps for free.'

'They let her go alone?'

Robertson frowned. 'Apparently this Madison can be a bit of a stickler. Not that it should be a risk taking a walk up a side of a cliff in broad daylight with officers patrolling the area. Anyway, they saw her heading up the steps. They were worried so decided to call her parents.'

'That's something.'

'Yes, but they waited three hours to do so. We've been to the house and have officers there in case she returns.'

'Does she have a phone?'

Robertson frowned. 'Yes, it rings through to answerphone. We've tracked a location for it. I have a team up there now with DS Ireland. From what we can see it's located along the cliff walk going in the opposite direction from the village. About half a mile from the lookout tower.'

Louise shrugged off a mental image of the girl – lying among the trees, a wound across her throat – that immediately formed in her mind. Although the walk had been shut off, there were other ways to and from the clifftop. Louise checked her phone, hoping for a message from Thomas. She didn't want to speak to the parents until they had news of the location of Madison's phone.

The FLO walked over, leaving the girl's parents to their embrace. 'Hi Louise,' she said, adjusting the woollen hat pulled down over her brow. 'They're ready to speak to you. They're both a bit fragile as you would imagine. The dad keeps breaking down in tears.'

'Any home tensions that I should be aware of?' asked Louise.

'Nothing that is apparent at the moment. The parents appear to get on well together but obviously it's too soon to know. Madison is in year seven at the local comprehensive. She had a bit of trouble settling into the new routine but, according to the parents, is pretty happy and well adjusted.'

'Go ahead. We have a PolSA en route from headquarters,' said Robertson, answering his radio.

PolSA stood for police search adviser. They would co-ordinate the search for the missing girl. Louise heard Thomas's voice on the other end of Robertson's radio. 'Looks like we have the phone. Still intact and has power. I've cordoned off the area while we wait for the SOCOs, but no sign of the girl.'

'Okay, let's speak to the parents,' said Louise to Alison.

Neil Pemberton's eyes were red raw. They had a glazed look about them and he looked at Louise as if he'd pinned all his hopes on her. Claire Pemberton was more stoic. She was taller than her husband and stood straight as Louise addressed her. Louise sensed the woman's intensity as they spoke. Louise was worried that she was containing her emotions and that the revelation about the phone might set her off.

Louise wanted to offer reassurances, but it wasn't her role. She needed to get as much information as possible in the shortest time. 'I apologise if I'm repeating questions you've already been asked but anything you tell me, however minor, might help us find Madison quicker,' she said.

'What do you want to know?' asked Claire.

'We have a list of numbers of Madison's friends?' said Louise, receiving a nod from Alison.

'Do you know if Madison may have made any new friends of late?'

'Not that I'm aware of,' said Claire.

'Please don't take this the wrong way, but would she necessarily tell you? Maybe a new boy, or some friends in school?'

'She doesn't always tell me everything, and she's been a bit more secretive since starting secondary school, but I haven't noticed anything out of the ordinary.'

'We told her not to walk along the cliff walk,' said Neil, receiving a short glare of reprimand from his wife.

'Does she often walk that way home?' asked Louise.

'Sometimes. It's not really a short cut but it's a beautiful walk. It's quite a populated area and we like to give her some personal responsibility . . .'

'Of course. I quite understand. Do you have a picture of her?'

Mrs Pemberton showed Louise some images from her phone.

'She's eleven?' asked Louise, moving through the images. Madison appeared to be quite small for her age. She was thin and looked more like she would still be in primary school.

'Yes, she's not twelve until July. Youngest in her class.'

'In the school,' said Neil.

Louise paused. What she had to say next would be hard for any parent to hear. She recalled how helpless she'd felt the day she realised Paul had taken Emily on holiday without telling anyone. That had been with the security of knowing that Paul had his daughter's best interests at heart.

Alison edged towards the parents as if sensing what Louise was about to say. The husband shifted on his feet, his eyes glancing nervously between Alison and Louise.

'It's nothing to get worried about, but we've found Madison's phone on the walk.'

'Nothing to worry about?' said Claire, as her husband's legs went.

Alison put her arm around the man and managed to keep him upright.

'The majority of the time there is a simple explanation. From what I understand, the phone is intact and was found close to the pathway,' said Louise.

'What are you saying?' said Mr Pemberton, trying to regain his composure.

'Chances are the phone fell out of Madison's pocket as she was walking home,' said Louise, doubting her own words.

◆ ◆ ◆

Louise had admired the steely determination she'd seen in Mrs Pemberton's eyes. She sensed the panic bubbling beneath the surface and it must have taken great strength to keep things together. In most circumstances, the parents would have been the first potential suspects. The majority of crimes – murders, abduction, abuse – involved close family members. The Pemberton house had already been searched for signs of Madison, yet although Louise was far from ruling it out, the recent events in the village brought a different perspective to things.

The PolSA, Sergeant Ray Clarke, had arrived and was organising the search effort. Drones with heat-seeking radar had been deployed and a helicopter was on its way, while dog teams were scouring the cliff walk and the surrounding land.

Louise had remained at the foot of the steps until the SOCOs arrived – having sent the Pembertons home with Alison Eabrook – before taking the walk up Jacob's Ladder alone. As the PolSA had the search in hand, she wanted to take the route Madison would have followed back to her house.

Tension ripped through her calves and thighs as she took the steps, her legs still sore from the recent climbs. It was pitiful she'd let herself get so out of shape that the repeated walk was painful, and as she reached the top, breathless, she promised herself she would start exercising again even if it was simply running to the station every day.

The sky was a dense black, dotted with the occasional star breaking through the light covering of cloud. Louise tried to picture the area as it would have been when Madison walked the steps. When she'd been there that morning with Emily, the sky had been a haze of varying shades of blue. She imagined Madison taking these same steps, unaware as to what would happen next. For a second, it was as if Emily had been the one walking the steps on her own, the one who was missing. Louise had to suck in a breath to banish the thought and bring herself back to reality.

At the summit, Louise experienced a profound sense of isolation. It was a beautiful but vast area. To the north was the clifftop route and, further inland, the Mendip walk. Thousands of trees stretched off into the distance of the Mendip Hills and already the possibility of finding Madison in this wilderness felt improbable.

Dragging herself back into the present, Louise headed along the track back towards Madison's house. It was a precarious walk in the dark. Even with the torchlight she tread carefully, more than once tripping on loose rocks. Descending the path, she reached Lynch Lane and the back gardens of the local houses. As she made her way down the road she glanced at her phone, hoping to see the message that Madison had been found – that this was all a complete waste of time. It was impossible not to imagine Emily in this situation, and that made her admire the Pembertons all the more. She understood how the father had broken down. She'd experienced the unknowing before, but never on this kind of scale. She fought the desire to call her parents, to check in on her niece. It was hard to focus, but all her energy had to be given to finding Madison.

Once she hit the main road she returned to Lynch Lane and retraced her steps until she reached the top of Jacob's Ladder. Behind her, the lights of the village blinked in and out of view. Above her, the police helicopter had arrived. It whirred and floodlit the immediate area where Thomas and the team had found the phone. The SOCOs had cordoned off the area and were busy filming and photographing the site. One of them walked over to Louise. She removed her mask and Louise saw it was a long-standing colleague, Janice Sutton.

Louise nodded a muted greeting, in no mood for pleasantries.

'Hi Louise,' said Janice, pointing to a marker where the phone had been discovered. 'It's so close to the pathway that it could have dropped out of the girl's pocket. Obviously, we've only just started. But with all this . . .' she said, pointing to the open space.

'I understand,' said Louise, potential scenarios rushing through her mind. It would have still been light when Madison made the walk. Perhaps she'd made along the cliff walk and realised later that she'd dropped her phone and had returned to retrieve it. Louise had passed enough hiding spots on the walk here. If she'd returned in the dark, then it was feasible that an abductor could have taken her.

Louise thanked Janice and returned back along the cliff walk. Another possibility was that Madison had dropped the phone on purpose in the hope of it being discovered.

It wasn't much of a positive but it lifted Louise as she began the descent into the village. The flashing lights of the emergency services guided her to the Pemberton house. The streets were eerily desolate, the lights throwing shadows over the buildings. Louise checked her phone again as she approached the house, the front door guarded by two uniformed officers. Claire Pemberton was outside smoking, standing in silence with Alison Eabrook, the husband not in view.

Louise exchanged small talk with her colleagues on the door, before moving inside where she found Neil Pemberton in tears. He was being awkwardly consoled by Robertson.

And behind them, further down the hallway, she saw a man she'd hoped never to see again.

Chapter Eighteen

DCI Finch was leaning against the hallway wall, a broad smile on his face. Louise ignored him, pleased to see her old colleague DI Tracey Pugh approach her before she was forced to exchange words with Finch. 'Louise, I was wondering where you were,' said the woman.

'Tracey,' said Louise. She gave her friend a brief hug, the wild tangle of Tracey's hair brushing her skin.

'I bet you're pissed to see us here aren't you?' said Tracey.

Aside from Finch, Tracey was the last of Louise's old team remaining after Finch had disbanded them one by one following his promotion to DCI. It was a wonder Tracey had survived the cull. Her friendship with Louise was self-evident but somehow Finch had allowed her to remain, and Louise was grateful for the fact. Ever since moving to Weston, Louise had struggled to shrug off the attention from MIT. She'd had to fight not to lose every major case to their team, and their arrival at the Pemberton house meant she would soon have another fight on her hands.

'Not all of you, Tracey,' said Louise, with a sardonic smile. 'What's Finch up to?' she said, under her breath.

'Honestly, I don't know. We were told to get here to help. Greg is about somewhere as well.'

Mr Pemberton walked by them, his eyes faced to the floor, as Finch joined Robertson in the living room.

'See you in a minute,' said Louise to Tracey.

She could smell Finch's aftershave the second she entered the living room area. The over-application of the vile citric spray he called aftershave – a pathetic habit he'd developed since becoming DCI – lingered in the air. That she knew he did it on purpose was of no comfort. He wanted it to be overpowering. He was marking his territory, and everyone was too scared to mention it. It made her retch. It was hard for her to rationalise why they'd once been lovers.

'DI Blackwell, so good to see you,' said Finch, who'd taken up residence on one of the sofas.

'Don't you have your own cases to be working on, Tim?' said Louise.

Robertson squirmed. To his credit, her boss had always backed her and she understood that her continued feud with Finch put him in a difficult position.

'You know us, always here to help. Looks as if this might be turning into a major investigation after all,' said Finch.

It would sound paranoid to air it out loud, but everything Finch said seemed intended to annoy her. His allusion to a major crime was his less-than-subtle way of suggesting the case be handed over to his department. Unfortunately for him, he'd tried the same trick on two previous occasions with Louise, and even though he'd managed to sneak his way into her investigations she'd always managed to retain a semblance of control. Due to her recent successes, it would prove even harder for him to wrestle this case away from her.

That didn't mean he wouldn't try. She understood Finch for what he really was, and with her still on the job, he could never relax.

'I have accepted DCI Finch's offer of assistance, Louise,' said Robertson. 'As I told him, you will continue to be SIO on the case.'

Louise noticed the slight twitch in Finch's left eye at the words. That Louise would remain the senior investigating officer would be another slight against him. In a perfect world, she would have no use for MIT's involvement but in reality she welcomed their assistance. If Madison Pemberton was missing then their help wasn't only welcome, it was necessary, and she was willing to endure Finch's company if it meant they could find the girl.

'Thank you, sir,' she said. 'Of course, all help is welcome.'

Finch puffed out his cheeks as if deciding how much energy he was prepared to exert on his campaign against her. 'We'll give you Pugh and Farrell. What uniformed officers you need you'll have to get from local stations,' he said, seemingly impatient to leave.

'Thank you, Tim,' said Robertson, holding out his hand.

Finch grabbed it, making eye contact with Louise as he did. 'No problem, Robbo. Let's just make sure we all stick to our own, active cases,' he added, before leaving.

Louise stood, eyes wide, fighting the urge to confront Finch over his less-than-subtle dig. Robertson looked at her and she was pleased when he didn't say anything.

'I took the route back from the village. The same one Madison would have taken if she'd gone along the cliff walk,' said Louise, ignoring the hint of citric aftershave still festering in the air.

Robertson rubbed his chin. 'It's a large search area,' he said, shaking his head. 'I'm getting in help from everywhere. We've another dogs team arriving from Wiltshire,' he added, with a hint of hesitancy as if he wanted to discuss the continued feud between her and Finch.

The potential discussion was curtailed by Farrell's arrival.

'Sir, ma'am,' he said.

Robertson pursed his lips. He looked annoyed at being interrupted, and Farrell glanced at Louise as if in search of an explanation.

Eventually her boss nodded and walked off. 'Something I said?' asked Farrell.

'Looks like I can't get rid of you,' said Louise, deflecting the conversation. Her relationship with Farrell had initially been strained but she'd learnt to trust the man over the last three years. With Thomas and Tracey also involved, she felt as if she had the strongest possible team working on the case.

'I'll be back at HQ before you know it, ma'am.'

'If I say "I hope so" I presume you won't take it the wrong way?' said Louise.

'Wouldn't cross my mind.'

Louise kept her face neutral. She wanted to ask Farrell about Paul's relationship with Jodi Marshall but now would be professionally inappropriate. 'Anything for me?'

'I've some details on the parents. Neil Pemberton is a local councillor, the mother, Claire Pemberton, works as a commercial solicitor in Taunton.'

Farrell showed Louise his phone. 'They've been quite vocal over the planned developments in the area,' he said, handing her the device.

The screen displayed a local newspaper from last year. Louise scrolled down the piece that quoted Claire Pemberton:

> 'We must, at all costs, stop the proposed development. The commercialisation of our beautiful village is already a major concern. We must not let its natural beauty be destroyed by these monstrous newbuilds.'

The article went on to say that Neil Pemberton was unavailable for comment. Scrolling down further, Louise alighted on a photograph captioned: 'Development king, Stephen Walsh.' Louise zoomed in on the image, her interest not on Walsh but the man standing next to him, Richard Hoxton. She'd thought seeing him at the cave earlier that day had been a coincidence, now she wasn't so sure.

'Thanks, Greg,' she said, handing the phone back to him.

'There seems to be a lot of bad blood in the area about this development,' said Farrell.

'I'm beginning to understand that,' said Louise.

◆ ◆ ◆

The mounting despair of the parents was hard to watch. As the hours passed, what brittle hope they had of Madison walking through the door as if nothing had happened faded. Louise was pleased Alison was there; making cups of tea and coffee, offering assurances to the parents that everything that could be done was being done.

Louise thought again about the coincidence of seeing Hoxton. With the resources Walsh had to hand, it wasn't inconceivable that he had Hoxton monitoring her movement. But why?

◆ ◆ ◆

Claire Pemberton broke down in the middle of the night.

Louise had been working in the Pembertons' dining room, collating the reports from the door-to-door searches, organising the extensive questioning of known sex offenders in the area and trying her best to co-ordinate the extended search, planned for that morning, with the PolSA. She heard a cry from Claire Pemberton, and then Alison trying to placate her. The next thing Louise knew, the dining room door had been flung open and Claire was standing before her, shouting.

It took a few seconds for Louise to tune the hurried words into some sense.

'Why the hell are you sitting at your computer?' screamed Claire. Alison stood behind the woman, the look on her face a mixture of compassion and a muted apology to Louise.

Louise stood up. Despair had invaded every inch of Claire Pemberton. She stood rigid, her face distorted. Worry lines were carved deep into her forehead, her eyes squinting as if in concentration. She was a slim, athletic woman and Louise saw the slight bulge of muscle as she tensed her arms, the tendons on her neck pronounced. 'Please, Claire, take a seat,' said Louise.

'What's a seat going to do?'

'Please,' repeated Louise, turning her laptop around so the woman could see the screen. Some of the tension eased from around Claire's face. 'I know it might not look like it but I assure you, we're doing everything in our power to find Madison. Here,' said Louise, pointing to the screen. 'It probably won't mean much but we have every available officer in the region working on this. We're conducting door-to-door searches, we have drones and now a helicopter working through the night. Our dog teams are searching the area, and at first light we will be sending more officers out. We've been speaking to all Madison's friends, their parents, her teachers, everyone from the swimming club she belongs to. I promise you, I know what I'm doing,' she said, omitting the fact that the majority of their attention was currently focused on known paedophiles in the local and extended regions, which had been their first action point.

Claire nodded, momentarily placated. Louise noted her keen intelligence, the way she studied the information on the screen before accepting what she'd been told.

'I know about you,' said Claire, after looking away from the screen.

There was no accusation in the words but it wasn't the friendliest of comments. The solicitors' practice Claire worked for had a criminal division, and Louise hadn't been a stranger to the front page of local newspapers. Nowadays all it took was a few clicks on the internet and most of her career was laid bare for all to see. Louise didn't know if Claire was alluding to a specific part of her past, and she wasn't about to get into a conversation about it with the woman. 'Then you know I've headed up a number of successful high profile cases,' she said. She considered offering the woman further assurances that she was the best person for the case, but she wasn't there to sell her services. She was there to do a job.

As Alison led Claire back to the living room, Louise took another tour of the house. Cold air leaked through the front door and with no central heating in the hallway area, Louise shivered as she climbed the stairs. The walls of the upper landing were uncovered grey stone, cold to the touch, but the bedrooms were wallpapered and the floors were covered in thick, lush carpeting.

Along with the rest of the house, Madison's room had already been searched, her belongings filmed and photographed. Little numbers adorned the room where inventory had been recorded and prints taken for future analysis. Louise took out her protective gloves and entered the room. The numbers gave the place an ominous feel, giving the impression of a crime scene. The walls and carpet were a tasteful mix of light pastels, not what she would have expected for an eleven-year-old girl. There were no posters or pictures in the room, the majority of wall space taken up with overflowing bookcases.

Louise flitted through the titles. Among the children's books, Louise found a large number of titles that were more aimed at adults. Madison seemed to have a strong interest in science fiction and Louise uncovered some horror titles hiding behind the outer layer of books, including a pristine copy of *The Rats* by James

Herbert. Louise smiled to herself, remembering reading the book as a teenager and being equally repelled and enthralled by the story of a plague of rats taking over London.

One of the tech team had begun searching Madison's laptop and had printed up some recent documents. Louise picked up the pile of notes from the desk and began reading through Madison's latest piece of homework, an essay called 'Myths and Monsters'. The essay centred around the discovery of an ancient set of bones beneath Madison's school. Madison wrote well and had expanded the essay to a number of pages which had presumably exceeded the remit of the homework. It included details of Cheddar Man – the oldest known recovered human fossil in the UK, found in Gough's Cave in 1903 – and even gave a quick mention to the internet hoax featuring the plastic goblin creature in Cox's Cave. More intriguing were the mentions of cannibalism and witchcraft that had reputedly occurred within the local area in the past. To Louise's eye, the essay was highly advanced for someone of Madison's age. The young girl clearly had lots to say and Louise hoped she would get the chance to speak to her one day.

At the end of the essay were printouts of Cheddar Man, and another of the imp, alongside an impressive bibliography. Louise took a photo of the printout and was flicking through the bookcases for some of the titles when the bedroom door opened.

A head peered around the door. 'Hello, ma'am. Not bothering you am I?'

'Simon,' said Louise. 'I didn't know you were here.'

Simon Coulson was one of the senior tech guys from headquarters. He'd been invaluable on her most recent case and she was pleased to see he was here helping. 'I heard about the missing girl and had the weekend off so thought I'd come and help.'

'Thank you, Simon. We can always do with your help.'

Coulson held up a laptop in front of him. 'I've been working on this since I got here. She's too young for some of the social media outlets but she's been logging on to some chat sites.'

Louise lowered her eyes, not sure she wanted to hear what Coulson had to say next. 'Tell me,' she said.

'I've started reading some transcripts. It looks like Madison was in conversation with someone she shouldn't have been talking to.'

Chapter Nineteen

Hoxton glared at his computer screen trying not to betray his unease as the man on the screen stared back at him. It was rare for Walsh to demand a face-to-face conference call and seeing him again now, for the second time in as many days, his face taking up nearly every pixel of the screen, Hoxton thought he understood why. Consciously or not, on-screen Walsh had a death stare that would have unnerved the strongest of people. Hoxton was rarely intimidated but he caught himself looking away every now and then from the unblinking gaze of his boss.

'It's less than two weeks until the council vote and we now have a missing girl to contend with,' said Walsh, leaning towards the camera. 'Jennings called me directly. That's why I employ you, Richard, so I don't have to talk to anyone directly unless it's absolutely necessary.'

'I'm sorry, I didn't know. What did he say?' said Hoxton.

'I'll tell you what he said, Richard. He said he was considering pulling his investment.'

Hoxton was used to being in no-win situations with Walsh. He was paid handsomely to put up with such shit, but he wasn't sure what the man wanted to do in this situation. 'I'll talk to him,' he said.

'Too goddamn right you will. It's the least you can do.'

The least he could do. Some poor schoolgirl had been abducted, or worse, and Walsh expected him to smooth it all over like it was some kind of financial blip. Hoxton had spent much of the last few years wondering what the hell he was still doing in this industry. With the right type of investments, he could probably retire early if he was willing to temper his lifestyle. He didn't need to work for and with people like Walsh and Jennings any more; the type of people who considered a missing girl to be an inconvenience that needed to be overcome. Yet on he continued, some ingrained form of professionalism driving him forwards.

'You've spoken to the police, I take it?' said Walsh.

'On a couple of occasions,' said Hoxton, momentarily lifted by the thought of seeing DI Blackwell again.

'What do they think is happening?'

'A girl has gone missing, Stephen. There's a limit to my powers of persuasion,' said Hoxton, regretting his impatience.

'I realise that, Richard,' said Walsh, pausing either for dramatic effect or to control his rising temper. 'But do they think it's linked to that sheep thing, and the man who was attacked?'

Hoxton's main contact was based out of Bristol, so his information came second hand. He knew DI Blackwell was running the case and that a full-scale search was already in progress, but had no inkling yet of motive or links to the other attacks. 'It would seem likely,' he said, uncommitted.

'This could be a means to sabotage us. I thought you had everyone under control, Richard.'

By everyone, Walsh meant the councillors and politicians, the local resident groups and the press. 'I'm not sure even our fiercest critics would kidnap a girl to stop some building work,' said Hoxton.

Walsh scratched his nose, for the first time looking away from camera. 'Don't be so sure.' After an indeterminable time, Walsh stared back at him. 'What about them?' he asked.

'Them?'

'That crackpot group.'

Hoxton placed his hand on his forehead and stifled a laugh. When the plans had first been unveiled, Walsh had received something in the post with a warning note. Such things happened on occasions, usually the result of a local resident drinking too much. The note had told them that the land didn't belong to them and that there would be dire consequences if they went ahead with the developments.

Hoxton was convinced the note had been sent by a group of environmentalists, who lived in a sprawling commune based in the Mendip Hills not that far from Cheddar. Hoxton had managed to meet with them and, although they denied sending the message and painting the increasing amount of graffiti on the cliff walls, he was convinced they were responsible for the note. They were a ragtail group, living mainly in decrepit trailers and tents. Whispers around the village suggested they were involved in some strange ritualistic practices but Hoxton had seen little to suggest a threat from them and he couldn't believe they were involved. 'They haven't anything to do with this.'

'Famous last words,' said Walsh. 'Let's not rule anything out. Speak to them, offer them some money if you have to, but I want something positive to tell Jennings soon,' he added, shutting his laptop before Hoxton had a chance to argue.

Walsh was so far removed from day-to-day life that he sometimes forgot how it worked. He expected to click his fingers and for everything to be fixed to his liking. Hoxton sighed, pouring a slim bottle of cheap whisky from the mini-bar.

He could go and see the group tomorrow morning, he thought, swigging the drink in one. Or maybe it was a piece of information, albeit mostly useless, that he could share with DI Blackwell.

Buoyed by the thought, he took the last bottle out of the fridge and downed it in one before collapsing on to the bed.

Chapter Twenty

Coulson handed Louise the laptop. 'She'd been talking to him via a bespoke app I haven't come across before. Looks similar to WhatsApp but better encryption. Probably innocuous but you never know.'

Madison appeared to have been in conversation with someone called Ben. As Coulson suggested, the conversations seemed innocuous, Louise's interest only piqued when she saw mention of the attacks on the sheep and a link Ben had sent the girl. 'Do we know who this Ben is?' asked Louise, opening the link.

'Ben Collins,' said Coulson.

'Oh yes,' said Louise, reading Collins's name at the beginning of a short story. The tale was about ritual killings on the Cheddar clifftops. Some of the details were unnervingly accurate, though Louise supposed the author could easily have found out such details from the newspaper articles. In Collins's story, the sheep were killed by a group of witches who lived in caves deep into the Mendip Hills. 'You have more than a name for me, I take it?'

'Ben Collins goes to the same school as Madison. He's seventeen and in the lower sixth form. They've been chatting to each other for the last three months. It seems they have a shared interest. From what I've read I wouldn't say the macabre exactly, but they're both interested in myths and legends. They point each other to various articles on Cheddar Man and the history of the caves and the surrounding area.'

'Anything untoward?'

'Not that I can see,' said Coulson.

It was a precarious situation. In basic terms, there was nothing wrong in the two schoolchildren talking. As Louise read through more of the exchanges, she could see there was a naivety between the interactions which, as Coulson stated, centred around a shared fascination on the more supernatural elements of local history. She'd read some of the quotes forwarded by the boy in Madison's project and couldn't see anything inappropriate. That didn't mean she shouldn't act. Right or wrong, the boy was six years Madison's senior, and with the girl missing, Louise had to act now. 'You have an address for me?'

Coulson nodded.

◆ ◆ ◆

The Collins house was three streets down from Madison's. Louise took Coulson and Thomas with her. The streets were empty. A lone bedroom light glowed from one of the houses along the street, the Collins house cloaked in darkness. It was 3 a.m. but she had no qualms about ringing the doorbell.

She was surprised when the outline of a figure approached the front door seconds later. 'Who's there?' it said.

'Mrs Collins?' asked Louise. 'I'm so sorry to disturb you at this time of the morning. My name is Detective Inspector Louise Blackwell. I'm investigating the disappearance of Madison Pemberton. I was wondering if I could come in to talk to you. I am here with two of my colleagues, DS Thomas Ireland and Simon Coulson.'

Louise held out her warrant card as the door opened. 'Sarah Collins,' said the woman, who was wrapped in a dressing gown. 'I couldn't sleep,' she said, as way of explanation.

'Can we come in?' said Louise.

Sarah lowered her eyes, through confusion or guilt. 'Come in,' she said, leading them down the hallway to a kitchen area. 'Can I get you some tea?' she asked, pointing to an old-fashioned kettle sitting on the hob of an Aga cooker.

'We're fine,' said Louise.

'Sorry, I'm not with it. Why are you here at this time of the morning?'

Louise told her what they'd discovered about Ben and Madison. 'We were hoping to speak to Ben,' she said.

'At this time of night?'

'If he can help in any way then it would be worth it,' said Louise.

'He doesn't know anything about Madison's disappearance,' said Sarah.

Louise nodded. Time would come soon when she would have to insist on speaking to the boy but she wanted to keep things cordial for now. In her experience, most parents would be distraught if they knew the number of things their children kept from them, and she doubted Ben was any different. 'Did you know Ben was talking to Madison?'

'Yes, actually,' said Sarah, with a hint of impatience and annoyance. 'They are in an after-school club together. He's devastated by her disappearance, as am I. That's why I'm still up.'

Louise exchanged looks with Thomas and Coulson.

'Claire called me,' said Sarah, as way of explanation.

'I understand, this is very traumatic for everyone. May I ask what the club is they are members of?'

'It's an after-school writing club. They get together and work through themes. According to Ben, Madison is quite the talent,' said Sarah, her eyebrows furrowing as if a thought had just come to her. 'Listen, this is nothing to do with age is it? There are other people in Ben's class who are in the club. The school is very inclusive and encourages all age groups to mix together. Ben and Madison were working on a story together so . . .'

Louise understood the woman's defensiveness. 'We just want to find Madison. May we speak to Ben? You would be present at all times.'

'Are you sure it's totally necessary? With all that's happened, I'd much rather he got a good rest.'

Louise didn't answer. She smiled politely and waited. In the end, the mother's decision was made for her. Her husband and son appeared in the room wearing matching dressing gowns. 'It's okay, Mum, I don't mind speaking to them,' said the son.

'You must be Ben,' said Louise.

'Yes,' said the boy. Louise hadn't quite pictured what the boy would look like but it hadn't been this. He looked closer in age to the missing girl than he did to a seventeen-year-old. He was thin and wiry, his thick glasses only increasing his boyishness. Louise wouldn't have given it a second thought if she'd seen him with Madison, and she had to wonder if that was the reason he'd befriended the girl.

'Please take a seat, Ben. Mr Collins?' she said to the man.

'Andy,' said the dad. 'I heard your conversation with my wife and thought it best to get this over and done with,' he said, clearly unhappy to find himself in this situation.

'Thank you, this won't take long. Ben, sorry to wake you. I just need to ask you a few questions about Madison. You're not in any trouble. In situations like this, the more we find out – and that can be the simplest things, things you might think quite irrelevant – the better the chance of us finding the missing person. Does that make sense, Ben?'

Ben looked at his father before nodding his head.

'That's great, Ben. I understand from your mum that you are in the same after-school club as Madison. Is that correct?'

'Yes.'

'Can you tell me about the project you've been working on together?'

Ben looked at his mother this time. He appeared reluctant to speak but eventually answered. 'Our plan is to write a number of interconnected stories regarding Cheddar and the surrounding areas.'

'That sounds very interesting. Is there anything specific about the theme or content of the stories?'

Ben scrunched his eyes, as if sensing Louise knew more than she was saying. 'The stories are more about the legends of the area. I guess they're fantastical in nature. You might say supernatural.'

The boy had a very clear way of speaking, his word choice and mannerisms in stark contrast to the way he looked. 'Could you be more specific?' said Louise.

Ben sighed. 'I've recently written a story about Cheddar Man.'

'Cheddar Man?' said Louise. Louise had read about the skeletal remains that had been in the caves but wanted to keep the boy talking.

'The skeleton discovered in Gough's Cave. It's the oldest fossilised human in the country. We thought it would be fun to write a story about what had happened to him. To imagine at least.'

'Yes, I remember. Wasn't he bludgeoned to death?'

'What is this?' asked Mr Collins.

'Please, sir,' said Thomas. 'Let them finish.'

Ben hesitated, looking at both parents before continuing. 'It was Madison's idea. She knows loads about these things.'

'Is that why you chose to work with her?' asked Louise.

'Yes. The others . . . the others just want to write space operas, or gaudy police stories.'

'Well, we are very gaudy,' said Louise. She was pleased the boy was beginning to relax a little, and hoped it would make him more responsive.

'Madison is different. She's much more mature than her friends. She knows things and we have the same interests, so . . .'

'You don't have to defend yourself, Ben,' said Sarah.

The boy's mother was right but Louise wondered if there was a reason for his defensiveness.

'I'm not,' said Ben, raising his voice, hinting at the teenager behind his mature demeanour.

Louise wanted to keep him talking. 'Do you write the stories together?' she asked.

'No, we write separate stories and then edit each other.'

'We found your story at Madison's house but haven't found any of her stories yet. Has she sent you anything?'

Ben blushed. 'Yes, I have one of her stories. It's in my room.'

'Could you?' said Thomas to Mr Collins.

'You'll have to bring my laptop down,' said Ben, as his dad walked off.

'While we're waiting, can you tell me the last time you saw Madison?' asked Louise.

'I saw her yesterday. She was in the village with her friends.'

'What were you doing?' said Louise, careful to keep her tone as light as possible.

'I was going to the shops for some milk.'

'You spoke to her then?'

Ben shook his head.

'Did she see you?'

Ben lowered his eyes.

'It's okay,' said his mum.

'We saw each other but didn't say hello. You just don't do that,' said Ben.

'I understand,' said Louise, as his dad returned and gave him the laptop.

Louise could tell the boy was embarrassed and didn't push him any further.

'Do you mind if I have a quick read?' said Louise.

Ben puffed out his cheeks. 'Here,' he said, handing her his laptop. 'I've been doing some editing.'

The story was three pages long. Ben studied her intently as she read. When she'd finished she gave the laptop to Thomas to read. 'When did Madison write this, Ben?' asked Louise.

'Friday. She's a quick writer. I let her borrow my laptop at school as she'd forgotten hers.'

'You're sure she wrote this on Friday?'

'How else would she have known about the sheep?' asked Ben.

'The sheep?' asked Mrs Collins. 'What sheep?'

'Thomas, show Mr and Mrs Collins when you're finished,' said Louise, noticing Ben sink back into the sofa as if wanting to disappear.

The story centred around a group of people who sacrificed the wild sheep on the Cheddar hills. Madison didn't directly allude to it in the tale, but the suggestion was that the group was made up of modern-day witches. They believed sacrificing the sheep would ultimately protect the environment of the Mendips.

Louise waited for Ben's parents to stop reading. His mother stared at her as if the revelation about Madison's story was Louise's fault, before speaking to her son. 'Ben, do you know something we should know?'

'No. Like what?' said Ben, his politeness seemingly reserved solely for Louise.

'It just seems coincidental that Madison would choose to write a story about the cliffs, and the . . . sheep, the day before she disappears.'

'She was interested in what happened to them,' said Ben, more to Louise than his mother. 'She'd already been studying those things so when it had happened to the sheep, it made sense for her to write the story. I don't know.'

'Those things?'

'All the weird stuff that used to go on around here.'

'But she wrote this story purely from imagination?' asked Louise.

'Yes, of course.'

'She didn't know this was going to happen?'

'No, I promise,' said Ben, close to tears.

'But there is something, isn't there?'

'I didn't think she would do it.'

'Do what, Ben?' said Mr Collins.

'She said she was going to go and find out who was responsible.'

Chapter Twenty-One

Mornings like this were rare for Hoxton. He was usually awake at some ungodly hour, nursing a hangover. But the two slim bottles of whisky he'd downed just after midnight had lulled him into an unusually restful sleep. He was awake, now, feeling like all he'd drunk the night before was water. With renewed energy, he'd set off for the Mendip Hills straight after breakfast and now was the only car driving through the narrow country road.

He passed a signpost for an army training base in Yoxter before, further inland, taking a turn down a single-track road. Such journeys always uplifted him. He enjoyed the remoteness of the area, and the fact that such places still existed. He understood the direct contradiction with the work he did for Walsh but if it was up to him, such areas would remain undeveloped.

In part, it was how he justified his work. Walsh would go ahead with his developments with or without him. But being in his employ meant that Hoxton could occasionally steer Walsh in the right direction.

Not that the group Hoxton was driving to meet would agree with such a brittle justification. They'd made it clear last time that he wasn't welcome and had all but driven him off the site. And as he pulled up to the farmland he grew concerned that he'd been sent on another fool's errand.

Trailers and caravans dotted the entrance to the land. The farm was no longer in working use. The previous owner had bequeathed it to the environmental group and now they lived together in some form of collective.

The faces of the residents were always changing. Hoxton received some stares as he pulled up and made his way across the mud to the main building. Cold, musty air drifted his way as he opened the front door of the main building. With concrete floors and high ceilings, it felt colder inside than out. Tables with long wooden seats were arranged in the open space, a number of people were eating breakfast. The walls were adorned with flags and posters of dizzying colours. Hoxton knew many of the group travelled the country attending protests; many had been arrested in London during a recent climate change protest.

Hoxton had sympathy for their cause. The world was undergoing an environmental crisis and things were likely to get much worse in future years. It was easy to dismiss the protestors. They didn't fit in easily with an often indifferent society, and Hoxton didn't need to work in the system to know that, however loud they shouted, they would always be drowned out by the sound of big money.

He did the small things. Recycled when he could. Ate organic. But when you worked for a man who used a private jet on an almost daily basis you didn't really get to have an opinion on such matters. It made him think once again that he should look for another career; made him regret the fact that he couldn't think of anything he was remotely passionate about.

In his suit, Hoxton felt woefully overdressed. Breakfast was laid out canteen-style, and he poured himself a coffee from a large metal urn, regretting the decision after the first sip of the mud-coloured water. From behind the serving counter, a woman who must have been in her sixties studied him with interest. She wore the collective uniform of well-worn jeans and colourful fleece, her grey hair a matted mess of dreadlocks.

'Can I help you?' she said, a hint of amusement in her eyes.

'I'm here to see Sam.'

'Are you now? And which Sam would that be?' Her accent was an odd mix; Hoxton noted hints of Mancunian and the West Country.

'Sam Amstell.' Hoxton had tried calling earlier, but Amstell hadn't picked up.

The woman nodded. As far as Hoxton could tell, Amstell was as close a thing to a leader the group had. With a double first from Oxford, the man had given up a lot to live as part of the collective. Hoxton had met him on a couple of occasions. Amstell was one of many who opposed Walsh's developments, but he was also amenable and had liaised with Hoxton on parts of the project. It was more than just lip service. Walsh knew the benefits of keeping the protestors at least half on side, and Amstell had given them some sound advice and even put them in contact with a sustainable timber supplier from Cornwall. From Amstell's perspective, he didn't want the project to go ahead but if it was inevitable, he wanted it to be as environmentally sound as it could be.

'And what would you be wanting with Mr Amstell?' said the woman, her accent veering more towards the West Country this time.

'Please could you just tell me where he is?'

The woman sighed, her eyes running up and down his body. The verdict didn't seem positive. She scowled. 'You could try his hut,' she said.

Hoxton smiled when he wanted to scream. 'Would you be able to point that out to me?' he asked.

'Don't want much, do you?' said the woman.

Beyond his suit, Hoxton was at a loss as to the reason for the woman's animosity. 'Please, I would really appreciate it.'

The woman sighed once more and took a piece of paper and scribbled down a rudimentary map. 'You'll have to walk,' she said.

Hoxton thanked her and took the map. 'How far are we talking?'

'A good three miles,' said the woman, with an ungracious smile.

◆ ◆ ◆

Hoxton tried Amstell's phone again before retrieving his walking boots and rain jacket from his car. Initially, he'd thought the woman had been joking, but looking at the map and the layout of the land the estimate may have been on the conservative side.

Hoxton made sure to turn on his phone's GPS before setting off. The map was at best rudimentary, but the entrance through a copse of sycamore trees was easy enough to find. Stepping through the threshold of the woodland, Hoxton had a sudden urge to turn back. The overhanging trees changed the light and, for a second, it was as if he was back in the caves in Cheddar. As he crunched deeper through the undergrowth, he strained his hearing. Behind the birdsong and various rustling sounds, he thought he caught snippets of the ragged breathing he vaguely remembered from that night with Jennings and the others.

He stopped and closed his eyes. The only sound he could hear was his own laboured breathing. He'd never suffered from claustrophobia and was surprised by his reaction. The open space of the commune was less than a few hundred metres behind him so it was irrational to feel trapped. His hand reached for his phone and he double-checked that his progress was being monitored before continuing.

His mind played tricks on him. Although he was all but certain that Amstell and the commune had nothing to do with the recent events in Cheddar, something or someone had been responsible. And in his current paranoid state, it wasn't a stretch to imagine them following him now. If something was after him then all he would have to defend himself with was his wits, and in his current mindset they would be next to useless. Every fifty or so metres he stopped and turned, cursing his irrationality as he pictured someone or something following him.

The pathway began to narrow, his way hindered by low branches and brambles. Hoxton had seen the aerial view of this area from the cliff walk in Cheddar. The cover of trees stretched for miles in all directions. Although he'd only been walking for thirty minutes or so, it was easy to imagine how easy it would be to get lost. He didn't have even the most basic of survival skills; couldn't even begin to work out which way was north, even if that would have been a help to him. Again he checked his phone, dismayed both by his reliance on it and the forty-three per cent power that remained on the device.

'Fuck,' he shouted, his voice carrying in the deserted area.

He was about to turn back when a voice called out to him, spiking his pulse rate so quickly that he fell to his haunches. 'I didn't think you'd give up so easy,' it said.

Hoxton felt as if every hangover he'd experienced in the last month was crashing down on him. He was nauseous and dizzy. He wanted to sit down but feared he was about to be attacked.

'Here, have some water,' said the voice. A figure emerged from the trees in front of him and held out a flask.

Hoxton blinked and looked up at him. 'What the fuck is going on, Sam?' he said.

'Abi radioed to say you were on your way to me. You were taking so long I thought I'd come to check on you,' said Amstell, who was standing over him with his arm outstretched.

Hoxton grabbed the water from the man. 'She said it was three miles.'

'Give or take a mile,' said Amstell, pulling Hoxton to his feet. 'You really should have called.'

'Funny,' said Hoxton. He drank the water, some of his energy returning as Amstell led him through the woodland area to a clearing where a small wooden hut was situated.

'Tea?' said Amstell, pointing to a pair of rusted garden chairs outside the hut, which had the appearance of an extended garden shed.

Hoxton nodded and took a seat. He couldn't comprehend how anyone could live so remotely. Yet, as he waited for Amstell to return, he began to appreciate the tranquillity of the area. They were only a mile or so away from the normal world but they may as well have been a hundred. The only sounds were the hum of the wildlife, and the gentle rustle of the wind through the trees. Maybe it would be good to occasionally lose himself in a place like this he thought, but as the wind whistled through the branches and something unidentifiable scurried through the undergrowth, he conceded that maybe a few minutes would suffice.

'So what's this all about?' said Amstell, returning with two chipped mugs and handing one to Hoxton. Amstell wore oversized cargo trousers and a fleece. Like the woman in the kitchen area, his hair was long and matted, though unlike hers it was thick and jet black.

'I'm here about what's happening up the road,' said Hoxton.

'And what's that?'

'You don't need to play dumb with me, Sam. I realise you all like to live as one with the land or whatever, but I know you're hooked up to the internet. I even know you have a phone despite it never being switched on.'

Amstell chuckled. He had an easy way about him and with a change of clothes and a clean shave, Hoxton could picture him working in the same circles as Jennings and Walsh. 'I heard about the missing girl. Tragic business.'

It was tragic and Hoxton realised he hadn't truly acknowledged the fact. He'd been too busy doing Walsh's legwork to consider that somewhere the girl's family would be enduring the worst time imaginable. It made what he had to say next meaningless, yet he proceeded. 'It's partly why I'm here.'

Amstell frowned but didn't comment.

Hoxton took a breath, and it felt like the longest he'd ever taken. He sucked in the air of the clearing, the dank smell of the grass and mud, the wet leaves mulched on the ground. 'We would love to help the authorities find this girl. To stop whoever is committing these attacks. We thought . . .'

'You thought?' said Amstell, his mouth tightening.

'Look, Sam, I wouldn't for a second suggest you had anything to do with this . . .'

'That's something I suppose.'

'But you, more than anyone, know what goes on around here.'

'You think I know who's responsible? You want to check my hut, Richard? See if the girl's in there?'

'No, of course not,' said Hoxton, thinking once again about his fool's errand. 'Stephen sent me. He'd like to make an offer. He just wants your help.'

'You people just don't get it, do you?' Amstell turned away and stared towards the woodland behind his hut where the trees were denser. He stayed that way for a few minutes, Hoxton content to sip at his tea as he waited. Eventually, Amstell turned back to look at him. 'You don't honestly think we would stage something like this to distract from your developments do you?'

'No, that's not what we're saying.'

'We care about the land, Richard, about the wildlife, about the air we breathe. But we also care about one another. You think we would slaughter those sheep, attack a man and abduct a girl?'

Amstell was growing angry. Hoxton feared he'd wasted his time. 'No one is saying that, Sam, believe me. It's just that if anyone knows something about what is going on, it would be you. You're all but worshipped by the people in these parts, you know that.'

'I'm sorry, I can't help you.'

'Walsh is keen to make a contribution to your work here,' said Hoxton, handing him an envelope.

'One, you can't buy me off. Two, I don't know anything,' said Amstell, not letting go of the envelope.

Hoxton had thought the conversation would unfold along these lines. It was true what he'd said about Amstell. Not only was he revered by the people in the commune, his influence spread further across the Mendips and surrounding countryside. Amstell was a man in the know and he would have, at the very least, heard rumours. Hoxton had one further hand to play and he did it reluctantly. 'I'm sure there are other people who would like to speak to you about this?' he said.

Amstell smirked. 'It would be much easier for all of us if you showed your true colours to begin with, Richard.'

'I just want some help, Sam. Think of the girl's poor family.'

'Shame on you, Richard. You come here and threaten me, and then have the audacity to suggest you're here for the girl's family. I don't have anything to hide so send who you want. You'd be surprised by the people I know, Richard.'

Hoxton sighed inwardly. Amstell had relationships with the press and the local police. Walsh's investigation into him had revealed that, and now he felt foolish for his idle threat. 'The offer stands,' he said, getting to his feet.

'The way out is back through there,' said Amstell. 'You'll find it much easier to leave.'

Amstell was right. Once Hoxton found the track, the way back out of the woodland was much easier, his progress aided by his speedier pace. He didn't once look back, but it was only when he reached the clearing and his car that he was fully able to shake the feeling that he'd been followed all the way.

Chapter Twenty-Two

He remembered the man.

The man had been in Cox's Cave the other night, drunk with his idiot friends. He'd meant to scare him then and it had worked. He detested the men and all they stood for. They wanted to destroy the land, and the man had been all too willing to help, but had it been the right way to go about it? He couldn't shake the feeling that it had been a mistake and that his actions had led to his current situation.

After watching the man leave the commune, he had hiked back through the countryside. It would take hours but would give him the chance to think. He avoided the tracks as much as he was able, navigating his way through the woodlands on instinct. He revelled in the earthly smells and the sound of the teeming wildlife. When he did encounter other people he avoided eye contact, fearing his guilt would be evident.

Taking the girl had been an obvious error. For a glorious moment he thought Jack had returned. In the gloom, he'd mistaken her for a boy, her narrow shoulders and frame so reminiscent of Jack, and he hadn't understood his error until he'd taken her to a safe place. Now, he needed to get back to her. It wasn't her fault and he didn't want her to suffer. But letting her go wasn't an option.

He wouldn't be able to find Jack from a prison cell.

He hid in the undergrowth as a family walked along the cliff walk that led back to Cheddar. He withdrew his knife as their dog, a slobbering Dalmatian, stopped metres away. He covered his mouth with his hand as he began to cough, his palm coated by a thick gluey substance. The dog tilted its head to one side. It didn't look mean but he couldn't risk being found. 'Go,' he said, wiping his hand on the undergrowth.

The dog's ears pushed back against its skull. 'Go,' he repeated, relieved as through the brambles he saw the dad summon the dog back to the path. He was holding hands with a child.

This time he was sure the child was a boy.

He held in another cough, a ray of sunshine catching on the blade of his knife as the dog ran back to its master. The mother grabbed the child's other hand as if alert to the unknown danger.

It could all be over in a few seconds. The family were strangers to the land and he could move undetected. He could take the boy before they'd even realised he was there; could take the boy to his wife, and they could start again.

But it wasn't Jack.

He coughed, breaking the spell. The dog barked and the parents upped their pace as a group of ramblers came into view from the opposite direction. The coughing intensified and he retreated further back into the undergrowth, his chest stinging as a loose vine ripped open the skin on his forehead. In the background the ramblers were talking to the family as the dog stuck its nose further into the undergrowth having caught his scent.

The dog's snuffling nose came closer, its fur catching on the brambles. Maybe it was the sign he needed. He could give himself in, let the girl be rescued and put all this foolishness behind him.

He placed the knife back in its sheath, his hand about to reach for the dog, when its owner shouted out to him again. Ears pricked, the dog made one last grasp for him, its snout only inches away, when its master reached in and yanked it back by the collar.

He lay that way for some time, watching the family and the ramblers move in opposite directions, the dog looking back every now and then as if to check it wasn't being followed.

Chapter Twenty-Three

By the time they reached the cliff walk, the sun had already burnt through the early morning mist though the ground was still solid underfoot. The community had come out in force. The mood was sullen but optimistic as Louise organised the various factions. The search began at the foot of Jacob's Ladder. On the cliff walk, teams were sent in various directions. The helicopter and drones were backup, and following her conversation with Ben Collins, Louise had doubled the number of the dog teams tracking for Madison through the Mendips. There was a three-mile circular route at the top of the cliffs, but the path also extended deep into the hills. The area was over seventy square miles, much of which was sheltered beneath trees.

Louise held a copy of Madison's short story in her jacket. The sheep attack had been widely reported in the local media, but the details in Madison's tale were very specific and detailed. It was as if Madison had witnessed the attack, despite assurances from both parents that she'd been home that night.

Of greater concern to Louise had been Ben's final revelation – that Madison had intended to find out who was responsible. Louise tried to view it as a positive. It was feasible that Madison had gone searching for the attacker and had become lost or injured. Despite the cold, it was likely the girl would have managed to survive the night in the thick woodland. She wouldn't have been able to travel too far afield in the darkness, and sooner or later the dogs would be able to pick up her scent.

Yet the more likely alternative really troubled Louise; that Madison had got her wish and found out who had killed the sheep and attacked Mr Tabart, and was now either under their control, or had suffered at their hand.

Hard as it was, the only way forward was through procedure and process. Starting from the foot of the pathway in the village, she followed the path taken by the search teams. She tried to place herself in Madison's position, mustering a sense of curiosity and outrage at what had happened to the sheep. But when she reached the summit, it was impossible to know for sure where the girl would go next. Louise had walked the same path last night and the only difference now was that Madison's motivation may have changed.

Even that was fanciful. What could the girl really have hoped to have achieved on her own, even if by some miracle she'd come across the attacker? Louise's best guess was she'd made the journey in the relative comfort of knowing it was daylight and there were plenty of other people on the walk.

And then something had gone wrong.

She stood in the area where Madison's phone had been discovered. In daylight, the extent of the surrounding area was intimidating. The limestone hills stretched as far as the eye could see. It was hard not to be despondent, but Louise couldn't let her team, or Madison's parents, sense any hint of negativity.

Louise split the rest of the day between the incident room and the Pemberton household. She began sending her team home for rest. Many of them had been on shift for close to twenty-four hours and although she admired the way they all wanted to continue, rest was essential if they were to do their job properly.

Despite this, she resisted taking her own advice later in the day when Thomas found her close to sleep on the sofa in the Pembertons' living room.

'You won't thank me for this, boss, but you're looking tired. Even in this light,' he said.

'Charming,' said Louise. She couldn't deny the fatigue in her body. She'd been on her feet all day. The muscles in her legs were tight and she had to keep stretching to banish the pain in her lower back. She would have loved to return home for a few hours but the sight of Madison's parents kept her in place.

Both parents had insisted on helping the search. Through the day, Louise had witnessed the painful snatches of hope in their eyes every time a piece of information was radioed through to her. And now that night was drawing in, Louise saw the dawning realisation on their faces. Leaving now would be abandoning them, and she wasn't prepared to do that.

'Remember what you told me this morning?' said Thomas.

'That your tie didn't match your shirt?' said Louise, not ready to listen to her colleague.

'Yes, there was that. But you also said I was no good to anyone tired. I'm rested up now and can take over. Leave your phone on and if we get anything I'll call you immediately.'

Louise sighed, a heaviness to her breathing she hadn't expected. 'Make sure you do,' she said, reluctantly making her way to her car.

◆ ◆ ◆

She was back home in thirty minutes, driving on autopilot. She managed to set her alarm before collapsing fully dressed on her bed. Her sleep was punctuated with uneasy dreams of the gorge interspersed with images of Paul and Emily at the caravan site in Cornwall, and the fire on the old pier.

When her phone rang, it took a few seconds to orientate herself. 'Yes?' she said, still not fully awake as she answered.

'DI Blackwell?' The voice on the other end was familiar but she couldn't yet place it.

'Who is this?' she said, pulling the duvet over her.

'Apologies for calling you this late, and on a Sunday. It's Richard Hoxton.'

Louise blinked as if doing so would banish the tiredness. Remembering she'd seen Hoxton in the village a couple of hours before Madison went missing, her tiredness vanished. She sat up in bed, alert as if she'd just finished the day's first coffee. 'Mr Hoxton, how may I help you?' she said, hoping for the man's sake that he had something worthwhile to tell her.

Hoxton paused as if preparing his next words. 'I was wondering if you would be free to meet up for a drink tonight?'

Louise's grip on her phone tightened. She pulled it from her ear and read the time on the screen. It was 9.30 p.m.. Admittedly, she'd been rather taken with Hoxton on both the occasions she'd met him, but she'd been clear when he'd asked her out. 'Mr Hoxton, you do know what has happened in Cheddar, don't you?'

'I apologise, you misunderstand me. This isn't a social call. I need to speak to you.'

'This is about the missing girl?'

'I'm not sure, but there is something I think you should know.'

Louise felt like she was crashing, the initial surge of adrenaline she'd felt fading and making her more tired. 'Could this not wait until tomorrow?'

'I imagine it could, but I thought in cases like this every second was precious,' said Hoxton.

'Whatever you need to tell me you can say on the phone,' said Louise.

'I'd rather meet face to face. This is going to sound a little far-fetched,' said Hoxton.

'Believe me, it would take a lot to surprise me at this point.'

Hoxton told her of his visit to the commune in the Mendips earlier that day; his trail through the woods to the secluded hut. Louise made a note of the names, underlining the mention of Sam Amstell, but wasn't sure what Hoxton was hoping to achieve with his disclosure. 'Do you think this organisation has anything to do with Madison Pemberton's disappearance, Mr Hoxton?' she asked.

Hoxton was flustered. Louise was sure he'd been drinking but didn't mention it. 'I don't know. Something weird is going on down there. I'm sorry, I shouldn't have called,' he said.

Louise agreed with his sentiment. She'd been asleep for less than two hours and doubted she'd be able to return to sleep. However, at this point every bit of information, however minimal, could prove to be vital. She thanked Hoxton and hung up before calling Thomas. 'Have you heard of this group?' she asked, after relaying details of the call.

'There was a drugs bust there I believe but that was two or three years ago. I could pay them a visit now?'

Louise checked the time again. In normal circumstances she would wait until the morning but the girl had been missing for over twenty-four hours. 'I'll head down there now,' she said.

'You're supposed to be resting,' said Thomas.

'I won't be going back to sleep so I might as well be useful. Get me a number for this Sam Amstell when you can,' she said, hanging up and stumbling to the kitchen where she switched on the coffee maker.

She'd worked on missing person cases before during her time in MIT. Disappearances were more common than the general public would imagine. Only a few ever made the front page or national news. People disappeared all the time.

Sometimes they came back, sometimes they didn't.

As she waited for the coffee to brew, she forced down some cereal. In her living room, she pinned up photos of Madison Pemberton and her parents. Below Madison, she pinned up a photo of Ben Collins. She'd all but ruled the boy out of the investigation but wasn't yet ready to eliminate him completely. On the opposite wall she frowned at the picture of her dead brother. She'd seen her parents and Emily yesterday, but it felt like a lifetime ago. Finding Madison was a priority but that didn't ease her guilt every time she thought of her family. The investigation into Paul's murder had stalled; if she didn't get it back on track it would be shelved and forgotten, and here she was focusing all her attention elsewhere. But there was a missing girl here, and she had to be the priority.

From the kitchen she heard the steady drip of the coffee falling into the pot. Her eyelids began to lower and she shook to stop herself falling back to sleep. Coffee brewed, she poured a cup before filling a flask for a journey. It was going to be a long night.

◆ ◆ ◆

The torchlight acted as a beacon, guiding Louise to a stop in the commune's car-park. The journey had been a surreal one – she'd only seen three other cars, each going in the opposite direction – and if it hadn't been for the torch, and the man holding it, she would have doubted she was in the right place. The man appeared to be standing in the middle of a flat plain, and it was only as she approached the light and stopped her car that she made out the distant shape of a large building fifty metres behind him.

Thomas had called ahead, but she wasn't taking any chances. She opened her window a few inches and introduced herself.

The man nodded. 'Sam Amstell,' he said. 'If you like you can come into the main building.'

Amstell wasn't like she'd imagined. She'd pictured some twenty-something eco-warrior but the man was closer to her own age. She locked up and followed him to the main building, light spilling into the fog as he opened the heavy door.

The temperature didn't ease as Louise stepped inside. The interior of the brick building had concrete floors and high ceilings where the air was as cold as it was outside. It would be expensive to heat so it appeared its owners hadn't bothered.

Amstell led her to a long trestle dining table and they sat facing each other. If he was annoyed at having to see her at such an unsociable hour, he hid it well. 'Sorry, no heating,' he said, realising her fears. 'We have a wood fire but we restrict its usage.'

'That's fine,' said Louise. 'Hopefully this shouldn't take long. You spoke to my colleague?'

'DS Ireland, yes.'

'You know about recent events in Cheddar?' said Louise.

'Of course. That's why I agreed to see you, but why do you want to speak to me?' said Amstell.

'Thank you for understanding, Mr Amstell. It is appreciated. What can you tell me about your group? How many people live here? Is this building occupied?'

Amstell frowned. She wasn't directly answering his question – and didn't have any intention of doing so just yet. 'No one lives in this building. We can't get the safety certificates. We own the land and people can come and stay. Contribute what they can. We have about sixty-five on site at present.'

'And that's how you fund yourselves. Contributions?'

'Mainly, yes. We work the land together. Fortunately we have a few wealthy sponsors who help out.'

Louise nodded. She quizzed Amstell further about the group and he provided the standard answers about their environmental activities. 'We try to be law abiding at all times but sometimes that isn't possible,' he said.

'In what way?' said Louise.

'Some people are more equal than others in the eyes of the law.'

'Is that so?'

'Our protests are always peaceful.'

'But sometimes disruptive?' said Louise.

'As I said. Just because something is made illegal because it inconveniences a few people it doesn't make it morally wrong.'

Louise wasn't there to debate the intricacies of morality and the law. 'And as a group, you're opposed to the planned developments in Cheddar Gorge?'

Amstell smiled and nodded. 'I thought as much. Richard Hoxton has been on to you, hasn't he? Man, to think he's one of the ones I can get on with. You think they care about that missing girl? All they care about is the delay to their building projects. Listen, I would like to help you, Inspector, but this is absurd.'

Amstell stood but Louise remained sitting. 'I understand your frustration, sir, but we have to investigate these things.'

Amstell crossed his arms, his voice rising as he spoke. 'You don't think we would kidnap a girl just to try to stop that development, do you? If it was the other way around, if I'd accused Hoxton or Walsh of doing something like this, would you have taken them seriously? I don't think so.'

'No one is accusing anyone of doing anything, Mr Amstell. My only concern is finding the girl.'

Amstell unfolded his arms. 'My apologies. I understand what you're saying and I'll do anything I can to help. You can search every inch of this land and we'll give you all the assistance you need. But you must understand my position. Every time there is a hint of a crime, the finger is always pointed at us. And the real criminals,

Hoxton and Walsh, and the others who want to destroy our land, get to do what they want.'

Louise regretted her decision to answer Hoxton's late night phone call. Whether Amstell liked it or not, she would have to send a team to the area at first light. It wasn't something they could risk overlooking, even though she was all but certain she would be wasting her time.

◆ ◆ ◆

It was two in the morning by the time she reached the Pemberton house in Cheddar. The stillness in the area was foreboding; the lack of helicopter in the night sky disquieting, as if they were admitting defeat.

Thomas was in the dining room staring at his laptop screen. He slowly lifted his head as Louise crept into the room, a frown forming. 'You should have gone back for more sleep,' he said.

'Where are they?' she asked.

'In their bedroom. Alison somehow managed to get them to try and sleep. She's trying to get some rest in the living room.'

Louise doubted the parents were resting. They would see it as a sign of betrayal. The next time either of them would sleep would be through sheer exhaustion. Louise hoped she could get them some answers before then.

Pouring coffee from her flask, she updated Thomas on her meeting with Amstell. The tiredness in her colleague's eyes was unmistakable. No doubt he would have spent some of his time thinking about his young son, and imagining the same thing happening to him. However detached you learnt to be in the job, it was impossible not to transfer events to your own personal circumstances. 'Why don't you try and get some rest?' she said. 'I'd rather have you fighting fit first thing in the morning than sitting up here all night.'

Thomas rubbed his eyes. 'I'll try and find a quiet spot,' he said, moving into the living room area where the FLO was sleeping.

Louise took his place in the chair and closed her eyes. The sounds of the house – the water in the pipes, the creaking of the wooden boards – played through her head as she tried to assess the situation. It was over twenty-four hours now since Madison had gone missing, and already they were being dragged in too many different directions. She made a mental note of the tasks she wanted to complete. She'd already ordered Thomas to arrange a search of the commune. Now she wanted to speak to Hoxton again, as well as Madison's friends and teachers, and members of the council. Each of them would have already been contacted but Louise wanted to speak to them personally.

If there was an answer to be found – and the stark reality was this wasn't always the case – then she had to declutter the distractions.

A theory had been playing at the periphery of her thoughts. They'd been working under the assumption that the attacker's behaviour was escalating. First the sheep, then Tabart, and now the girl.

But what if the child, or *a* child at least, had been the target all along? What if the sheep and then Tabart were mistakes borne out of frustration at not finding the right target?

This uncomfortable thought accompanied Louise into an uneasy sleep.

Chapter Twenty-Four

The search continued the following morning, Louise splitting her time between Cheddar and the incident room in Weston. Officers and volunteers covered the cliff walk, their search extending further and further into the Mendips. No one dared mention it, but Louise knew what her fellow officers were thinking. Each passing hour reduced the chances of ever finding the girl again. The fear galvanised the team, and Louise couldn't recall a time she'd seen so many fellow officers working around the clock.

Louise spent the day conducting interviews. She met with Madison's teachers – the school's headteacher having returned from a holiday abroad to assist with the search – her friends and extended family. No one was ruled out as a suspect – around half of all abduction cases were committed by family members, or those known to the victim – but Louise struggled to obtain anything significant from the interviews. The earlier incidents on the cliff walk were an added variable that confused matters. It was still impossible to decipher if the abductor's behaviour was an escalation or, as Louise had considered last night, that Madison had been the target all along.

From the interviews, a clearer picture of Madison was forming in Louise's mind. It was hard to be certain of its accuracy, as her disappearance distorted the way people viewed her, but Louise's impression was of a young girl, small for her age, reasonably popular, who had a close group of four or five friends. Her teachers suggested she was hard working, introverted but not averse to offering her opinions when called upon. Louise had skimmed further through the books she'd found in Madison's bedroom. She had a passion for fantasy and horror, and Louise was surprised that Madison's parents allowed her to read some of the titles on the bookcase.

'We tend to give her a lot of leeway when it comes to reading,' Madison's mother had told her, later that day at their house. 'I check each title and get guidance. As long as the books are not gratuitous, we allow her to read them. She's a very advanced reader and we don't want to stop that. And however hard we try and monitor it, she is only a click or two away from viewing things much worse on the internet. If I'm being honest, I'd rather she was reading books.'

Louise thought about Emily reading *The Sleeping Bug*, and disappearing into the fantasy world where she could forget the harsh realities of her life; maybe somewhere, Madison was reading a book of her own. The comparison brought feelings of guilt. She was so focused on finding Madison that Paul's case was currently an afterthought. It was the way it had to be but it didn't make it easier, and every day the investigation continued her guilt magnified.

◆ ◆ ◆

The rest of the week was spent working through MAPPA – the Multi-Agency Public Protection Arrangements – in the extended area, and narrowing down their searches in line with what had happened.

Louise was increasingly concerned that the attacker had succeeded in their goal, and that they may never hear from them again.

Tomorrow was Good Friday, and Madison had been missing for five days. The teams had scoured much of the Mendips but it was impossible to cover every square inch, and with nearly a week gone, both the attacker and Madison could be anywhere in the world.

And that was working on the presumption that Madison was still alive. But for now, that was the only approach they could take. The alternative was unthinkable. Louise was working closely with MIT who were busy cross-referencing all the missing cases over the last few years, searching for the merest hint of a connection to Madison's disappearance.

◆ ◆ ◆

Louise spent Thursday night at her parents' house. Although Cheddar was equidistant between Weston and Bristol, she felt a pang of guilt being away from the village. She'd been working eighteen- to twenty-hour days all week and as she sat on the sofa next to Emily, watching an animated film, she could barely keep her eyes open.

'Come on, sleepy,' she heard her dad say. She opened her eyes, surprised to see he was talking to her and not Emily who was wide-eyed watching the screen. 'Get some rest while you can,' he added, pulling Louise to her feet.

'Thanks, Dad,' she said, climbing the steps to her old bedroom where she was hit by the same feeling of nostalgia she always experienced when back at home. As it always was of late, the warm memories were tainted by Paul's absence, and she wondered if she would ever be able to remember her childhood again without the cloud of her brother's death hovering over her.

She double-checked her phone was switched on, the volume on maximum, before retreating under the covers. The strain was evident in her body. She felt like she was in mid-hangover. Nothing quite made sense and the swirling thoughts plaguing her mind were intensified by being in the surroundings of her childhood. She desired sleep but wanted to think about Madison Pemberton as well, as if letting the girl slip from her attention for even a second would condemn her to never being found.

As she played over the details she'd considered hundreds of times before, Louise reflected on the underlying reason why she was spending the night in Bristol. Yes, it was Easter weekend and she wanted to spend time with her niece and parents, but if she was being truthful to herself she was here for another reason. However hard she'd been working on the missing girl case, the investigation into Paul's murder still burnt away in the periphery of her thoughts. She'd tried telling herself that she should put it to one side until they'd found Madison, but there would always be something. If she didn't act soon then the investigation would be shelved. Someone had to keep the investigation alive, and although she shouldn't be anywhere near it, she intended to make her contribution the following morning.

In the end, sheer exhaustion dragged her to sleep. She was surprised to see it was 7 a.m. when she next opened her eyes. Heart beating fast she grabbed her phone, fearing she'd missed some important contact during the night, but the screen was devoid of messages.

With the rest of the house still asleep, Louise crept downstairs and made herself coffee. She yawned despite having had the best night's sleep since returning to work. Wanting to get back to Cheddar as soon as she could, she poured the coffee into her flask and left a note for her parents before leaving.

Fifteen minutes later, she pulled up outside Jodi Marshall's house. The terraced house was one of hundreds of identical buildings that covered the area. Each was adorned with grey pebble-dash and red-tiled roofs. Louise couldn't imagine anyone being able to design an estate more dreary looking. The dank colours bled into the grey sky, and Louise instinctively pulled her coat tighter as a shiver ran through her body.

There was movement behind the downstairs window in Jodi's house. Louise wasn't sure why she was there. She wanted to speak to the woman to find out how close she'd actually been with her brother, but it would be a risk. Chances were high that it would get back to Farrell, and therefore Finch. After Robertson's reprimand she wasn't sure it was a risk worth taking. She hadn't asked Farrell if he'd spoken to the woman before. If Tania knew about her, then Farrell would be aware. She trusted his judgement, and it was conceited to think she could gather information Farrell had missed. So what was the real reason for her being there?

Until she'd returned to work and questioned Everett, no one in the family had known about Paul's supposed affair with the woman. Her parents still didn't know, and maybe that was why she was sitting outside the stranger's house. Louise had grown apart from Paul over the last few years and maybe by speaking to Jodi, she could catch a glimpse of what his life had been like before he'd died, and could take a small dash of comfort from it.

In the end the decision was made for her. Louise had been sitting in the car for ninety minutes, co-ordinating events back in Cheddar by phone, when the front door opened and Jodi Marshall stepped out. Wrapped in a beige dressing gown, her hair dishevelled, the woman tiptoed to the end of her front path and deposited a bag of recycling in a green plastic box. She didn't know she was being watched and scratched her face as she filled the container with plastic and glass.

As she stood back up, she gazed out to the street revealing a pattern of red bloodlines that spread from her bruised eye and took up half her face.

Chapter Twenty-Five

The Clifton Suspension Bridge was visible from Richard Hoxton's hotel suite. Such was the density of the early morning fog it appeared that the crossing stopped halfway, swallowed by the swirling mist.

It was Easter weekend, and Hoxton had treated himself to a break at the five-star hotel. He needed to escape the cloying atmosphere in Cheddar. The week had crawled by, the girl's disappearance hanging over the village like the fog draping over Clifton, and Hoxton wasn't sure it would shift until they found Madison.

Amstell's accusations had resonated with him through the week. He was glad to have shared his concerns with DI Blackwell, but he couldn't shake the feeling that Amstell was correct in his assertion that Hoxton was part of the problem. Of course he wanted the girl found, but what he really wanted was to escape the whole situation. He was getting it from all sides. Walsh, or one of his many underlings, was a constant presence on the phone and Hoxton had spent the week pacifying the investors, in particular Jennings, who was trying to exploit the situation to his own ends.

Hoxton would have washed his hands of it all if it weren't for the fear of what it would do to his professional reputation. He'd seen it before. Walsh could, and would, ruin people and without the considerable bonus waiting for him at the completion of the project Hoxton wasn't in a position to leave the man's employ.

After breakfasting in his room, Hoxton changed and headed outside. It was Good Friday, the city resting. Hoxton walked to a mini-market on the Triangle. He stared at the rows of alcohol, a line of cold cider bottles calling to him. The assistant behind the counter gave him a sly glance and Hoxton looked at his watch, dismayed to see it wasn't even 10 a.m.. He purchased a newspaper and some chewing gum, coming close to explaining himself to the man who handed him his change.

He hurried back to the hotel. Ever since visiting the commune, he'd been unable to shake the feeling of being followed. It was pure paranoia, a legacy of too many late nights that had left his nerves shattered, but he only began to breathe easy when he stepped back through the glass threshold of the building.

As long as Walsh didn't call, he planned to spend the rest of the day within the safety of his hotel suite. With movie channels, a mini-bar and room service, he didn't want for anything. He lifted his paper in greeting to the hotel receptionist who proceeded to stop him as he headed over to the lifts.

'Mr Hoxton, excuse me. I was about to take this up to your room,' said the woman, who was holding a brown envelope in her hand.

Hoxton walked over, taking a subtle glance at the woman's name badge before accepting the letter. 'Thank you, Melanie,' he said.

It wasn't until he was back in the suite, biting down on the complimentary pastries that had been delivered in his absence, that he looked at the envelope again. It was nestled inside his newspaper and he hadn't given it a second thought until he saw the envelope had no postage information and must have been hand delivered.

He rubbed his forehead and considered the small number of people who knew he was staying at the hotel, before tearing at the opening.

He dropped the letter seconds after reading the opening lines.

The panic set in long before he'd finished the note. He wanted to call the police, to ring down to reception to see who'd dropped off the note, but did neither. Instead he emptied three small bottles of vodka from the mini-bar into a glass and downed the burning liquid in one. The relaxing effect was immediate. The shock from reading the note dissipating, he picked up the single piece of paper and took it all in again:

> Dear Mr Hoxton,
> As an associate of Mr Stephen Walsh and his company, Walsh Investments, we are writing to you specifically to let you know that we have the missing girl, Madison Pemberton. No harm has come to her and we would like to return her to her parents. That is where you come in. To secure Madison's safe return, we demand that you withdraw all current planning applications into Cheddar Gorge and the surrounding areas with immediate effect.
>
> Do this and the girl will be returned safely.
> Yours,
> Concerned Citizens

With the vodka in his bloodstream, Hoxton's initial panic faded. He was sure the note was a fake. He couldn't believe anyone would stoop to such lengths to stop the development going ahead. His logic was admittedly distorted by the alcohol, but he thought that anyone willing to return the girl wouldn't have taken her in the first place. She'd been gone six days now, long enough to be severely traumatised by the situation for the rest of her life even if she did return. If the writer, or writers, of the note had taken the girl then why wait until now to make contact? Not that they weren't being clever. Hoxton would have to take this to the police and chances were high that the authors of the note would receive the publicity they craved.

And how could he do otherwise? Even if there was the slightest chance that the girl's safety depended on him revealing the details of the note, then he had to notify the authorities.

Still he hesitated. He would have shown it to Walsh first but Hoxton wasn't sure his boss could be trusted. By the time he'd run it by his lawyers and various advisers, precious time would be lost.

Hoax or no hoax, there was only one person he felt he could trust with the note.

Chapter Twenty-Six

The woman tilted her head to the side as she answered the door, the bruising still visible to Louise. 'Jodi Marshall?' said Louise, flashing her warrant card.

The investigation into Paul's death was Farrell's case. All Louise's focus should be on Cheddar. But staying at her parents' house, and seeing Emily had made her snap. The simple truth was that although she trusted Farrell, the same could not be said for Finch. The investigation was all but over and if they stood any chance of finding Paul's killer, she had to get involved. It was easy to justify her actions as the majority of the constabulary's force were currently in Cheddar. Maybe it was a brittle lie she was telling herself, but it helped ease the guilt and she was sure the investigation wouldn't grind to a halt just because she was absent for an hour.

'If this is about last night, that's over and done with,' said Jodi.

'No, this is about Paul Blackwell. What happened last night, Jodi?'

Jodi closed her eyes as if she'd been caught out in a deception. 'Nothing. Come in if you want. You'll have to excuse the mess,' she said, the front door opening directly into a living room. Signs of a recent fight were evident throughout. Empty bottles of alcohol were discarded on the carpeted floor, dirty clothes and takeaway cartons strewn across the room. 'Is your husband in?'

Jodi shook her head and sat back on a cloth-covered sofa that creaked as it accepted her weight. 'He left last night,' she said, as if that was all the explanation needed.

Louise moved a pizza box from an armchair and sat down. It wasn't clear if Jodi expected her husband back anytime soon but she didn't push the woman on the point. She looked about her and wondered if Paul had ever been in the room. Jodi caught her looking and frowned. Beneath the swelling on the side of her face, Louise could see the woman was attractive. She was younger than Paul had been, her hair dyed a dark shade of blonde. 'You want to tell me what happened to your face?' asked Louise.

'Walked into a door,' said Jodi.

Louise had heard the clichéd refrain too many times before. 'I can help you,' she said.

Jodi lifted up her hand. 'I've heard it all before. You said you were here about Paul?'

Louise had prepared roughly what she would say to the woman but now she was here she was momentarily lost for words. She saw glimpses of Paul's wife Dianne in Jodi. Perhaps she was imagining it but they had similar ways of holding themselves. Jodi sat to one side, her arms folded, a slight downturn to her lips Louise had seen countless times on Dianne's face. Again, she wondered if Paul had been in love with this woman, and the thought filled her with melancholy. Had he known that Jodi's husband had been hitting her? What had the woman thought when Paul had taken Emily to Cornwall? They were questions she couldn't ask. Instead, she asked about Jodi's whereabouts on the night Paul had died.

'I've told you all this before. I was with Nathan all night. We were out at the bar until closing time, then home.'

'Does this happen a lot?' asked Louise.

'What?' said Jodi.

Louise pointed to the side of Jodi's face. She was veering off topic, shouldn't have been here in the first place, but couldn't move past the woman's injuries.

Jodi paused, a slight tremble to her lips. Louise waited without speaking. She wanted the husband to return. At that moment she didn't care that she would get into trouble for being there, she just wanted to see the look on his face when she questioned him.

'What did you say your name was again?' said Jodi, her eyes reddening.

'Louise.'

Jodi nodded, wiping the tears from her face. She smiled. 'He said you were beautiful,' she said.

Louise fought the threat of her own tears. 'Paul said that?'

'He loved you very much,' said Jodi.

Louise was disarmed by the words. She couldn't remember the last time Paul had told her he loved her. Probably some distant time in childhood before sibling differences got the best of them. She wondered how she would have responded had he told her that when he'd been alive. 'How long were you seeing him for?' she asked.

Jodi hesitated. 'About six months.'

Louise leaned back in the chair. She couldn't believe Paul had hidden the relationship from her so successfully. During the last months of his life, he'd failed to pick up Emily from school on a number of occasions due to his drinking. It seemed incongruous that he could have been dating someone without anyone, especially her, knowing.

'You aren't here officially are you?' said Jodi, when Louise didn't respond.

'No, but have you told the investigating officers about your relationship with Paul?' asked Louise.

Jodi shook her head. 'They did ask, but I didn't want to get Nathan into trouble. He's a bastard but he didn't . . .'

'He really was with you the night Paul died?'

Jodi nodded. 'We were at the bar until closing time. Loads of people saw us.'

'He knew about Paul though?'

'He found out. He'd been away on duty until that last month.'

'Stupid question, but how did he respond?'

Jodi's laugh was dry and hollow. 'Something along the lines of this,' she said, displaying her bruising.

'Did he threaten Paul?'

'He tried to get his address from me but I wouldn't tell him. I promise,' said Jodi.

'Paul knew he was back, though?'

'I told him to go away. I didn't want . . .' said Jodi, through tears. 'I didn't want something to happen to Paul, or for Emily to somehow become involved.'

The mention of Emily was like a punch to the stomach. Breathless, Louise asked, 'You met Emily?'

Jodi shook her head. 'We decided it was best if I didn't but . . .'

'What?'

Jodi bit her lip. 'Paul wanted me to go to Cornwall with them.'

Louise couldn't believe what she was hearing. 'Permanently?'

'I don't know. His mind wasn't straight. It surprised me as much as I imagine it surprised you when he went. He called me and asked me to come down. He was looking for places to live.'

'And what did you say?'

'I was all set to join him when Nathan saw my suitcase.'

'He stopped you going?'

'At first he begged. That was why we were out that night. He wanted to take me out, as if ten pints in the local fleapit was going to turn my head. It's only when we are out of the public eye that this happens,' she said, pointing to her face.

'Why didn't you tell the officers when they questioned you?'

'What difference would it make? Nathan was with me all that night, all that week.'

Louise didn't argue. She wondered how hard Farrell had pushed the woman. Jodi had caved in quickly to her but that was probably due in part to her being Paul's sister. 'Where's Nathan now?'

'He left last night. Away with his mates for a week. He gave me this as a going-away present.'

'Someone is going to come and speak to you again, Jodi. And you're going to tell them exactly what you told me. Do you understand?'

Jodi nodded.

'In the meantime I'm going to find you somewhere safe to live. Would you do that for me? For Paul?'

Louise saw hesitancy in the woman's eyes. The first step in a domestic abuse situation was an acceptance of what was happening. 'Okay,' said Jodi, finally. 'I think it's time.'

◆ ◆ ◆

Louise was reluctant to leave Jodi alone at the house. The woman must have confirmed three or four times that her husband was definitely away before Louise was ready to leave. She would have called support already if her career wouldn't have been in jeopardy. She didn't want to leave Jodi this way but she needed to speak to Farrell before she took things further. She had uncovered a lead that had evaded everyone else, but there were still potential repercussions. She was interfering in his investigation and needed to clear things with Farrell.

She called him as she took the A370 back to Weston and he agreed to meet her back at the station. Stopping for petrol, she purchased an early edition of *The Bristol Post*. A snippet of a longer article on Madison's disappearance was on the front page, written by Tania Elliot. Louise had spoken to the journalist on a couple of occasions in the last week, and was glad to see the disappearance was still prominent. She wanted it to be front and centre news. The most minor thing could unravel everything, and for that to happen she had to keep Madison in everyone's thoughts.

Farrell was already at the station. The whole building was still swarming with officers. Authorised overtime was on-going and Madison's disappearance was the highest priority. Although he'd been working out of headquarters, Farrell had remained a significant part of the investigative team. He'd spent the week with Tracey and Thomas, interviewing everyone identified by MAPPA. He welcomed her with a coffee and news of a recent arrest in Blagdon where a random house search had uncovered a stash of illicit material.

A look of surprise came over him as Louise told him to find an interview room, but he didn't comment. She noticed the changes in him every time they met. He'd matured so much in the last three years that it was hard to equate him with the smirking officer she'd encountered on her first day in Weston. She considered him a colleague now and it made what she had to say all that more difficult.

'I'll get straight to the point, Greg,' she said, taking a seat opposite Farrell in interview room three as if he was a suspect. 'I went to see Jodi Marshall this morning.'

Louise watched the information settle, Farrell's eyes blinking as he recalled the name, his brow furrowing in anger. 'With all due respect, Louise, was this wise?'

Louise understood his concern but didn't regret her decision. 'As it turns out, yes,' she said, relaying the information Jodi had given her.

'You think she was telling the truth?' said Farrell, the strain not leaving his face.

Normally the question would have annoyed her but she understood Farrell asking. It was natural for him to suspect she was too close to the case and willing to see things that weren't there. 'She's scared of him, Greg. I need your help to get her to a refuge.'

'We have a number of eyewitnesses stating that he was at the bar on the night Paul . . .'

'I realise that. That doesn't mean he isn't involved. He beats his wife, Greg, and Jodi was having an affair with Paul. That should change things.'

'That doesn't mean he stabbed someone seventeen times.' Farrell looked away. 'Sorry, Louise.'

'I'm not saying he did, in fact I concede it couldn't have been him, but you need to look into him more closely. He definitely has motive.'

'I'll speak to Mrs Marshall and I'll get on to social now and see if we can find a refuge for her,' he said, hesitating. Louise sensed his conflict. She knew he was still loyal to her but Finch was a dangerous foe. 'What do I tell Finch though?'

It was the question she had expected. Finch was the reason she'd had to interfere in the first place. When she'd first moved to Weston, Finch had sent her anonymous texts on a daily basis. He'd been trying to play with her mind, his goal to get her to quit the police. And although she'd finally overcome that, Paul's case was the perfect opportunity for Finch to mess with her further without getting directly involved. He would know how much it would pain her to see the investigation fade away, and it was only a matter of days before that happened.

'Look, Greg, I don't want you to lie and you shouldn't. It was wrong for me to go and see Jodi but I'm willing to face up to any consequences on that front. Best that she is safe and we now have a lead on this than the alternative.'

Louise meant every word. From a point of procedure she shouldn't have gone to see Jodi, but if it was necessary she could argue that her visit had been personal. By Jodi's admission she'd been having a long-term relationship with Paul, so Louise felt justified in speaking to her. That the meeting had resulted in a new avenue of approach into Paul's murder should only be viewed as a positive, but she wasn't naive enough to think that Finch wouldn't at least try to turn it to his own advantage. It had occurred to her that her involvement was what Finch had wanted all along. It could turn out to be exactly what he needed to get rid of her. Even if her actions weren't enough to warrant disciplinary charges, he could argue that she wasn't focused enough on events in Cheddar. That was partly why she was glad to have everything in the open with Farrell. Maybe now, she could trust him with the case and she could focus on finding Madison. It all came down to what he said next.

Farrell scratched his chin. Even deep in thought he looked like he was smiling. 'I'm not happy about this, Louise.'

'I know, Greg. I appreciate your help. It's not something I'll forget.'

Farrell hesitated again and she wondered if he was going to change his mind. They stood that way for some time, Louise not wanting to speak; needing Farrell to reach the right conclusion on his own. When he eventually did speak, it came as a relief. 'He was discharged from the army,' he said. 'Did she tell you that?'

'No she didn't. When did this happen?'

'Five weeks ago. A group of five men from his regiment. I had another look following our last conversation. The army are reluctant to share more than the basic information. He still had five years left on his contract.'

'Jodi says he is away on a jaunt with some of his friends now.'

'I'll look into it. I know an MP in Aldershot. See if he can point me in the right direction.'

Louise thanked him. 'You need to get her out of that house immediately.'

'Will do.' Farrell hesitated. 'If you don't mind me saying, boss . . .'

'I won't interfere any more, Greg,' said Louise, saving them both any further embarrassment.

◆ ◆ ◆

Thirty minutes later, Louise was back in Cheddar standing on the cliff pathway, gazing out towards the village and the alien-like reservoir.

She'd come here to clear her mind. Meeting Jodi Marshall that morning, and her subsequent conversation with Farrell, had been a distraction, albeit a necessary one. Now that Farrell had the information, she hoped he would run with it and that her involvement could be minimal. There was still a missing girl out there, she thought, trying not to be overwhelmed by the never-ending sight of the countryside stretching out in all directions.

As she stared out at the mound of land to the east where the commune was situated, a small flock of the brown-coated sheep skipped past her and drank from the pallets of rainwater next to the wooden fence. As Louise edged closer to the animals, they froze, poised to flee. Not for the first time, Louise wondered at the speed of the attacker. How was it possible for them to have snuck up on the sheep without being noticed, she thought, as the sheep fled.

What troubled her most was the lack of sightings of the girl. They'd set up a special hotline and received a number of calls, but nothing specific to Madison. The difference between Madison's abduction and the other incidents was telling. Previously, the attacker had been careless, or at least unconcerned about leaving evidence of their actions. The sheep had been left where they'd been slaughtered and the attacker had retreated after slicing Tabart. If not exactly proud of their work, they'd been willing to display it. So why the different approach with Madison?

Louise battled down the rocky pathway towards Lynch Lane, losing her footing a number of times, wondering – like she had on that first day – if Madison had reached this far. On a couple of occasions she heard rustling sounds in the undergrowth and, rather than fleeing, chose to investigate. It felt like overkill but she had her baton ready as she moved into the dense foliage near a particularly steep drop. With her heightened pulse, she willed an imagined attacker to emerge from the shadows, but it was a foolish notion. She returned to the muddy path, a group of teenage boys, their white flat-soled trainers unsuitable for the walk ahead of them, greeting her as she walked past. Louise warned them to be careful, before moving down the incline.

She was exhausted by the time she reached the road, annoyed that her trip to the top of the gorge had been a waste of time. A man in biking leathers was dismantling his bike engine as she made her way towards the car-park. He nodded to her as if she was a tourist returning from a walk. Louise's first instinct was to view the man with suspicion, but everyone in the local vicinity had already been interviewed. He looked away. She sensed despondency in the gesture, in the way his shoulders sagged. Madison's disappearance had irrevocably changed the village and everyone in it. No one had given up on the idea of finding Madison, but her disappearance meant the place would never be the same again.

And like them, Louise wasn't even entertaining the idea of giving up, and by the look of it neither was the man loitering by her car.

Chapter Twenty-Seven

By the time Louise reached the car-park, her greatest concern was how Richard Hoxton had tracked her to the spot. No one at the station would have dared give her location, even if they'd known it. It wasn't the first time he'd surprised her. She'd thought seeing him in the village on the day she'd visited with her family had been a coincidence, but now the detective in her was becoming increasingly suspicious of Hoxton's motives.

'Mr Hoxton,' she said, her tone neutral as she opened her car door and retrieved her radio.

'DI Blackwell. I know what this must look like,' said Hoxton. The man was scratching his beard, clearly agitated. 'I tried to find you at your station but they said you were out. I thought you might be here, and when I saw your car I thought I'd wait for you.'

'This isn't very appropriate, Mr Hoxton. How can I help you?' said Louise, trying to recall when Hoxton would have seen her car before.

Today, Hoxton was a different character to the man she'd met on the other occasions. His confidence and charm had faded. As he handed her an A4 sheet of paper protected by a plastic covering, his hand was shaking. She held his gaze before taking it.

'I didn't know who else I could trust,' he said, looking away.

Frowning, Louise took the sheet and read the note. 'When did you get this?' she asked, reading the note three times.

'It was handed into reception at my hotel in Bristol this morning. At least I think it was this morning, I haven't checked. They gave it to me at 10.30 a.m. but I didn't open it straight away.'

'Is this how the note came?'

'No, it was in a brown envelope. When I realised what it was I got these plastic files from the hotel to protect the letter so you could test it for prints or whatever. Here,' he said, retrieving the envelope from his car.

Louise read the note again. Her initial reaction was that the letter was an opportunistic hoax. It had been almost a week since Madison disappeared, and it didn't make sense to wait this long to send it. Furthermore, the validity of kidnapping someone to stop the development, combined with the previous attacks on the cliff walk, didn't ring true to her, but she couldn't ignore the glimmer of hope the note offered. 'Why didn't you hand this in to the local station?'

Hoxton frowned, his hand still shaking. He was dishevelled and uneasy, and as she took the crudely addressed envelope from him, she understood why. Smelling the sour tang of alcohol on the man's breath, she recoiled, trying her best to hide her revulsion.

'How do you think you'd fare if I gave you a breathalyser test now, Mr Hoxton?' she asked.

Hoxton turned away. 'I wanted to bring this to you. I feel shit enough as it is with all this happening. If I can do anything to find this girl . . .'

Louise sighed. A few days ago she'd considered going to dinner with the man, now she couldn't help equate his current state with her brother's alcoholism. 'You better get in my car,' she said, before calling the station.

◆ ◆ ◆

By the time she reached Weston twenty-five minutes later, officers had already been dispatched to Hoxton's hotel in Bristol. Louise shared the note with her team before rushing it through to processing. Louise decided to let Thomas interview Hoxton while she spoke to Robertson.

'I've seen this type of shit before. Shameful, taking advantage of a situation like this,' said her boss, who shared her opinion that it was a hoax. 'You think that commune would do something like this?'

After speaking to Sam Amstell the other evening, the team had conducted a detailed search of the commune but aside from obtaining numerous illegal substances, they'd hadn't found anything to aid their investigation.

'Hopefully we'll get a hit on the CCTV images in Bristol. Could be a rogue member trying to make a name for themselves.'

'We need to try and keep this in-house,' said Robertson. 'Whoever sent it wants the publicity. If it gets to the papers they'll have succeeded.'

In principle, Louise agreed. She didn't believe the note was from the attacker, but had to approach the situation as if they had sent it. Their actions up to this point had been disjointed so she couldn't rule it out. From what Hoxton had told her, the development project in Cheddar was already strained. If the sentiments in the note were true, then maybe it was better to share it with the wider world.

Robertson wasn't convinced. 'It would seem like we were playing sides,' he said.

'I don't think we should sit on it though, Iain. What if someone spots something in the note? You know how these things go. Someone could spot a turn of phrase, or recognise the handwriting.

However unlikely it is, if this note is genuine, making it public could lead us to the attacker.'

'Or make them retreat further.'

'Let's see what the team at the hotel come back with,' said Louise, not ready to dismiss the notion of going public with the note yet.

'And the parents?' said Robertson.

Louise frowned. 'My next stop.'

◆ ◆ ◆

Alison Eabrook, the family liaison officer, met Louise outside the Pemberton house. By the time Louise returned to Cheddar, the CCTV images at Hoxton's hotel had already been secured and were being examined. Louise showed the printouts of the note to the FLO. 'How are they coping?'

'As well as can be expected. The lack of sleep is still a problem.'

Louise had been to the house on a daily basis. The same stilted atmosphere greeted her as she stepped through the door. It was as if the house existed out of time. Both parents were sitting on armchairs in the living room, neither looking up as she entered the room. They were doing their best to remain positive but Louise saw the creeping doubt in their actions, the occasional slips where the façade of denial vanished and they were left to face the horrible realisation that they may never see their daughter again.

The animation Louise saw on their faces as Alison explained the note to them was hard to endure. Unless something came from it, it felt cruel to show them the note and to create what was more than likely to be false hope.

The parents read the note together. Louise studied their ever-changing faces, the movements of lips and eyes as they scanned the note and tried to make sense of what they were reading.

'Who sent it?' asked Claire, as her husband sat next to her trying to hide the fact he was on the verge of tears.

'We're not sure yet. It was delivered to a hotel in Bristol. We're checking CCTV cameras, interviewing everyone in the area as we speak.'

'You must have an idea. What about those crackpots from the commune? They've been protesting for months. Surely they could be responsible?'

Louise shivered at the memory of the cold farm building where she'd met Sam Amstell. 'I can assure you that everything that can be done is being done. I was wondering if there is anything you can spot in this note. Anything about the way it is written, the paper, the envelope?'

Claire shook her head, and glanced at her husband who mirrored the gesture. Louise hoped to have some results back from headquarters shortly, the processing taking precedent, but there appeared to be nothing out of the ordinary about the letter or envelope.

'You mentioned the commune. I know we have asked you about this before but did Madison have anything to do with the protestors? Anything that may have come to mind now?'

'She didn't show much interest,' said Neil, clearing his throat, his eyes red. 'To be honest, the proposed developments have been going on for so long now that it's hard to keep interested in it. If it's not this, it's something else.'

Louise wondered if that was how these developments got completed. Continual attrition until everyone was so disengaged that the developments slipped by almost unnoticed. 'And either of you. What's your viewpoint?'

Claire scowled. Louise could see her thinking, weighing up the question for its real meaning. 'We're quite neutral about it,' she said, after some thought. 'There is real concern about the effect it would have on the local area. And once these things start who knows where they will end.'

Louise had admired the way Claire had remained stoic throughout the ordeal. She didn't think it was an act but would never rule anything out. She hadn't been working on the case herself but four years ago in Bristol, a couple had staged the kidnapping of their young child, only for the child to be discovered a few weeks later in a relative's house in Newcastle. During this time, the couple had amassed a small fortune from well-wishers and media rights. Although it seemed highly unlikely, what if the couple were working with a larger group, possibly the commune? It would have made the disappearance all that easier to stage.

After leaving, she shared the idea with Thomas and instructed him to look at any links between the parents and environmentalists in the south-west area, and in particular the commune.

She bought a coffee from the petrol station – the dank liquid hot and flavourless – and prepared herself for another long night in a week of long nights.

Chapter Twenty-Eight

It felt like days since Madison had last seen the monster but she had no way of knowing. Time was different in the cave. The light was the same – the constant darkness alleviated by the lamp pinned high to the cave wall – as was the temperature. She'd learnt that long ago during one of the first visits to Cox's Cave where she'd seen that stupid goblin. The temperature of the caves was a constant eleven degrees centigrade. It never got colder or hotter. And although she believed that, it didn't stop her shivering sometimes when she was trying to sleep.

She called him a monster but he wasn't like the monsters she'd read, and sometimes written, about. She hadn't really seen him properly, and there was something weird about the way he breathed, as if he was always gasping for a last bit of air, but he was as real as she was.

She couldn't believe she'd been so stupid. Mum was always warning her that her bravery would get her into trouble and here she was. But she wasn't really brave. Every time she walked along the cliff walk on her own, she was scared. In fact, she was always a little bit scared whenever she was alone. That was why she did it, really. She hoped that if she walked home that way enough times or was able to walk alone more often than not, then one day she would stop being afraid.

Dad liked to tease her about her wild imagination and the way she liked to scare herself. He often joked that he was too scared to read some of her books. Madison would see Mum roll her eyes but she'd heard them argue before about some of the novels on her bookcase. Madison had started reading the books for the same reason she walked along the cliff path by herself, so she didn't need to be afraid any more.

But this wasn't like reading a scary book. This was real and there was nothing remotely fun about it.

The shock of her abduction still resonated through her body. She'd heard noises, the sounds she now knew belonged to the monster, but had thought it was the wildlife or the wind playing tricks with her. He'd grabbed her with such speed and force that it had been impossible to fight. One second she was standing on the cliff walk, the next her face was covered, her hands and legs bound, as she was carried away.

She stayed conscious during the journey. Her stories had told her to pay attention, that anything, however minor, could be of importance later, but all she could recall from the journey was the monster's rapid breathing and the earthy, sour smell of the cloth he'd put over her mouth.

Madison still didn't know what he wanted from her. He'd dumped her in this inlet within the cave, a solitary lamp nailed high on the cave wall. He'd left her with a mattress and blankets, food and water. Every now and then he would return and change the lamp. He always left more food and water, and took away the buckets she hated to think about. His face was always covered and Madison would hide beneath her blanket whenever he returned, fearing the worst.

And although she was relieved he'd wanted little to do with her since he'd taken her, the situation reminded her of a Korean horror movie she'd stayed up late to watch on television one night without her parents knowing. The monster in that movie didn't have a human form. It took people and saved them for later. In the film they were kept for food, but Madison was worried that her own monster had even more sinister plans in store for her.

She wrapped the blanket tighter against her shivering body. The furry material shared the same dank smell as the face cloth and Madison worried she wasn't the first to hide beneath it. She thought about her mum and dad and how worried they would be. She wished she'd been nicer to them. The last time she'd seen her mum she'd shouted at her. She hadn't meant anything by it but she would give anything to turn back time and to say sorry.

The light from the lamp seemed to be getting dimmer and she feared he would be returning soon.

On her first night in the cave, the monster had stopped her trying to scale the cave walls to retrieve it.

'Even if you have the light you would only get lost in here,' he'd said, his voice throaty and deep. 'And even I wouldn't be able to find you.'

She'd screamed then, her high pitched wail echoing across the cave walls, and he'd stopped talking. Madison had sensed his confusion.

'What is your name?' he'd asked, as if the question had only then occurred to him.

She almost didn't hear the question through the sound of her wailing. Even when she closed her mouth, the noise continued as if another child was trapped within the caves mimicking her. It had been hard to contain herself – her body moving of its own accord, shaking and trembling – but she'd known that if she could befriend the monster then maybe he wouldn't go ahead with whatever grisly plan he had in store. 'Madison,' she'd said. 'What's yours?'

The monster's lips had then moved beneath his mask, but it was a few seconds before any words escaped his throat. 'Madison,' he said, forming the word as if it was the first time he'd ever said it; as if he'd made the gravest of errors.

'If you take me back, I promise I won't tell anyone,' she'd said, but the monster had already started backing away as if somehow he was afraid of her.

Chapter Twenty-Nine

He remembered him.

He was easily spotted on the pathway but he didn't care. Things were starting to come together.

If anyone questioned why he was holding the binoculars, he would explain he was bird watching. Not that anyone approached. The ramblers and families kept a clear distance, offering the occasional nod in his direction as he hid in the long grass, his head poking through the brambles as he relished the earthy smell of the land.

He pointed his binoculars towards the trees and sky, but every now and then he would turn his attention to the farmhouse and what lay within.

The girl was safe. He changed her light every day, made sure she was fed and warm. It was a mistake but he couldn't think about that for now.

It could and would be rectified.

He'd been looking for the wrong thing. Jack had returned but he was different from the last time they'd been together. Now he understood that, everything else made sense. He took one last look at the window before heading back, the long blades of the grass whipping his skin as he took the short cut away from the main track.

For a time he was a boy again enjoying the endless freedom of the hills, the despair of seeing his ex-wife obliterated. He ran over the muddy paths, skipping over the rocks that jutted out of the ground at strange angles, and before he knew it he was back in the village, walking down the path at the side of his house to the small lock-up the landlady let him keep his stuff in.

His ex-wife had wanted him to throw most of it away but he hadn't been able to bring himself to do so and now he'd been proven right. A putrid smell greeted him as he opened the garage. The dust reached his lungs and he began coughing, droplets leaving his mouth at an alarming speed, but he refused to let the trapped air bother him. Boxes fell as he bulldozed through his meagre belongings, the sound of scurrying insects and his rapid breathing catching in the confined space until he found what he was looking for.

The metal was cold, coated with a fine fuzz that clung to his skin as he dragged it through the upturned boxes into the twilight outside. He retrieved the other sections and took it to the house where he washed and assembled it.

He didn't need to close his eyes to picture Jack in the crib.

He could see the boy, his boy, lying there as clear as he'd seen him earlier that day through the farmhouse windows.

Chapter Thirty

Farrell was mainly present as a courtesy to Louise. He was sure the Nathan Marshall route was a dead end but Louise had convinced him to take a second look. When she'd first joined the team at Weston, Farrell hadn't known how to take her. She'd come across as aloof and he'd had the impression she thought Weston-super-Mare was beneath her and he'd resented her for a time.

Now he understood. He'd snapped up the opportunity of joining MIT and knew better than anyone how the transition must have been for her. But he'd changed his opinion of her long before leaving Weston. He'd worked on a couple of major cases with her and experienced first-hand her diligence and bravery. In her own way, she instilled a sense of loyalty in the people she worked with, and Farrell's devotion had only increased since his move to headquarters.

In part that was also due to one man, DCI Tim Finch.

Finch had contacted Farrell a few weeks before Louise had joined Weston, and Farrell conceded now that he'd given the man too much credence. The fallout between Finch and Louise following the Walton case was legend in the region, and when Finch had warned him to keep a close eye on Louise he'd accepted it as good advice.

Now he appreciated it for what it truly was, a way of Finch manipulating events to his own end.

Finch had an iron-clad hold on the division. The type of hold that should have been impossible in the modern police force. It was the subtle way he manipulated things that made it possible. On the surface, everything was above board but look deeper and the department was run on the basis of fear. Finch had demonstrated on more than one occasion that the risk of going against him was great. As well as Louise, the majority of the MIT team from the last three years had moved on. In Farrell's opinion, Finch was creating a team of yes men and women and that made him even more dangerous.

Which was why he'd made no official record of his journey to Aldershot.

Captain James Ross was six foot two of pure muscle. He had the type of assured self-confidence Farrell associated with two types of people: those with private educations, and those from the armed forces. 'DS Farrell, this way please,' said Ross, releasing Farrell from his vice-like handshake.

Ross led him to a wood-panelled office adorned with military memorabilia. Farrell noticed Marshall's file on the desk. 'Please, sit,' said Ross. 'This is about Marshall?'

Farrell nodded, explaining in detail his investigation into Paul Blackwell's murder.

'And Marshall is a suspect?'

'Not as such, I'm just getting some background information on the man. I understand he was discharged.'

Ross tilted his chin upwards, frown lines crossing his forehead. 'This murder took place a few months ago. Marshall was still with us at this point.'

'That's correct. New information has come to light which I need to follow up on. I'm sure you understand.'

'I can confirm that Marshall was on leave at the time of the murder; beyond that there isn't much I can help you with.'

Farrell had expected some resistance. The armed forces sometimes behaved as if they were on a different legal basis to the rest of the country and although they usually worked well with the police, they could sometimes be reluctant to share information. And discharged or not, the last thing they wanted was bad publicity for one of their former members. 'There was an altercation. Reports of bullying. I believe five men were discharged,' said Farrell.

'You've been doing your homework,' said Ross.

'Aren't these things usually dealt with in-house?'

'Believe me they were,' said Ross, a sardonic grin spreading over his face.

'Yet, you still saw fit to let these men go.'

'Things have changed,' said Ross, clearly lamenting a different time. 'Certain behaviours are no longer tolerated. Haven't been for some time. The men appeared before the Court Martial. Everything is on public record.'

'Nothing on the record states the name of the accusers.'

'In this case, anonymity was a necessary precaution. The men pleaded guilty. Case closed.'

'Do the person or persons involved still serve?'

Ross folded up the papers on his desk. 'Listen, I'm not sure what you are hoping to achieve here, Greg. I can only share with you what's public knowledge.'

'I was hoping you could save me some time. Give me some insight in to what these men were like.'

Ross shook his head, as if Farrell was beyond understanding. 'These men are highly trained and disciplined soldiers. They made some mistakes and were punished for it in a way you probably wouldn't understand. I read about the case. Seventeen stab wounds? Come on, Greg, sounds like a crime of passion to me.'

'There are rumours that Paul Blackwell was sleeping with Marshall's wife,' said Farrell.

Ross's lips twitched. 'Even so. I don't believe for a second Marshall, or any of them for that matter, would be capable of cold-blooded murder. But say, for argument's sake, they were, this wouldn't be the mode of attack. Seventeen stab wounds would be overkill. I'm sorry you've wasted your time,' said Ross, standing to indicate the meeting was at an end.

◆ ◆ ◆

Headquarters was deserted by the time Farrell returned. One of the civvies told him about the note delivered to Richard Hoxton. He called Tracey to get an update and was about to leave for Cheddar to assist when Finch arrived.

'What are you doing here, Greg? Thought you'd be manning the ships in Cheddar by now.'

Farrell sensed the underlying tension in Finch's words. He wouldn't have been surprised if Finch already knew about his meeting with Ross. 'Just on my way now, sir.'

'What were you up to earlier?'

It was a strange question. Finch didn't usually micromanage his team. Such was the nature of the job, they were often away from their desks. Farrell decided he couldn't risk getting caught in a lie and told his boss about his meeting with Ross.

Finch grimaced, his tongue darting out from his lips. 'Marshall,' he said, as if deep in thought. 'Doesn't ring a bell to me.'

'Yes, Guv. I found out recently that the victim may have been having an affair with Mr Marshall's wife.'

'I see. So Marshall was in Cornwall on the night of the murder?' said Finch.

'Unfortunately not. There are a number of witnesses placing him in Bristol that night.'

Finch scratched his head. 'Well, you know what you're doing, son, but sounds like a dead end to me.'

'Sir,' he said.

'I'll leave it up to you then, Greg. Whatever you think is best,' said Finch, walking away.

Farrell sighed, lacing his hands behind his head as he sat back in his chair. One of the things he'd learnt in his time in MIT was to listen very carefully when Finch spoke to you. Not necessarily to the words he used, more the way he used them. In this case he didn't have to think too hard. Finch was all but telling him to drop the line of enquiry. The case was supposed to be shelved in the next few days. As it was technically Devon and Cornwall's case, shelving it wouldn't have a detrimental effect on Finch's figures.

Louise hadn't come out directly and said it, but Farrell had understood the underlying message. She believed Finch would scupper the investigation if he could. He didn't blame her for her paranoia after the way she'd been treated, and his recent conversation with Finch had done little to persuade him she was wrong in her beliefs.

In the end it was Farrell's decision, but Finch would be on to him now, and there would be no way of hiding his movements should he continue looking into Marshall.

Farrell typed up his meeting with Ross before leaving for Cheddar. He printed up details on the five men discharged at the same time as Marshall, having decided that there was one person who should get to see them.

If Finch was going to keep him under scrutiny then maybe someone else could take a closer look in his absence.

Chapter Thirty-One

The letter brought a different dynamic to the case but the last few days had stumbled by with no developments. It was the Tuesday after Easter weekend and tourism in the village was all but dead. Cheddar was caught in a state of limbo and there were concerns from all sides about what to do next.

Finch had surprised Louise by rushing through the checks on the note. A number of fingerprints had been identified on the envelope but the only fingerprints lifted from the letter itself were Richard Hoxton's. That meant either Hoxton wrote the note himself or whoever had written the note had been meticulous in its preparation.

The former seemed unlikely. Hoxton was back in Cheddar, and she would see him later at the emergency council meeting. She wanted to speak to Stephen Walsh but short of getting a warrant issued that was proving impossible. Walsh was allegedly somewhere in the States, and placed Hoxton in charge of his UK operations.

It was early morning, and Louise found herself back on the cliff walk in Cheddar. It was hard not to enjoy the sense of solitude whatever the reasons for her being there. She wanted to believe the note was real, and that something as simple as denying planning permission could bring the girl back, but things were rarely – if ever – that simple. The local council had agreed to the emergency meeting that afternoon and Louise already hated the thought of it; that a group of self-interested adults somehow held the fate of the young girl in their hands was hard to bear.

Walking past the lookout tower, and the exit down the steps of Jacob's Ladder, Louise once again imagined Madison taking this walk back home. She recalled the sound of something following her the last time she'd been here, and listened for the sound now, willing it to materialise, but all she could hear was the rustle of the leaves, the sound of her footsteps squelching in the mud, as she headed towards the back route and the line of houses that led on to Lynch Lane.

◆ ◆ ◆

Thomas Ireland met her outside the village hall later that afternoon. He wore the same hounded look as the majority of the investigative team. However hard you tried to act professional and detached, cases involving children were always the hardest. It was impossible not to imagine your loved ones being in the same situation, which made it twice as hard for those officers with young families.

'This place is eerie when it's quiet,' said Thomas, a cigarette in his hand. Louise couldn't recall seeing him smoke before but didn't mention it. 'All these cliff faces give me the creeps.'

Louise understood what he meant. With the absence of the regular tourist trade, she felt like an interloper in the village. The lack of people made her feel smaller, the gorge running through the village appearing narrower as if it was trying to squeeze the humans out of the area where they were no longer welcome.

Together they watched the attendees arrive. The councillor Annette Harling arrived at the same time as Sandy Osman from the National Trust. The other councillor she'd met, Robert Andrews, was not long behind and Louise wondered about Madison's dad. Also a councillor, he would have been present at any other time.

Richard Hoxton was the last to arrive. He looked sheepish as he glanced over at them, the pale skin above his unkempt beard dotted with red bumps that matched the bloodlines in his eyes. 'I wasn't sure if you'd be joining us, Mr Hoxton,' said Louise.

'I'm here on behalf of Walsh Associates,' said Hoxton, his usual light charm missing.

Thomas turned to Louise and frowned as Hoxton walked inside. 'I think he's still pissed that he had to go through all that questioning,' said Louise.

'Poor lad.'

'Shall we?' said Louise, heading into the village hall.

Four tables had been set up in the middle of the room. Louise counted twelve people, fourteen with her and Thomas. The room was used for various activities during the week. Smells of gym socks, nappies and stale food competed with one another, the cloying aroma intensified by the number of people in the room. Louise introduced herself and circulated copies of the letter, studying the response of each person like a professional poker player.

Louise checked her notes and an elderly man at the end of the table spoke. Charles Liddle was head of the planning authority for the area. 'Forgive me my ignorance, but isn't this a no-brainer?'

'How so, Charles?' said Annette, as if humouring an old relative.

'We simply delay our decision on the final planning deeds until the girl is released. Once she is back nothing is to stop us starting again and I'm sure the boys, excuse me, persons, in blue will do their best to catch those responsible.'

'I'm afraid it isn't quite that simple,' said Hoxton, with a lack of conviction.

'And how is that, young man?' said Liddle.

'You know as well as I do what's at stake here, Charles. The money involved,' said Annette.

Louise was impressed with the woman's command. She'd struck Louise as confident the times they'd met, but now she was showing an extra dimension to herself. When she spoke, the men, for they were all men, listened.

'Ah, money, of course,' said Charles, exchanging a knowing look with Louise.

'You must understand the time and energy that has gone into this,' said Hoxton, coming to Annette's aid even though she didn't need it. 'Even a short delay would . . .'

'Would what?' said Charles, growing irate. 'What could possibly be more important than a girl's life?'

'We don't even know if this is a legitimate letter,' said Annette. 'What do you think, officers?'

Louise felt the attention focused on her and she mirrored it back, searching for a twitch or flicker, anything that would suggest someone knew more than they were letting on. 'We wouldn't be here if we weren't taking this seriously.'

'It's that bloody kibbutz,' said Osman, as if that was the end of all conversation.

'By kibbutz you mean the commune?' said Thomas.

'They can barely organise a demonstration let alone a kidnapping. They're using that poor girl as a way of distracting us. Come on, we all know that. What have you done about that?' said Osman, directing his ire to Louise.

Louise glared at him and ignored his question, pleased when the man shrank back in on himself. 'Obviously, the decision will have to be yours. I believe the final decision is made next Wednesday?' she asked.

Annette nodded. 'The thing is, even if we postpone it, or even pretend to cancel it indefinitely, is that going to be enough?'

'My guess is that those responsible, whether they have taken the girl or not, want to cause as much disruption as possible. They will know that nothing is irreversible but are working on the principle that we will walk away if things are prolonged enough,' said Hoxton.

'And is that a possibility?' said Louise.

Hoxton paused, considering his answer. Louise wasn't sure where his hesitation came from. She hoped it was from consideration for Madison, rather than his business interest. 'I want to see the girl found as much as anyone. I hate to speak this way but we have investors who are obviously shaky about all this. Things move quickly, and if things aren't resolved soon then I can't guarantee what will happen.'

At least he had the good grace to look embarrassed thought Louise, as the meeting fizzled out.

'I feel dirty,' said Thomas, lighting another cigarette outside.

'I know how you feel,' said Louise. The meeting had drained her with its lack of humanity. They'd discussed Madison as if she was a business interest, and whether or not they could reach an agreement, the girl was still missing.

◆ ◆ ◆

The thought stayed with Louise as she made her way back to the bungalow and it made her think about the time Paul had taken Emily away to Cornwall. She hadn't really spoken to anyone about Emily disappearing with Paul beyond the mandatory sessions with the police psychologist. That in itself was something to be sad about. She'd spoken to Tracey and Thomas but they were work colleagues and had been with her on that night. Outside of work, Louise had no one she could turn to. Maybe if it hadn't been a family matter she would have found it easier to talk to her parents.

Once again she worried that if she didn't find Paul's killer, it would remain a burden that would stay with her forever.

A large brown envelope was waiting for her on the door-mat. She opened it as she made her way to the living room and realised the package was from Farrell.

Louise's tiredness was so acute that she had to fight to keep her eyes open as she read through the case notes on Paul's murder. The file included details of Nathan Marshall and his former army colleagues. It wasn't something he should have shared, and they both could get in trouble if it ever came to light. It was too late to call Farrell and ask why he'd left this for her so she added the photographs to the crime boards on the living room wall.

By the time she'd finished she felt as if she was back at work. Everywhere she looked were images from either Madison's disappearance or Paul's murder. She lay down on the sofa, too fatigued to walk to the bedroom.

Her last view before she closed her eyes – the picture of her brother's corpse from his murder scene – guided her into a night of disrupted and haunted sleep.

Chapter Thirty-Two

Louise woke fully dressed, her neck stiff from sleeping on the sofa. She rubbed her eyes and alighted on the image of Paul she'd fallen asleep to last night, vague images of fires and caves from her dreams already slipping from memory.

If anything, the sleep had made her feel worse. Brewing her daily pot of coffee, she had to fight the call of her bed. Not that she would have been able to fall back to sleep. Despite her exhaustion, her mind was already in full flow mulling over the various aspects of Madison's disappearance and Paul's murder.

By the time she reached the station, she'd begun to put things in order and used her debrief to organise her thoughts into actions. For all the talk yesterday at the emergency council meeting, nothing had been resolved. It seemed that, at the moment, the final decision on the application process would be going ahead. Louise asked Thomas to look deeper into the various council members, while for now her focus was to remain on Richard Hoxton's firm – in particular his boss, Stephen Walsh.

Louise had always despised the political aspect of her work. It was probably among the reasons for her effective demotion to Weston three years ago. She wasn't one to bow down easily to authority, and unlike Finch she wasn't an effective networker. She'd understood all the underlying nuances she'd seen in the interactions at yesterday's meeting, but would never be comfortable in such an arena.

Trying again to make contact with Stephen Walsh, she wondered at the extent of his influence in the whole planning process. The days of brown envelopes exchanged under the desk were supposedly in the past, but it would be naive to think that corporate incentives had no part to play in what was happening in Cheddar.

After speaking to Robertson about a possible warrant to force Walsh to speak to her, and being all but laughed out of his office, Louise went to the car-park and retrieved the files Farrell had left at her place. After suggesting she should keep clear of the case, it was strange for him to have dropped off the files.

She shut the car door and called him. 'You're not handing this case over to me are you, Greg?'

Farrell's voice boomed back through the speakers. 'Not exactly but maybe this is an avenue you would be best exploring. Perhaps from the personal angle,' he said, updating her on his meetings with the army captain. 'There's a former colleague of Marshall's who lives locally. Perhaps you could speak to him yourself?'

'What aren't you telling me, Greg?'

'Hang on a second,' said Farrell, sounding as if he'd just stepped outside. 'Right, that's better. Listen, I'm not sure what's going on here but Finch is on my back about it.'

Louise moved her phone away from her mouth and swore under her breath. 'What's he said?'

'It's not what he said but what he didn't. I get the feeling he wants to wipe this off the board and leave it with Devon and Cornwall.'

Louise wasn't surprised even though she suspected there was more to it than massaging Finch's conviction rate. 'He told you to stop investigating?'

'Not quite, but if you spoke to this Goddard guy first then we could keep it off Finch's radar. But if you'd rather I go, I will.'

She was sick of Finch's games. It could be that he'd manipulated his conversation with Farrell to force Louise to get involved. If he could prove her interference in the case was prejudicing the investigation then he would have the leverage he needed. But if she did nothing then she risked Finch getting directly involved and shutting down the investigation completely. 'Okay, leave it with me,' she said, taking Goddard's details before hanging up.

Goddard answered her call and agreed to meet with a surprising enthusiasm, and she called Thomas as she made the short journey to Clevedon to meet the man. It was hard not to feel conflicted but she could trust Thomas in her absence.

North of Weston, and south of the headquarters in Portishead, Clevedon was a mini-replica of her now hometown with its sand, muddy water and truncated pier. The man she was waiting for, Troy Goddard, had been keen to speak to her. All it had taken was the mention of Marshall and he'd jumped at the chance.

As she waited for Goddard to arrive, Louise read an early edition of *The Post*.

The paper led with the on-going story about Madison. Louise was not surprised to see Tania Elliot's name on the by-line. As she read it was easy to imagine Tania extending the article into a book. Some of the details – Madison's interest in storytelling, the area's gothic history – were so vague that they cried out for further exploration.

Louise wondered with a sardonic smile if it was about time she started asking the journalist for a percentage of her royalties. Since moving to Weston, Louise had become something of a meal ticket for her and in the article Tania alluded to Louise's two most recent cases, the phrase 'celebrated detective' making Louise wince.

She looked up to see a labourer standing by the entrance to the coffee shop looking around like a lost dog. 'Mr Goddard?' she called over.

The man turned towards her, raising his right hand. Louise remained sitting as he approached, noting the prominent tattoo of a skull and crossbones on his forearm.

'DI Blackwell?'

'Can I get you a coffee?' asked Louise.

'No thanks, don't touch the stuff,' said Goddard, sitting down.

'Thank you for seeing me on such short notice.'

'No problem. I know who you are. I was reading about you earlier actually. You want to speak to me about Nath?'

'You were in the army together?'

'We were, yes. Tight as, until the end.'

'The end?'

'I'm sure you know we were discharged, so you can cut out the games.'

'What happened?'

'What's he been up to?' said Goddard, ignoring the question.

'I'm just trying to get some background on him.'

'It's nothing to do with that girl going missing is it? I mean, he's a wanker, but he wouldn't do anything like that.'

'So you're no longer friends with him?'

'Am I fuck,' said Goddard, hardness in his eyes. 'Sorry, shouldn't swear. No, not now.'

'Is he to blame for you being let go?'

Goddard laughed. 'Let go, that's a laugh. I gave the army twelve years of my life and it was gone in a flash.'

'And that was Nathan's fault.'

'In part, yes.' Goddard sighed. 'There was an altercation. Not the first. I got caught up in it and that was that. I think they were glad really. When you reach a certain age, your usefulness can wear thin.'

'An altercation?'

'With an officer. It was off barracks. It was Nathan. Absolutely no control any more. Taking too much shit if you know what I mean. Anyway, this officer starts mouthing off and Nathan takes offence. Next thing we know, there is a full brawl and the officer is out cold. There are lots of things the army will forgive you for, but going against rank isn't one of them.'

'There'd been trouble before?'

'With Nathan, yes. Truth is he could have kept us out of it if he really wanted to but he didn't.'

'Wouldn't the officer have identified you?'

Goddard scowled. 'Yes, but Nath could have said we were bystanders or something. But he didn't and now I'm cleaning out shitty gardens for a living.'

'Have you been in contact with him since leaving?'

'Have I hell. If I see him again, I'd . . .'

Louise studied the man, already tired of his aggressive stance. 'Have you ever seen this man?' she said, placing a picture of Paul on the counter.

Goddard looked from her to the picture a couple of times. 'That's your brother, isn't it?'

'Fame spreads quickly around these parts.'

'What's this about?'

Louise told him about Paul's affair with Jodi Marshall.

'Wow. I see. You think Nathan killed him?'

'Do you think he's capable of that?'

Goddard frowned and rubbed his face. 'We're trained soldiers. Nath has seen action and he's a hothead. But this?' He scowled again, deep creases forming around his eyes. 'Sorry to ask, but your brother – he was stabbed lots of times?'

'Seventeen.'

Goddard shook his head. 'Nah. No way. I hate Nath now but he would never do that.'

'Actually he had quite a strong alibi for the night in question.'

'So why are you asking me about this then?'

'You must see that there is a potential motive here, Mr Goddard. And given Nathan's history of violence . . .'

Goddard shook his head. 'Can't help you.'

Louise wasn't sure how to take the man. He'd been so willing to meet with her but was now backtracking. 'I met Jodi the other day,' she said.

'She's a nice girl.'

'She is. What wasn't so nice was the large bruise on the side of her face.'

Goddard shook his head again. 'Fuck me. What an arsehole. Look, I can't believe he would have done anything to your brother but maybe you could try a guy he used to know. Nasty piece of work. Bryan Lemanski. He used to be in our unit. Spent five years in Colchester.'

'Colchester?'

'The military prison. I think they call it a rehabilitation centre or some such shit but I've been there and it's a prison. Nathan was good friends with Lemanski. I presume you're thinking along the lines that someone did the deed for him?'

Louise stared straight at Goddard until it dawned on him that she wasn't going to answer the question. 'Well, if anyone was going to do something like that it would be Lemanski. Him and Nath were tight as before Lemanski was put away.'

'What did he do?'

'He killed an unarmed soldier in Iraq.'

'You only get five years for that?'

'Mitigating circumstances. We were at war, remember. But . . . I don't know, let's just say no one was surprised when it happened.'

'Okay, thank you for your help Mr Goddard.'

'Actually, just thinking about it, it was Cornwall where your brother . . .'

'Yes, that's right.'

Goddard nodded as if he'd solved the case for her. 'I'm pretty sure that's where he's based nowadays.'

◆ ◆ ◆

Louise watched Goddard leave before calling Thomas. As she waited for him to answer, she scribbled Lemanski's name in her notebook over and over. It was way too early to jump to any conclusions but it annoyed her that it had taken her interference to reach this stage.

When Thomas picked up, she tried to put thoughts of Paul's case to the back of her mind. She had to focus on Madison. The letter had rejuvenated the investigation but that would only last so long. She needed to squeeze everything she could from the renewed hope it offered. They were at a pivotal time and although no one wanted to give up, the statistics were not encouraging.

She heard the tiredness in Thomas's voice. Like her, he was getting by with only a few hours' sleep a night. She wanted to confide in him about her meeting with Troy Goddard but it would be wrong to get him involved. Instead, they had a conversation she'd had a hundred times before in the last week. The updates on potential suspects felt meaningless, as if they were treading water waiting for something to happen.

'I have to go,' said Louise, hearing the weariness in her voice as a second call came in from her mother. 'I'll aim to be back at the station in an hour,' she added, accepting the new call. 'Mum?'

'Hi Louise.'

'What is it?' asked Louise, sensing the emotion in her mother's voice.

'I know you're busy, Louise, but could you come over?'

'What is it, Mum, you're scaring me.'

Her mother sounded on the verge of tears. 'It's nothing really. Emily is playing up and I think it would be good if you were here.'

'Mum, what's happened?'

'Louise, please,' said her mother.

'Mum, I am working on a missing persons case. I can't just drop everything, especially when I don't know what it is you want.' She'd been shorter than she'd wished and regretted speaking that way.

Her mother went quiet. Louise hated the feeling that somehow she was being manipulated and, despite herself, she wondered if her mother had been drinking. 'I'm sorry, Mum, but I'm under so much pressure at the moment.'

'I realise that, Louise,' said her mother, matching Louise's impatient tone. 'I just thought you might be concerned about your dad's health.'

'Jesus Christ, Mum, how can you say that when you haven't even told me what has happened. What's happened to Dad?' said Louise, her impatience replaced with a mounting panic.

'It's nothing, I don't want to worry you but he was injured. Emily was . . . involved.'

Don't want to worry you, thought Louise. 'Okay, I'll leave now,' she said.

'You don't need to,' said her mother, but Louise had already cut her off.

◆ ◆ ◆

There was no sign of Emily when she arrived. 'Mum?' said Louise, opening the front door.

'Through here, Louise.'

As Louise entered the living room, her heart sank. 'Dad, what's happened?' she asked.

Her father was sitting on the armchair, his leg stretched out in front of him. His ankle was badly swollen, her mother fussing over him with a bag of ice. 'Nothing,' he said.

'Looks like nothing,' said Louise.

Louise's mother gestured to her, nodding towards the kitchen.

'God, you don't have to treat me like a child, Sandra,' said her dad.

'What the hell is going on here?' said Louise.

'Come and sit down,' said her mother.

'Just tell me what the hell is going on. What happened to Dad?'

Her parents exchanged looks. Under her breath, her mother whispered, 'It was Emily.'

Chapter Thirty-Three

It was like every nightmare she'd ever had, every scary story she'd ever read. Sometimes the stories had happy endings but occasionally they didn't.

Madison's parents didn't like her reading newspapers but they didn't actively stop her. The newspapers she'd read contained more horror than any of the books in her library, even the adult novels she snuck past her mum and dad. People died all the time, and bad people committed crimes. The papers had taught her she was lucky to live in this country. The majority of the horror was to be found in the foreign news sections where people were dying, or starving, or being put in cages.

But bad things still happened here and she tried not to imagine what the monster would do if he caught up to her.

It had been hours since the monster had changed the batteries in the lamp. For now, Madison was glad of the dim light. The skin on her hands and knees was shredded. She felt the warmth of the blood dripping down her legs but had no desire to see the wounds she'd inflicted on herself.

She was getting closer.

She began again, taking a deep breath before scaling the cave wall once more. She told herself it was like being at Climb Zone, the climbing centre her parents took her to on special occasions, and tried her best to ignore her mind's counter-arguments – that in the cave there was no harness, there were stone walls and hard ground where usually there were cushioned pads waiting to catch you if you fell.

With each attempt she neared the top. She was starting to understand the wall. A pathway to the top existed, she was sure of that. Maybe it was her desperation, but she felt as if the wall wanted her to reach her goal. All she had to do was concentrate and hold on.

She made the first few feet with little difficulty, reaching for the grooves and rocks as she had many times before. Her journey slowed the higher she got until she reached the position of no return. She was higher than she'd ever been before and couldn't risk a fall.

There would be no point getting the lamp if she couldn't walk.

For a time she hung on the cave wall, surprising herself by smiling at the thought that she must look like Spider-Man. As she moved her right hand to a little crack in the wall, she wished then that she had his superpowers. Even if she reached the lamp, she had no idea if she could dislodge it, and sometimes coming down was harder than going up. But she couldn't dwell on that. Anyone who wasn't brave rarely survived in her stories and she needed to focus on the positives. She was only feet away from the lamp now; if she could get it, she could get out of the cave; could escape and get back to see her parents.

She could say sorry.

Her hands felt red raw as she held on to the rock, her skin tearing as she eased her body weight up. She was inches away and could see much clearer now she was nearer the lamp. She studied the space above her, knowing a fall would potentially be fatal, and determined the best positions for hands and feet to move towards.

She hung that way for minutes, too scared to move. Her strength was fading and she needed to act quickly. The monster could return any second and he'd already warned her – in that ugly, breathy way – that he would take away the lamp and she didn't think she would survive this place in darkness.

Screaming with effort, the sound of her thin voice reverberating around the cave, Madison scrambled upwards until she was level with the lamp. She almost fell as she foolishly touched the outer glass. The heat, although meagre, burnt her raw flesh.

Up close Madison saw the battery was stuck crudely into a metal casing and with her left hand locked on to the cave wall, she managed to shake it loose.

As she descended she kept waiting for the monster to appear but she reached the ground without him returning. There was little time to waste. She didn't know how long the lamp would last but this would be her one and only chance. With no belongings to collect, she gave herself the once over with the lamp, running the light over her wounds and scrapes.

She'd only edged her way to the cave entrance once before, her eyes glued to the light. When she'd stuck her head out that time, all she'd experienced was darkness. Unable to see more than half a metre in front of her, she'd retreated back to confinement.

This time the light revealed a second corridor-like structure, much narrower than her cave. It presented two choices – left or right. She tried to recall which way the monster had led her but she'd been too disorientated then. Ignoring the voice in her head telling her she would get lost, she chose the left-hand path where the cave floor was slightly elevated.

The air remained still, the visibility restricted to the faint beam of the light as she crept forwards. She couldn't hurry. That was the mistake they always made in her stories. Running would make her panic and that would make her fall.

The corridor led to a larger open area, Madison was dismayed to see the multiple options available to her. The monster had told her she would get lost and now she understood. There were three routes out of the area and then who knew what awaited her. Still, anything was preferable to going back to her cave and waiting for him to return. She picked up a loose stone and scraped a mark on the entrance to the corridor she'd just left with a triangle and the number one, deciding she would take the first exit out of the cave and see where it led. She marked this entrance with two triangles and the number two, just as she heard the sound of the monster returning through the next corridor along.

Chapter Thirty-Four

Louise stared at her mother dumbfounded. 'What do you mean, it was Emily?'

'It was nothing,' said her father. 'An accident.'

'It wasn't nothing and I'm afraid it wasn't an accident, Danny. She was in one of her rages, Lou, and Dad tried to get her to go up to her room to calm down. He was on the stairs and she pushed him.'

'It was three stairs,' said her father. 'I landed awkwardly and hurt my ankle. This is all an overreaction.'

'Tell me exactly what happened,' said Louise, realising that, like her parents, she was talking under her breath. 'Emily is in her room, I take it?'

Her mother nodded. 'It was six stairs, and your dad was lucky not to have been hurt more severely. She's in her room and she won't speak to anyone.'

'What sparked the behaviour?'

'It was nothing. She wanted to go out but it was about to rain so we said it would have to wait until later. She . . .' Her mother hesitated, as if confused. 'She told us she hated us.'

Louise's skin prickled. She saw the genuine hurt in her mother's eyes and although of course Emily hadn't meant what she'd said,

Louise had never heard her say that before. 'She didn't mean it, Mum.'

'I know that, Louise,' said her mother, in angry defence. 'That isn't the point. The point is she stormed off and was so angry that she shoved your dad down the stairs.'

'I was off balance and she didn't shove me, she held her hands out.'

'Look, I'm not necessarily saying she meant to push you downstairs.'

'Well, that is something,' said Louise's father.

Her mother gave him the kind of withering look only a long-standing partner could give. It contained anger and exasperation, but also a hint of amusement. 'But she did push you, Danny, and it wasn't in a nice way. She would never have done such a thing . . . before.'

Louise sat on the sofa. 'It was the psychologist appointment today, wasn't it? I'm sorry, with everything that's been going on I forgot.'

'Don't be silly, Louise,' said her father, grimacing as he adjusted his position in the armchair. 'You have far too much on your plate as it is.'

'I should have made time,' said Louise, thinking back to that morning where she'd woken up on the sofa and her subsequent meeting with Troy Goddard in Clevedon. Her life was in such turmoil at the moment that something had to give. It was impossible not to blame herself for what had happened, and that was becoming a familiar refrain. If only she'd been there at the psychologist appointment, maybe she could have helped keep Emily's behaviour in check.

It was no wonder the girl's mood had changed after seeing the psychologist. However gentle and patient Dr Morris was with her, the sessions always provoked painful memories of Paul and the night of his death.

'I'll go and see her,' Louise said.

◆ ◆ ◆

Emily was sitting on her bed. As Louise knocked and entered the room, the girl pulled her knees up to her chest. The concentrated frown on her face was at once funny and heartbreaking.

'Can I sit?' said Louise, softly.

Emily shrugged and Louise moved to the edge of the bed. 'Bad day?' said Louise. 'I know how that feels.'

Emily pouted her lips. She was as close as Louise would probably ever come to having a daughter, yet sometimes she felt a distance between her and the girl. That in itself wasn't surprising. For most of her life, she'd seen Emily at most once a week and occasionally would go weeks without seeing her. In the past, the changes had been staggering – her first words, Emily learning to walk – and even now she saw little changes every time they met. It was this distance that made the changes feel all that more significant. The truth was that as the way things were, she would never truly be there for her niece. 'You know Grandma and Grandad aren't angry with you, don't you?'

Emily didn't respond. Her anger was palpable and Louise didn't know where that anger was aimed. 'Come on now, let's go downstairs.'

'No,' said Emily, surprising Louise by her calm forcefulness. Louise wanted to put her arm around her niece and was pained that it scared her to do so. She imagined Madison somewhere alone, and as she blinked her eyes she saw Emily in her place.

'Grandma and Grandad just want you to be happy,' she said, not knowing if she was doing the right thing.

'They hate me,' said Emily under her breath, standing. Her tiny hands were clenched in front of her, her body shaking.

Louise had never seen Emily like this before. She was only six but it felt like she was slipping away from her. It would probably have been best to leave Emily for a bit to calm down but she was spooked by her reaction and continued speaking. 'Of course they don't hate you, Emily,' she said, keeping her voice quiet. 'They just had a fright. Grandad is fine.'

She didn't know if she was doing the right thing. She couldn't believe Emily had meant to hurt her grandfather, but that didn't necessarily mean she shouldn't be disciplined for her actions. She wondered if parents ever really knew what they were doing. Emily had lost both her parents in the most traumatic of circumstances and Louise had no appetite to scold her for lashing out. She wondered what Madison's parents would do if their daughter ever returned. It seemed unfeasible that they would ever let her out of their sight again.

Emily began to cry and for now Louise didn't care if she was doing the right thing. All she wanted was to comfort Emily and to do her best to take her pain from her. 'I know, darling,' she said, moving over to the girl who climbed into her arms and began to sob.

When Louise returned downstairs to the kitchen, her mother was halfway through a bottle of wine. She sighed as she caught Louise glancing at the bottle, but had no time to object as Emily ran over and grabbed her by the waist. 'Okay, little one,' said Louise's mother, running her fingers through Emily's hair.

'Have you seen Grandad?' said Emily, clinging on to her grandma.

'Come on, I think he's through here,' said Louise, prying the girl away.

'Here she is,' said her father, as Louise led Emily into the living room where her niece promptly burst into tears again.

Louise had to reach and stop her father getting to his feet, the ice pack falling on to the floor.

'Don't be silly now,' said Louise's father. 'It's just a little bruising.'

'I'm sorry, Grandad,' said Emily.

'That's okay. You come and sit next to me. The good thing about having a poorly foot is that Grandma is letting us have dinner in front of the television.'

Louise returned to the kitchen in time to see her mother pouring another glass of wine.

'What?' asked her mother, before Louise had even opened her mouth.

Louise didn't understand how her mother couldn't see the parallels between what she was doing and what had happened to Paul. It was another thing to feel helpless about, but for now it was secondary to looking after Emily. 'Dinner in front of the television, then?'

'You staying?' said her mother, defensive even though Louise hadn't said anything.

Louise was about to accept the less-than-gracious invite when multiple messages began pinging on her phone.

Chapter Thirty-Five

Madison knew this was a time to be brave. If she became lost in the labyrinth of the caves, then so be it. Better that than being captured again. Her options were limited by the presence of the monster so she continued heading in the same direction, the lamp held low so she could see where her feet were stepping.

She heard him behind her. The strange sound of his breath, the awkward way his legs moved as he followed. She fought the fear that he was playing with her; that he could reach out at any second and drag her back into the caves. 'Keep looking forward,' she whispered to herself, as she rushed into another tunnel.

Quiet as she tried to be, the caves amplified the sound of her movement. She decided it didn't matter. The monster was following so her only hope was to outrun him.

On she went, deeper into the narrowing tunnel. She wasn't sure if it was her imagination but the air suddenly felt colder. It rippled along her skin, sending goosebumps over her flesh. And in the cold air wasn't that the scent of the grass, the trees, the outdoors she thought she would never experience again?

She was close but the monster was getting closer too. She didn't want to turn back less she see his misshapen face grinning at her, his mouth open wide in the rictus grin she'd imagined in her delirious nightmares.

As the air became fresher, the tunnel narrowed. She heard him behind her, the steady thud of his feet like the zombies she'd seen on Dad's television programme – always slower but somehow able to catch their much faster prey.

Her mouth opened but no sound came out. She was there. It was an exit but it looked too small for her to fit through and she couldn't see what lay beyond. All she could see was a slight modification of colour, the night sky illuminated by the partially hidden moon.

Madison placed the lamp through the opening and peered through but couldn't see any further. As she pulled her arm back in, her hand caught on the rock opening. She didn't usually swear – many of the kids in her year did – but she swore now as the lamp rolled away from her grasp.

He was coming, she was sure. She couldn't tell if the lamp had fallen. The wind was rattling against the rocks. Dad had showed her little inlets before in the rock face. If she could squeeze through the opening she could find herself hundreds of feet above the ground but even that sounded better than being trapped in the tunnel with the monster.

She screamed as the skin on her neck ripped as she snagged her head through the gap, the feel of the cold air on her skin making her want to cry with its promise.

Something touched her legs and she screamed and wiggled her body, ignoring the pain as the rock sliced through her threadbare clothes.

She was through, her body dangling mid-air as her right foot remained snagged on the cave opening. She would have searched for the lamp but she expected the monster to reach through any second and grab her. So she wiggled her leg with everything she had and eventually it was loose from the rock face.

And she was falling.

Chapter Thirty-Six

The police helicopter acted as a beacon, hovering over the site close to the hamlet of Charterhouse. As Louise rushed along the darkened bends of the country road, she caught glimpses of flashing sirens in the night sky. Her attention was being diverted by the conference call streaming through the car's speakers, the voices of Assistant Chief Constable Morely, DCI Robertson and Finch, all competing to be heard.

The emergency services call had come in thirty minutes ago. Louise had listened to the message over ten times and it echoed through her head. The choking sounds of a woman on the phone, her voice filled with a trembling panic and disbelief, trying to tell the operative that her baby boy was missing from his cot. A local uniformed pairing had reached the scene within fifteen minutes and had confirmed that there appeared to have been a break-in at the Bolton farm on the outskirts of Charterhouse, deep into the Mendip Hills, and if the mother was to be believed, a nine-month-old boy by the name of Aaron Bolton was missing.

It seemed Madison's abductor wasn't finished. It was inconceivable to think the cases weren't linked. What this meant for Madison, Louise wasn't sure. Her mind was racing with various thoughts, none of which were helpful. As the road narrowed, a set of flashing lights blinked in her rear-view mirror.

'Get a move on, Blackwell,' said Finch, over the radio, flashing his lights behind her.

Louise was already close to sixty and the lane was narrow and dark. 'Let's try and both get there in one piece, Timothy,' she replied, purposely using Finch's hated first name.

'Both get there safely and report to me the minute you do,' said the Assistant Chief, signing off.

The courtyard of the Bolton farmhouse was already dotted with emergency vehicles. The lights of the solitary ambulance and three police cars pierced the night sky, their sirens silenced. Although she would rather have dealt with this alone with her team, Louise accepted Finch's presence was necessary. Madison's disappearance was already a major case, but with a baby being abducted from a house the inclusion of MIT was now unavoidable. Her only priority was finding the missing children and she was willing to put aside her differences with Finch to achieve that goal.

A different FLO, a young constable Louise knew as Rachael Maher, introduced herself to Louise as she parked up and walked into the stone farmhouse. The place had the same cold feeling as the commune, which Louise had noted was less than ten minutes' drive away.

'The mother is through there,' said Rachael, pointing to a kitchen area. 'Ellie Bolton. As you can imagine, she's beside herself. I've only just managed to stop her screaming. I had to drag her in from the fields.'

'Is there a husband?' said Louise, as Finch arrived, preceded by the smell of his citrus aftershave.

'Sir,' said Rachael to Finch before continuing. 'Yes, Liam Bolton. He's been notified. He was doing a weekly shop and is on his way back.'

'Thanks, Rachael. I'll come through now,' said Louise, turning to face Finch. Even with the place swarming with officers, she hated being in such close proximity to the man. He'd lied, tried to get her dismissed with the possibility of jail time, and when he hadn't succeeded had spent months harassing her by anonymous text messages. And now she had to work with him directly, when she couldn't trust him in any way.

'Look, Tim, I don't want to get into a thing about this but I am SIO on this case so would appreciate it if I led with no interference from you,' she said.

Finch was the higher ranked officer and could make things very difficult for her. Louise studied his reaction, the smug way he scrunched his eyes together as if in thought when the only thing he would be thinking about was how to come out of this on top. 'Okay, it's your show, Lou. My team and I are at your disposal.'

'Thank you, Tim,' said Louise, not buying a second of Finch's act.

◆ ◆ ◆

Ellie Bolton sat staring at the corner of the kitchen. Ghost-pale, she was rocking on a wooden dining chair that was scraping against the stone floor.

'Ellie, this is DI Louise Blackwell,' said the FLO.

'Mrs Bolton, I'm Louise. May I call you Ellie?'

The mother turned towards Louise, the blankness in her eyes unsettling to see. 'Ellie?' repeated Louise, her voice as light as a whisper. 'I know how hard this is for you, and this will be hard to hear, but we must act now if we are to find Aaron. Do you understand?'

Ellie's eyes flickered at the sound of her son's name, as if she'd just woken up. 'Aaron,' she mouthed.

'Can you show me where he was?' asked Louise.

Ellie nodded and stood, her chair falling to the floor.

'I'll get that,' said Rachael.

In the hallway, two SOCOs were suiting up. Louise nodded to Janice Sutton. 'Mrs Bolton is going to show me where Aaron was sleeping,' said Louise.

Janice frowned. Louise knew she probably didn't want the scene tampered with before she'd processed it. 'Take these,' said Janice, handing her some gloves.

'Ellie, if you don't mind?' said Louise, the woman placing the latex gloves on in a daze.

The bedroom light was on, and Ellie fell to her knees crying at the sight of the empty cot. 'He's only been sleeping here for two months,' she said, between sobs.

Louise had to concentrate to keep her emotions in check. She sympathised with the mother who was being led away by Rachael. She thought about Emily sleeping alone in her room and resisted the urge to call her parents to check in on her. She had to stay focused, and she began considering how the abductor would have got in the room unnoticed.

Janice was suited and began taping the scene. Louise put on foot protectors and walked across the room, the carpet plush beneath her feet. As she glanced in the cot, her breath caught at the sight of a lone teddy bear lying next to the space where Aaron should have been.

With Janice's permission, she pulled back the curtains to reveal a wooden-framed window. Louise pushed at the frame, the window opening. For the sake of the camera, she pointed to the part where the lock had been broken. A bitter wind billowed through the gap as she eased the window open, the space big enough for an adult to get through.

As she returned through to the other side of the room, Louise heard a commotion. Stepping into the hallway, she saw a man take hold of Ellie. 'What has happened, Ellie?' he demanded, his face red.

'Mr Bolton?' said Louise.

The man pulled Ellie closer to him and turned to Louise. 'What's happened?' he said, his wide eyes wet and staring as if he couldn't quite believe where he was and what he was seeing.

◆ ◆ ◆

Returning to the kitchen, Louise accepted the cup of tea from Rachael. Ellie and Liam Bolton sat next to each other at the dining table, their bodies fused together.

'I can't even pretend to know what you both must be going through,' said Louise. 'And I apologise for having to ask these questions but time is so imperative now.'

'We understand,' said Liam.

'It appears that the lock on the bedroom window is broken. Was it like that before?'

Ellie pushed herself away from her husband and turned to face him, rage in her eyes. 'I told you this would happen,' she said to him, before looking at Louise. 'I told him. How could we leave Aaron alone in that room? Look what we've done.'

'We're having some building work done upstairs so it isn't safe at the moment,' said Liam, his face ashen.

'But he should have stayed in with us,' said Ellie, her words so full of hate that Rachael had to place her hand on the woman.

'I'm sorry, but was the lock already broken?'

Ellie shook her head. 'No. I check it every time I put him down. I hate him being in there. Hate it,' she screamed at her husband.

'And obviously you didn't hear anything after you put Aaron down?' said Louise.

'No, of course not.'

'Any odd occurrences in the area? People you've never seen before perhaps.'

'Things have been a bit strange with what's happened in Cheddar but nothing has really happened here. Isn't that right, Ellie?' said Liam.

Ellie glared at Liam open-mouthed. 'Does this have something to do with what happened in Cheddar? Oh my god,' she said, realisation dawning on her. 'He's taken him like he took that girl.'

'Please, Ellie, let's not jump to any conclusions,' said Louise. 'You have that commune down the road, don't you?' she asked, matter-of-factly.

'Those fucking weirdos,' said Liam. 'What? You don't think they have something to do with it, do you?' He stood, anger washing over him, as if poised to set off towards the commune in attack.

'Please sit down, Mr Bolton.'

He sat back down with such little protest that Louise wondered if it had all been for show. 'Why do you call them weirdos?' she asked.

'God knows what they get up to there. Smoking all that shit, and that environmental nonsense. It's always been the same ever since I was a lad. Different guise but all the same.'

'What do you mean, the same?'

'My dad used to call them hippies. Always something weird going on. There used to be rumours of people going missing in the hills. Quite easy to get lost out there, and the stories would start, you know?'

'Not really, no,' said Louise.

Liam had warmed to his tale, and Louise wondered if, at that precise second, he remembered his son was missing. 'Weird stuff, like I said. I don't know, rituals, sacrifice, there used to be talk about cannibals having once lived in the hills going back hundreds of years. I know it's all horseshit but . . .' The change on the man's face was hard to watch. The flesh around his jawline began to wobble, as it dawned on him what he was saying. 'You don't think . . .'

Louise didn't want to know what images were filling his head. 'There is absolutely nothing to suggest that the commune are involved in any way, Liam,' she said.

Ellie broke the ensuing silence with a scream. 'The man,' she said.

Controlling the heavy burst of adrenaline flooding her system at the thought that the man could be the same person who took Madison, Louise asked, 'What man, Ellie?'

'It was a couple of days ago, I think. Do you remember, Liam, I told you about him?'

Liam looked at his wife as if he didn't recognise her.

'You never fucking listen. Sorry, I shouldn't swear,' said Ellie, abashed by the outburst. 'He was walking along the fields up top.' Ellie pointed to the back of the house. 'I didn't think nothing of it but I saw him a couple of hours later and he was still there and he was holding some binoculars.'

Chapter Thirty-Seven

There was no pleasure in what he was doing. If it was having an effect he'd long since lost the ability to acknowledge it. 'Another, please,' said Hoxton, from the comfort of the leather chair in the lounge.

The waiter loitered as if he hadn't heard the request.

'You're right,' said Hoxton, after the pause had grown uncomfortable. 'You're probably right.' He stood up, the bar somehow spinning in two conflicting directions.

'Can I help you to your room?' said the waiter.

Always keep the waiting staff happy was a mantra Hoxton lived by. 'I'll be fine,' he said, shuffling his way across the lounge. His fellow drinkers snuck glances at him. He could do without their pity but it was taking an extraordinary amount of effort just to stay upright.

Time slipped, and he was back in his hotel room. In the corner the television was playing the local news. In Hoxton's hand was a glass of something clear and alcoholic. He sniffed at it, wincing at the acrid smell, before taking a large gulp. The burning liquid tickled his throat and he tripped over himself as he found the source bottle.

He'd received news about the missing boy before it became public knowledge, one of his police contacts sharing the news by text message as if the abduction of a child was throwaway news. Hoxton's first reaction had been to reach for a bottle and he'd done little since but drink.

As far as Hoxton was concerned, the last couple of days had revealed to him the worst of humanity and he'd been more than complicit. It had started with the council meeting. The self-interest on display had made him despair and each time he'd spoken the company line he felt as if a bit of his soul had been eroded. And all of it in view of DI Blackwell.

He sank another drink. He thought the bottle might be tequila, but his taste-buds were no longer reliable. It was laughable to think he'd ever had a chance with the policewoman. It had been some time since he'd been so taken with someone and he'd managed to fuck it up in a matter of days. As far as he knew he was probably a suspect, and even if he wasn't, she'd seen enough of his bad side: his cowardice in representing Walsh and his inability to control his behaviour. He'd seen the dismissive way she'd looked at him at the meeting and could only guess at what she thought of him. And now there was another missing child.

Hoxton had a brother. They rarely spoke but he hadn't been able to stop thinking about him since hearing about the missing boy. It was pointless making resolutions when he was in this state – even if he did remember in the morning, he would dismiss any notion of change out of hand – but he promised himself he would call his brother tomorrow. He understood now that time was short and he was wasting it. He pictured the scene at the missing boy's house and tried to imagine what the parents were going through, the kind of panic and despair they were enduring. It made his chest tight and he tried to cry but nothing happened.

The disorientation was nothing new. One moment he was in the bathroom, confused by the dimmer switch and the lights above the bathroom mirror, the next he was outside, on the main street in

Cheddar, a bottle of wine in his hand, the tequila bottle seemingly having disappeared.

Hoxton blinked, trying to recall how he'd got there. Try as he might, the journey from bedroom to road was a blank. The only truth was the red wine and even that was a conundrum. It certainly wasn't anything from the mini-bar but its rusted taste soothed him as he stumbled through the meandering road of the gorge, the cliff faces crowding towards him from both sides until he was standing outside the hidden entrance to the caves.

It had all started here, that night he'd foolishly taken Jennings and his sycophants to see that ludicrous tourist attraction. If only he'd stayed home that night, maybe this whole sorry affair could have been avoided. Yet despite wanting to avoid the place, it kept calling him back as if the interior of the cave held the answers he so desperately sought.

His disorientation took on a greater scope as he slid through the opening into the enveloping darkness. Deprived of light, Hoxton was thrown into panic. He dropped the bottle, the deep waft of spilled alcohol filling the air as he desperately searched for a light in his pockets. Luck resulted in his fumbling fingers activating the torchlight on his phone and from there he managed to locate the torch he'd brought with him. He glanced down at the tragedy of the broken bottle and struggled to hold on to his own sense of reality.

Being with Jennings and the others in the cave had been spooky, but being alone was a completely different experience. Even the insensitivity that came from being drunk was absent as Hoxton tried to hold on to the reason he was there.

It was the noise they'd heard.

Everyone present had tried to write it off as group panic, a mild sort of shared hallucination, but Hoxton didn't believe that now. He'd heard something similar at the commune. And he was sure the answer was here, in the cave. If he could only solve the riddle of who or what it belonged to, then maybe he could redeem himself. Surely it wasn't too late for the missing boy, and hopefully the girl. If he could just work it out, he could tell Louise Blackwell and all would be well. He didn't want, or deserve, anything beyond that.

His courage returned as he followed the light beam across the cave wall, the only noise the clipping of his feet on the stone floor. When he thought about the sound he'd heard that night, his memory was jumbled and confused. He pictured the source of the sound as something deformed and monstrous hiding in the caves and even though it wasn't fully formed in his mind, he was worried that the thing was waiting for him deeper into the caves.

Feeling like prey, Hoxton bent down through the low ceiling and was presented once again with the cave imp. Even in his delirious state, Hoxton was able to laugh at the fibreglass figurine. It was beyond him how he could have ever seen anything menacing in the sight. Its soulless eyes glared at him but the threat was empty; as fake as he was. What had he expected? For the imp to find voice, to merge with the rattling breathing that haunted his dreams? Then what? Was he supposed to confront it, redeem himself by defeating the monster? 'Come on then,' he screamed, his voice reverberating around the cave. 'Show yourself.'

The cave remained quiet and Hoxton retreated. He'd been scared last time. Now he was desperate to hear the sounds again, wanted to will the monster into life, but the only thing he heard as he left the cave was his own ragged breathing, and in the distance the whine of police sirens.

Chapter Thirty-Eight

Louise kept glancing behind her as she battled through the gloom to the top of the hill, the Bolton farmhouse shrinking with every step.

'It must have been about here that I saw him,' said Ellie, who was all but wrapped fully in her husband's arms. 'It was lighter than this so it's hard to tell.'

Louise took a set of binoculars from Farrell, who she'd requested accompany her up the hill along with two uniformed officers. Two dog teams were already searching the area and the whine of police drones hung in the air.

Even with the binoculars, the mist and poor light made it difficult to focus on the house. It would be different in daylight but even now, both the living room and ground floor bedroom where Aaron had been taken were visible. 'It was just the one day you saw this man?' Louise asked Ellie.

'I think so. The walkway is up there,' said Ellie, pointing into the shadows. 'I see people all the time. Sometimes it's a strange comfort when you're alone. Sometimes it's a bit freaky but Liam is normally at home. As I said, it wasn't even the binoculars that worried me as we get bird watchers all the time. It was the way they were pointed at the farmhouse. If I'd known he was going to take Aaron . . .' Her husband grabbed her as her knees buckled.

'Is this necessary?' said Liam.

The question was more pertinent than Louise would have liked. Ever since that first day on the cliff walk there had been a sense of unpredictability to the investigation. The escalation was like nothing Louise had seen. The abduction, first of a pre-teen and then of a baby, was so random, and being on the hill in the middle of the night looking down on the farmhouse didn't at that moment feel like the greatest use of their time. 'Please, take Ellie back down,' said Louise, nodding to one of the uniformed officers.

'I've never seen anything like this,' said Farrell, as they walked back down the hill, the stumbling shadows of the Boltons in the distance.

'If it's the same person then they are getting more confident,' said Louise, almost to herself. 'If they were staking this place out then it suggests a certain premeditation that I'm not sure existed before.'

'You don't think the abductor targeted Madison specifically?'

'If we assume for now it's the same perpetrator, then why take an eleven-year-old and then a baby? It's horrendous to think but maybe Madison was a test run.'

Just saying the words made Louise feel uneasy. That someone could treat life so cheaply was horrendous, but Louise had seen it too many times before to be surprised.

'I know this isn't the time, but did you see Troy Goddard?' asked Farrell, as they made their way down the hill.

Farrell was right. It wasn't the time but every time she thought about Madison and the missing baby, her thoughts returned to what had happened to Emily and the threat looming for the case. Of course, they could leave it for now. Even if it was shelved, a case was never fully closed. But now that the Marshall line of enquiry had opened up, it was prudent that they explored it to its full extent. Goddard had given her Lemanski's name and it would be imprudent not to act on it. For that, she needed Farrell's help. She told him about the meeting. 'I think I've done all I can on this. I need to be fully focused on the case here, Greg. Can you do that for me?' She waited for Farrell to respond and when he didn't she said, 'Finch is still on your back?'

The uneasy silence seemed to last an eternity. Louise knew what was said next between them could forever define their relationship. It appeared Farrell was thinking along the same lines, his face twitching as he decided what to say.

'He's watching everything I do,' he said, eventually.

Louise shook her head. She was disappointed in him but he wouldn't be the first one to succumb to Finch's influence. 'You can't worry about that, Greg. No one had spoken to Nathan Marshall before I made that connection. Finch won't be able to stand in your way on this and if he tries, you have to question his reasoning. You must understand that?' She was sure he did understand, but he would also appreciate what going against Finch could do to his career.

Even in the gloom, Louise saw the remorse in Farrell's eyes. Despite the seriousness of their current situation, it was endearing to see him look at his feet. 'Did he tell you not to pursue that line of investigation?' she asked.

'Not explicitly. It was more a heavy suggestion, if you know what I mean.'

Louise knew exactly what he meant. Finch was too clever to be caught out by issuing a formal instruction that could later be called into question. A suggestion was nothing more than a suggestion and as Farrell was one of the lead investigators it was his decision how best to proceed. Something Louise reminded her colleague.

'You think I should stand up to the bully?' said Farrell, with a joyless laugh.

'Go see Lemanski, put it in your report. Finch won't be able to do anything then. You'll be doing the right thing.'

Farrell nodded but didn't look convinced.

'You're going to learn, Greg, that sometimes you need to make uncomfortable decisions. Sure it might piss Finch off if you do it but you never know, he might even respect you.'

'Or he might make me his enemy.'

Louise shrugged. 'It's a decision you'll have to make, Greg. Would you rather be on Finch's side or do the right thing?'

Farrell clenched his stomach in mock pain. 'Ouch, that's a low blow. I think I'd rather be his enemy than yours, that's for sure.'

'Go find this Lemanski character,' said Louise. 'Get it on the record as soon as you are able.'

'What about this?' said Farrell, looking down towards the farmhouse, still illuminated by the flashing blue lights.

Louise tried to convince herself she wasn't being selfish. They could do with all available officers, especially at the moment, but Farrell needed to pursue his own case before it was too late and Finch managed to destroy it. 'We've got ninety-five per cent of Avon and Somerset working on this. You're a good officer, Greg, but I'm sure we can survive without you for the day.'

◆ ◆ ◆

Finch was in the kitchen when they returned. He was nursing a coffee, his earnest focus on the young FLO, Rachael, who was busy detailing her previous work history. Farrell shot Louise a look before escaping out of the back door.

With a simple turn of his back, Finch silenced Rachael. Louise noted the familiar look of surprise on the FLO who processed Finch's snub before leaving to the living room, shutting the door behind her.

'You're doing a great job,' said Finch, approaching Louise.

She had to hand it to the man. He could say so much by saying so little. If she hadn't known him as well as she did, hadn't experienced his duplicity and lies, she would have felt flattered by the comment. Even now, she was forced to fight the part of her that had once sought Finch's praise and respect.

'Not sure Mr and Mrs Bolton enjoyed their little sojourn up the hill though,' he added, unable to maintain the pretence of positivity.

'If you'll excuse me, I have a search to co-ordinate,' she said.

Finch pretended to look at his watch. 'The PolSA has that in hand. Why don't we sit down and you can show me your action plan.'

Louise tensed, an ache spreading from her neck down her back. If it had been any other senior officer, she would have been obliged to accept their request but the last thing she wanted, or intended, to do was sit down with Finch and work on anything. He knew that as well as she did so she was surprised when he reached out and grabbed her as she began to walk away.

'Get the fuck off me,' she said, under her breath, shrugging off his hand and reaching for the expandable baton on her belt.

Finch held his hands up. 'Hey, calm down, Lou.'

Louise's pulse was so fast she felt dizzy. Her hand was still poised. No one had seen Finch reach for her but still she considered using the baton on him. He stared at her, his lips upturned, his eyes saying: *it would be your word against mine – just like last time.* She pictured the baton striking him in the mouth and wondered if she would be able to stop herself once she'd hit him. Finch raised his eyebrows willing her to attack – later she would realise this was what had stopped her.

'Where was Farrell off to in such a hurry?' asked Finch, stepping back, Louise's heartbeat slowing.

'I thought he reported to you, Timothy,' said Louise, receiving a grimace from Finch at the use of his full name.

'He's very sweet on you, isn't he?'

'He's professional, diligent and respectful. Things you haven't managed to grind out of him yet.'

Finch smiled. 'And loyal. Don't forget loyal. Like a little lapdog returning to its master.'

'Greg's his own man, Timothy. Maybe you should treat him as such.'

Finch looked over to the shut door. 'I shouldn't tell you this but we're friends so why not . . .'

'I'm not interested,' said Louise, interrupting.

'Oh, you will be. You see, once you fuck this up – and you will fuck this up – you'll be back to Portishead.'

Louise lowered her eyes. 'Whatever you say, Tim.'

'It's been in the pipeline for some time now. You've seen the local stations go. It beats me why we even need a CID department working out of Weston. And that's what I told the Chief. Why not merge the departments? Naturally, there'd be a bit of trimming necessary but I'm sure you can see how much more productive we'd be working out of one central location.'

Louise had heard such rumours before. It was true that other local departments had merged, or had become effectively community-policing centres. She didn't doubt Finch had the ear of the chief constable but she couldn't believe they would disband the team in Weston on his say-so.

'I know what you're thinking – all your recent success. But there is that small matter of your brother,' said Finch.

'Don't,' said Louise, her pulse rising again.

Finch stepped towards her just as the living room door began creaking open. 'What sort of man does that, eh?' he said, under his breath as Louise's hand tightened around the tip of the baton. 'Puts his daughter into danger like that?'

Louise moved forward towards Finch. Drops of spittle fell from his open mouth and it took all of her will-power not to smash his teeth in there and then.

'Ma'am,' said the FLO, waving a mobile phone in the air. Her voice was low, sensing the tension in the room.

As Louise walked over to her, Finch gave one last parting shot, the words so soft that they were almost inaudible.

'How is Emily by the way?' he said. 'It would be horrible if something happened to her,' he added, the humour in his smile not reaching his eyes.

Louise let the comment sink in. She had no idea what Finch meant by the threat, but her body tensed. He wanted her to react and she couldn't help herself. The years of betrayal and hurt she'd suffered at Finch's hands filled her with an uncontrollable anger. She made a step towards him, his grin widening, and was about to do something that would most likely have ended her career when she felt a hand on her shoulder.

She turned to face Rachael who was holding out a phone towards her. The FLO shot Finch a nervous look before speaking. 'I think you should take this, ma'am,' she said.

Chapter Thirty-Nine

Madison closed her eyes and waited for impact, surprised when it came almost instantly. Landing on her side, the ground as hard as the rock of the cave, she continued falling only coming to a halt as she stuck her hands out and dug her nails into the hard soil, her body crashing into jagged brambles.

She curled herself into a ball. She was freezing, but elated to be away from the monster, even if she wasn't completely free of him yet.

She opened her eyes and adjusted to her surroundings. Her hand went over her mouth as she gazed down at the drop ten metres further into the brambles. In the gloom, she couldn't see the bottom of the descent, only the jagged rocks which would have killed her long before she'd reached the bottom.

As she'd suspected, the tunnel had led to an opening in the cliff wall. On her hands and knees she crawled back up, past the cave opening where she imagined the monster was watching her.

She screamed at the scurrying noise to her left, and continued to do so even when she discovered the source of the noise was one of the wild goats that lived on the clifftops. It felt good to give voice to all her fears and anger. She hoped the monster was watching, trapped behind the opening too narrow for him to escape.

She was grateful that the goat appeared impervious to her cries. It continued sniffing the ground and allowed her to approach within ten metres before scurrying away.

Madison followed as best she could. The ground was worn, a path of sorts forming between the twisted brambles and bushes. She was desperate to run but kept calm, fearing that she would stumble into another descent.

And then from nowhere, heart racing, something miraculous appeared out of the clouds. She'd never been this high up before at night. As she stared at the lights of the village, the glow piercing the gloom and acting as a siren call, Madison began to cry, wondering if somewhere among those lights her parents were waiting for her.

◆ ◆ ◆

She wouldn't rest until she was home. She'd promised herself when she'd been taken that she would never walk the cliff path – alone or not – ever again, but she had to break her promise to get home. Telling herself the monster was still trapped within the cave, she kept her pace steady. It was hard not to run but the mud path was lined with jagged rocks and stones, the light still too dim to see properly. By now the monster would be unravelling himself and returning to another exit. He could be on his way, but if she fell and twisted her ankle she would be no use to anyone.

For a time, the lights didn't appear to be getting any nearer. She stumbled in the darkness as if trapped again in the never-ending tunnels of the caves. Every time she completed a descent, another appeared, her only companions the light breeze of the ice wind and the sound she hoped she was imagining – the footsteps of the monster in pursuit.

Only when she reached the lookout tower did she start to believe she might escape this nightmare. It was still night, the sun showing no inclination to rise, so she decided to take the stone steps of Jacob's Ladder. The exit would be closed but she could scale the iron gate by the shop. Better that than spend another second in the desolate woodland.

Two hundred and seventy-four steps. She'd counted them numerous times before both ascending and descending but there was no time for that now. She jumped them two at a time, never looking back, the end near enough to touch.

She almost cried when she reached the last step, but it wasn't over. The shop was closed and the thick bars barricading her from the pavement were higher than she remembered.

She forced a quick look back up the steps before climbing on to the railings. The freezing metal was hard to touch, her hands so numb that she struggled to get any leverage. The shadows from Jacob's Ladder – moving either from the breeze or the following monster – forced her up, the muscles in her shoulder tearing as she hoisted her body on top of and over the railings, landing with a thud on the pavement.

She was winded but able to stand up to face the man who'd appeared from the darkness. She tried to scream but no air was left in her.

The man looked more shocked than Madison felt. 'Are you okay?' he said, his mouth wide open.

Madison glared at him, momentarily frozen in place, before she recovered her senses, turned and ran.

As she ran, the cold air stung her lungs that were already close to bursting. For all she knew, the shocked man was the monster, so she continued running wondering if she would wake up at any second to find herself back in the cave.

And then somehow she was outside her house. The downstairs light was on and the front door open.

From the kitchen, she heard the faint sound of someone saying, 'Madison,' the words becoming more urgent, until they were being screamed and her mum was there, and her dad was there, and they were cuddling her, and everyone was crying, and she was home.

Chapter Forty

Hoxton was sobering up, but still experiencing slips of time. The flashing lights of the emergency services lit the village and the sirens raged in Hoxton's head, repeating over and over like a whiny mantra. Maybe it was his narcissism – maybe the alcohol swirling in his bloodstream – but he couldn't shift the idea that he had a role to play in finding the missing children. He wasn't the best of people – that much he conceded – but if there was even a slight chance that he could help, he was duty bound to do so. If it meant losing his job, so be it. Rather that than living the rest of his life with the knowledge that he could have done something but didn't.

However, that meant he had to go to the commune now.

The night receptionist offered him a cursory glance but didn't comment as Hoxton shuffled through the main area towards the lift. Snippets of the previous evening played through his mind as he waited for the lift to arrive, but he couldn't think about the apologies he may have to offer to his staff and fellow guests. He had a purpose now.

He winced at the state of the room as he retrieved his car keys. His clothes were strewn over his bed and the floor, the chair by the writing desk upturned. A second unopened bottle of red sat on the dresser and, after some indecision, he decided to take it with him.

'Everything okay, Mr Hoxton?' asked the receptionist, as he returned downstairs.

Hoxton searched for the man's name in his jumbled memory, fixing on Darren or David. 'Just getting some air,' he said, doing his utmost not to slur, the bottle of wine hidden in the rucksack hanging over his shoulder.

'Can I get you some water or something, sir?'

Hoxton shook his head, the action taking a surprisingly long time. 'Just some air,' he repeated, shaking his head again before heading outside.

Glancing around, like the criminal he supposed he was, Hoxton clicked open his car and got in, setting off before he had a chance to change his mind.

His focus was such that a sliver of pain ran across his forehead, his eyes blurring as he headed out of the village. Images of the last few days played through his mind as he concentrated on the winding roads, his headlights on full beam as he navigated the car through the darkness. Some were clear – DI Blackwell's cold stare at the council meeting, the hints of derision in his conversations with Walsh. Others less so. He was still haunted by that first night at the caves and the subsequent trip to the commune, his memory tainted by his drinking. Snippets returned to him but everything had a dream-like quality and he found it impossible to separate fact from fiction.

Resisting the urge to sound the car horn, he arrived at the commune and parked up. Fog hung in the night air that felt at least two degrees colder than back in Cheddar. Apart from the few beat-up cars and vans in the car-park, it was hard to believe the place was home to so many people. The portable homes and caravans were hidden beyond the canopy of trees and the main building sank into darkness as if derelict.

It was the last thing Hoxton wanted to do, but he needed to see Sam Amstell. That bastard definitely knew something. And this time, Hoxton wasn't going to be fobbed off. Unscrewing the cap on the wine, Hoxton drank heavily from the metallic tasting liquid and headed into the forest.

The alcohol in his bloodstream allayed his fears but he still took a second swig as he broke the threshold of trees. Torch held in his shaking hand, Hoxton shivered as his feet landed on the hard ground. The land narrowed as if trying to squeeze him out but he battled on, drinking every time he heard the air brush the hanging leaves or wildlife scurry behind him. He ignored the occasional hint of the breathing sound, telling himself it was all in his imagination.

His concentration was at its peak, his forehead throbbing from the pressure and dehydration. If he didn't keep his wits about him he could get lost, and in his current state that could prove fatal.

It was a relief when he saw the first battered campervan in the clearing. He peered through smeared windows to see the outline of two sleeping figures.

He screamed when something touched his shoulder but this time he remembered to hold on to the bottle of wine.

Chapter Forty-One

If it hadn't been for the news on the other end of the phone line, Louise thought it possible she would no longer be in a job. Finch was an expert in finding weak spots. She could take so much from the man but he'd crossed a line by mentioning Emily; had completely obliterated the line by threatening her niece.

The threat was vague but he'd known what he was doing. Louise saw it in the narrow smile that formed on his face after he'd taunted her. He'd been waiting for the right time and it had almost worked. Even with Rachael in the room, Louise had almost reacted to his subtle taunt – just like he'd wanted.

How far she would have gone, she didn't know. She could readily picture herself using her baton until the smugness faded from his face, imagined emptying her can of pepper spray into those taunting eyes. It would have been giving in to him but at that second it felt like it would have been worth it.

Thankfully, Rachael had insisted she take the call. And now here she was, siren wailing, making the short journey back to Cheddar where, somehow, Madison Pemberton had returned.

Louise would only believe it when she saw the girl for herself. So many questions whirled through her mind and already her thoughts were turning to what this meant for Aaron Bolton and his family. She left Thomas back in Charterhouse, the look of betrayal in the eyes of Ellie Bolton unmistakable as she'd driven away.

The Pembertons sat in a huddle on the living room sofa. It was a stark contrast to the last time Louise had been there. It was as if a light had been switched on again behind the eyes of Madison's parents. Their arms were locked around the girl, as if she would drift away if they let go.

Considering her ordeal, Madison looked in relatively good shape. She was covered in grime and scratches but was smiling and reciprocating the hugs from her parents. Unfortunately, Louise knew only too well that the real trauma was probably hiding out of sight. She thought about her father's fall, and the sullen look she'd received on entering Emily's bedroom the other evening, and wondered what demons lay behind the façade of happiness in Madison's eyes.

Louise bent to her haunches. 'Hello, Madison,' she said. 'My name is Louise. It's good to meet you at last.'

The girl tensed and her mother rubbed her shoulders. Louise glanced up at the FLO, who was hovering behind the door. 'I'm afraid we're going to have to ask you a few questions in a minute. Is that okay?' asked Louise.

Madison looked to her mother who offered her a thin smile. 'Do we have to do this now?' said the dad.

'I know it's difficult but these things are better done immediately, while the memory is fresh.'

'What if she doesn't want to remember?'

'Neil,' said the mum. 'Think about what else has happened.'

'What else has happened?' said Madison, alarmed.

'Madison, we'll talk in a minute. Your mum and dad too,' said Louise, trying to deflect the conversation away from the missing boy for the time being.

Louise took the FLO aside. The girl was wearing the same clothes she'd worn on the day she'd been taken and ideally she should have been processed by now.

'I haven't been able to separate them,' said the FLO.

'What have you asked her?'

'I asked if he'd hurt her.'

'And?'

'She suffered some cuts and bruises from the abduction itself and is complaining about toothache but says he didn't touch her beyond that. Says she saw him every now and then. He would bring her food and water and replace the batteries in a lamp.'

'Okay, we need to get her examined as soon as possible. Can you get her out of those clothes? You'll have to give her a suit until the medics arrive.'

The FLO broke the news to the parents. The mother looked apoplectic but eventually accompanied Madison to another room where the girl changed into one of the SOCO suits, her clothes placed in a bag for processing just as the medic arrived.

Louise was desperate to speak to the girl but the examination took precedence. She questioned the FLO again as she waited, insisting she replay every single line of the conversation. Teams were already back out on the cliff walk searching for the entry point into the caves where Madison had been imprisoned.

Finally the girl was checked over. Her face had been cleaned and she looked less bedraggled than before as she rejoined her father in the living room. 'Aside from some scrapes and bruises, she seems in pretty good shape considering,' said the medic.

'Any . . .' asked Louise.

'No obvious signs of trauma at all,' said the medic, a little too quickly. 'I'd like to take her in and run a few more tests but . . .'

Louise felt the relief as if the girl was her own. Either she'd been very lucky or her abductor had had different plans for her.

Louise glanced at her watch, waiting for the time when she could call Emily. Although her niece was safe at home, she had a desperate need to speak to her.

For now, her attention was all on Madison. The girl was sitting at the dining table, flanked by her parents and the FLO, Louise feeling like she was the one being interviewed as she sat down opposite.

The relief was still palpable on the faces of the parents, and although the worry had visibly lifted they still crowded their daughter.

Louise asked first about Madison's escape. The search team had yet to find the entrance she'd escaped from, and unless they did so soon, the time would come where they would have to take Madison back up on the cliff walk. The girl tried her best to explain, as she'd told the FLO on her return, but her escape had been in the dark and she was struggling to describe her route.

'This is going to be hard to hear, Madison,' said Louise, making eye contact with both her parents before continuing. 'But another child has gone missing.'

Madison looked distraught, and moved into her mother's arms. 'Who?'

'It was a baby,' said her mother.

'A baby? But why would he do that?'

'That's what we're trying to understand. You say he never spoke to you, Madison, but maybe you heard the baby crying at some point?'

Madison shrugged, her head falling into her shoulders, her eyes squinting as if she was either trying to remember or fighting to suppress a memory. 'When did he do it?'

'Sometime in the last eight hours or so,' said Louise.

'I didn't hear anyone else. I would say if I did.'

'I know that, Madison. When did you last see him?'

'I don't know really. It was always near dark in the cave. I had the small light but time was . . . it was funny. He left food for me and that felt like over a day ago. And I thought that maybe he was following me when I escaped but I could have imagined it.'

'Why did you think that, Madison?'

'I thought I could hear him. He has funny breathing.'

'Funny breathing?'

'It sounded like he is always out of breath.' Madison thought some more. Finally she said, 'As if he was about to die.'

Chapter Forty-Two

Hoxton screamed as he scrambled away from whatever had touched his shoulder. For a second he was back in the cave running from the goblin and it took him some time to reacquaint himself with his circumstances. That he appeared to be in a deserted forest wasn't much of a relief.

'You look like you've seen a ghost, Richard,' said a voice.

Pure relief hit Hoxton as he turned to see Sam Amstell.

'What are you doing out here?' said Hoxton, swigging from the bottle of wine he found glued to his hand.

'What am I doing? It's the middle of the night, Richard, and you're walking around the woodland with a bottle of red in your hand. Or what's left of it. Did you drive here in this state?'

Hoxton ignored him. 'What's going on, Sam?'

'What's going on is you clipped one of the cars when you arrived and have been causing one hell of a noise ever since.'

Hoxton stood straight. His muscles ached and weariness crept over him. He couldn't recall any collision, and didn't think he'd been making the kind of noise Amstell was suggesting. 'Someone else has gone missing,' he said.

Amstell looked at him with confusion and pity. 'What are you talking about, Richard?'

'A boy. A baby boy,' said Hoxton.

'I haven't heard about this. Are you sure . . . ?' Amstell glanced at the bottle in Hoxton's hand.

'I might not be sure of much at the moment, Sam, but I am sure of this.'

'But why are you here, Richard?'

'Because of the noise.'

'The noise?'

Hoxton felt helpless. He already wasn't thinking straight and had no idea how to explain himself. 'I heard it the last time I was here, and I heard it in the caves. Is he here, Amstell?'

'Is who here?'

Hoxton looked at the bottle. He was about to take a swig but decided against it. 'The baby.'

'Come on, Hoxton, let's get you inside before you catch your death.'

He'd been closer than he'd realised, Amstell's hut was behind the next copse of trees. Hoxton sat in the shadows as Amstell brewed coffee and made some phone calls.

Hoxton's eyes were heavy and he had to shake himself awake on a couple of occasions.

'It seems you were right,' said Amstell, handing him a coffee.

Hoxton wasn't completely sure he hadn't fallen asleep but it was still dark outside. He burnt his tongue on the coffee but continued drinking it anyway. 'About what?'

'About the boy. A nine-month-old; Aaron Bolton.'

'Jesus,' said Hoxton, his reason for being there momentarily forgotten.

'But there is good news as well.'

'Good news?'

'The girl. Madison. She managed to escape.'

Happiness stirred in Hoxton at the news. 'Really, that's such wonderful news,' he said.

'You look confused.'

'I am. The note.'

'The note?' asked Amstell.

'The ransom note. You must have heard about that.'

'I heard about that all right,' said Amstell. 'I had the police around here asking about it.'

'Louise?' asked Hoxton, his mind playing tricks on him once more as he struggled to recall where he was, and why he was there.

'Louise?' said Amstell, with disdain. 'Oh, you mean that woman officer. Blackwell, I think. Yes, you know her?'

'Yes. She was at the . . . meeting.'

'Jesus, man, will you make sense. What meeting are you talking about now?'

Hoxton stared at Amstell, struggling to focus on his features. 'Is he here?' he asked, unsure as to the meaning of the words.

'Look, you can use the room through there. Sleep this off and no one needs to be any the wiser. You're a decent bloke, Hoxton. I don't like who you work for, and what you do, but you're okay and I can see this is getting to you. Come on.' Amstell reached out a hand and hoisted Hoxton off the chair.

'I heard him the last time I was here,' said Hoxton, as Amstell led him to a bedroom the size of a shoe cupboard.

'The boy isn't here. And he wasn't even missing the last time you were here, Richard.'

Hoxton held his arm out against the doorframe. 'Not the boy. The man,' he insisted.

'What man?'

'The man with the breathing. I heard him following me when I left here last time.'

Amstell threw some jackets off the camp-bed and eased Hoxton down. 'Breathing?' he said, standing in hazy darkness like an apparition. 'You don't mean Ted Padfield do you? He helps out here sometimes. He's got some breathing issues, but I don't think he was following you, Richard. Try and get some sleep now,' he said, shutting the door.

Hoxton's eyes closed but not before a memory returned to him.

He knew Ted Padfield, and remembered where he'd met him before.

Chapter Forty-Three

It was another three hours before they got their first hit. Madison's parents had reluctantly allowed the girl back on to the cliff walk to retrace her steps at first light, heavy overhanging clouds lining their route up Jacob's Ladder.

On the day she'd been taken, Madison had walked up the same stone steps. Instead of heading towards Lynch Lane and home, she'd decided to walk along the cliff walk where she'd subsequently lost her phone. The details of her abduction had been vague except for that. She couldn't recall the monster – as she called him – harming her, but she had a recollection of a burning cloth being placed against her face and then waking up alone in the cave. Try as she might, the girl wasn't able to give a full description of the man. She claimed his face had stayed hidden behind a mask or balaclava, the only attribute she could describe being the man's strange and laboured breathing. The noise was like a rattling train, and when she'd told Louise that she'd begun to cry.

In the end it was a team of local potholers who found the site. The entrance to the cave was close to the cliff edge, and Louise shuddered at the thought of Madison emerging from the place in the middle of the night being pursued by the man she called the monster.

'She's not going back in there,' said her mother, before Louise even had a chance to speak. Madison was pressed up close to the woman, and a sting of guilt hit Louise for even bringing her back to the walk in the first place.

'No one is asking her to do that. I just need her to confirm that this is the place where she was being held captive.'

Madison looked at her mother, the pleading in her eyes making her much younger than her eleven years. 'It's okay,' she said. 'I think this is where it was but it was dark. I thought he was coming . . .'

'That's enough,' said the girl's dad.

The specialist search unit arrived thirty minutes later. Although desperate to access the area, Louise wasn't prepared to send civilians into the caves without the proper supervision. She introduced herself to the head of the team, Sergeant Sean Oldfield, a wiry young man who to Louise's eyes didn't look old enough to be in the police, let alone a sergeant.

Oldfield and his team conferred with the local potholers. The area was restricted and deemed unsafe and there was no record of anyone exploring the area in recent history.

Louise had already been considering how the abductor would have managed to navigate himself and Madison through the cave opening. Watching the team set up, and drop ropes through the slit in the rock, it was apparent that he must have great strength as well as a strong knowledge of the caves.

The rain finally came as Oldfield lowered himself into the gap, Louise receiving an accusatory look from Madison's parents as the FLO led them away to shelter.

Louise pulled up her hood, the rain bouncing off the material on to the compacted mud by her feet. The silence was palpable as a second member of Oldfield's team followed him in. Louise had decided not to share the information of the cave discovery with the Boltons yet. The thought that Aaron Bolton was being held within the cave provoked both optimism and fear in her, and the area was no place for concerned parents.

The rain stopped as abruptly as it had arrived, a blurred rainbow forming behind a backdrop of unseasonal blue sky. The FLO lifted her hand, and Louise nodded for her to take the family away. The last thing Madison needed now was to see her monster emerge from the caves.

Or something worse.

A buzz of static prickled Louise's skin and she picked up her radio. 'Ma'am, we've found signs of someone living here. There is a rolled mattress and a sleeping bag,' said Oldfield.

Madison had said she'd slept in a sleeping bag and Louise instructed the officer to leave the items until the SOCOs had analysed the scene. 'Signs of any other occupation?' she asked.

'Not yet. I realise the girl thought it was a maze of tunnels and caves but it isn't. There is only one way in and out. I'm one hundred per cent sure no one else is in here at present. We'll keep looking for anything that will help.'

Louise mumbled under her breath as she placed the radio back on her belt. She hadn't thought it would be this easy but couldn't fight her disappointment that Aaron wasn't in the cave, unharmed.

Thomas walked over, his hair ruffled by the wind. He stood next to Louise in silence as they looked out over the cliff drop. 'She did very well to get out of there alive,' he said.

Louise had been thinking the same thing. It was heartening to acknowledge the girl's bravery, but Aaron didn't have the luxury of bravery. He was helpless, and for every second that passed she felt they were failing the child and his family. 'It would help if we could get a fix on the abductor's motive,' said Louise, using Thomas as a sounding board. 'He's just so damn unpredictable.'

'Maybe this was his end game,' said Thomas.

The thought had occurred to Louise though she was struggling to find the logical jump. The attacks on the sheep and Tabart had been reckless. They didn't feel premeditated. Even Madison's abduction felt random. From what the girl had told them, he hadn't targeted her; she'd just been in the wrong place at the wrong time. But with Aaron it was different. It felt as if he'd targeted the family and the child. But why would he go to all the trouble of taking Madison in the first place, if it had been Aaron he was after all along?

'In a way I want that to be true,' said Louise. If Aaron had been the suspect's real target, at least no one else would be at risk. However, if the suspect *had* achieved their goal, then their chances of finding Aaron in the area were significantly decreased.

They both stared at the cave entrance, as if the answers were waiting within. 'Has to be someone local, with intimate knowledge of the landscape and area,' said Louise, almost to herself. 'Get the team to go back through MAPPA. Anyone with mountaineering, potholing, farming or any experience to do with the land we get back in for questioning. And get someone to supervise here as I'm going to pay another visit to the commune.'

◆ ◆ ◆

Louise called home as she made her way to the commune, her father answering the house phone her mother insisted on keeping. Louise was surprised by her reaction to the sound of his voice. Tears prickled in her eyes and she realised she hadn't slept for over twenty-four hours. 'Hi Dad, just checking in,' she said, trying to hide the emotion in her voice.

'I didn't know you checked in on us now. Is this a new thing?'

Louise ignored his attempt at humour. 'How's Emily?'

'She's fine. I don't know why we're making such a big thing out of this.'

'We're not, Dad, but we do need to take this seriously.'

'It was an accident,' said her father.

'I know she didn't mean to hurt you, Dad. But . . .'

'There're no buts, Lou.'

'Dad, she didn't mean to hurt you but she did push you. We can't go on ignoring it. She's suspended from school for heaven's sake. She bit someone.'

Her father dropped his voice to a low guttural growl she rarely heard. 'Don't you think I know that, Louise?'

Louise understood the pain and hurt in his voice. Try as she might, she'd yet to manage to get him to speak about Paul. What was happening with Emily was tearing him apart, and knowing her father he would be placing all the blame on himself. 'Okay, Dad, well I'm glad things are better.'

The line went silent. Louise pictured her father at home on the armchair, taking a deep breath. 'I heard about that missing boy. Is that your case now?' he asked.

'I can't talk about my work, Dad.'

'Okay, darling, I understand. You be careful, Lou. I love you.'

A tear fell from her eye this time. He didn't say the words very often and the fact he was saying them now suggested he was struggling emotionally. 'I love you too, Dad. Give my love to Mum and Emily. I'll try and pop over tomorrow,' she added, hanging up before she was no longer able to drive.

Oldfield updated her by radio as she entered the commune's car-park. A rolled-up mattress and a drink container had been recovered from within the cave and had already been processed by the SOCOs and sent away for further analysis.

Louise thanked Oldfield, catching sight of a car leaving the commune in her rear-view mirror. She turned around and tried to follow the vehicle as it left but it disappeared behind the trees.

Sam Amstell was waiting by the main building as if he'd been expecting her. 'Inspector,' he said, walking towards her as she left the car. He stopped short of blocking her but she didn't appreciate the closeness of his proximity and she took a step away from him.

'Mr Amstell,' she said. 'You may have heard about the latest developments in Cheddar?'

'Indeed. I'm very pleased for the parents of the young girl, naturally. It's such a shame that it coincides with the disappearance of the boy.'

Amstell was choosing his words carefully. Behind him, the commune was a hive of activity. 'Can we go somewhere to talk?'

'Have you eaten? It's breakfast time,' said Amstell, leading her to the main building.

The contrast inside the commune compared to the other evening was staggering. The long tables were full of people eating and talking, the air was ripe with the smell of food that reminded Louise of her old school canteen. She declined the offer of breakfast, accepting a lukewarm coffee in its place.

'May I ask, was the girl's reappearance linked in any way to the ransom note?' asked Amstell, as they took a seat at the end of one of the tables.

The note was no secret but it felt like an odd thing for him to ask. 'I can't get into the specifics at the moment.'

Amstell nodded. 'How may I be of service, Inspector?' he asked, the displeasure she'd seen cross his lips fading.

It was Louise's turn to choose her words carefully. The commune was less than ten minutes from the Bolton farm. She wanted to question everyone from the area, and it would be easier to have Amstell on her side. She studied his response as she made the suggestion.

Amstell interlinked his hands, returning Louise's gaze. He appeared to be weighing up the best way of answering. 'Is this something you're doing elsewhere? After all, you searched the place a matter of days ago,' he said.

'We're talking to as many people as we possibly can, Mr Amstell. Think of it from my position. You can reach the Bolton farm directly from here.'

Amstell shrugged. 'The whole of the countryside is linked one way or another.'

'I understand the disruption this may cause, Mr Amstell, but I'm sure I don't need to remind you that a baby boy has been abducted,' said Louise, purposely raising her voice. The background noise in the hollow room diminished, as they became the centre of everyone's attention.

'I'm sure we can arrange that, Inspector,' said Amstell, defeated.

'Thank you, Mr Amstell.' Louise took a chance and decided to share some information with the man. 'You may be able to help me if you'd be willing?'

'Whatever I can do.'

Louise told him about the cave structure in the gorge where Madison had been kept. Amstell didn't look that surprised. 'With your knowledge of the local area, I was wondering if you knew of any similar caving sites, perhaps closer to where the Boltons live?'

'You know these places are all mapped out?' said Amstell.

'Of course, we have our team studying sites as we speak but it's a huge job and we have limited resources to search. If there was anywhere you could think of?'

Amstell looked suspicious. 'You could just come out and say it, save wasting all this time.'

'Sorry, I don't understand,' said Louise.

Amstell frowned. 'I'm pretty sure it would appear on your records. There is an entrance to a cave structure on this land.'

◆ ◆ ◆

Louise called Oldfield before heading with Amstell into the woods. Thomas had updated her on the progress in Cheddar, and the progress on MAPPA. After Amstell had told her about the cave structure on site, she decided she needed to see it for herself.

As they battered through the woodland, Louise urging Amstell to walk faster, it became apparent where all the people in the hall had come from. Makeshift homes were dotted throughout the area as if purposely hidden. 'How many people actually live here, Mr Amstell? You said about sixty-five before but there seemed to be more in the main building.'

'Do you think we could do without the titles now, Inspector?' said the man, with a smile.

Louise didn't return the smile. 'Louise.'

'Sam. To answer your question, it changes. Not everyone you saw at breakfast lives here.'

'How much land is there?'

'Approximately three thousand acres.'

Louise tried to picture the size of the area but the number was meaningless.

'Ten square miles give or take,' said Amstell, as they passed through a clearing, Amstell pointing out the hut where he lived. 'The land has a rich history,' he added, leading her through to a second, denser, woodland area.

Louise's mind was awhirl with thoughts of Aaron Bolton and his family, of Madison and Emily. Every event and each relevant person played on a continued loop in her head. It was one of the ways she processed the information, studying it into submission; until an answer came her way. Amstell's comment about the land's rich history made her think about Hoxton, who'd said a similar thing to her once. 'You know Richard Hoxton?' she said.

It was subtle but she noticed the hesitation in the man's step. 'Did you see him leaving?' he said.

'This morning as I arrived,' said Louise, bluffing, thinking about the car she'd seen in her periphery earlier in the car-park.

'I didn't know when he left but I noticed his car was gone. He stayed at my place last night,' said Amstell. He told her about Hoxton's late night visit and the disruption he'd caused. 'I should have taken his keys. I didn't know he planned to leave so soon. I'd left him sleeping earlier when I went to open up the hall.'

Louise was disappointed by the news. Everyone handled uncertainty and crisis in their own way but she'd expected a bit more from Hoxton. She'd liked him from their very first meeting, finding his mixture of humour and confidence attractive, but in retrospect she could see a pattern in his behaviour. When he'd called her he'd sounded drunk, and during the council meeting he'd worn his hangover like a shroud. An image of Paul, semi-conscious on the sofa, empty bottles of wine by his side, flashed before her and she knew she would forever make a connection between the man and her brother. 'Why did he come here?' she asked.

Amstell hesitated. 'To be honest, I don't really know. He was rambling. It's not the first time he's been here. His boss blames us for everything that goes wrong with their development.'

'You do oppose it though?' Louise stopped short of asking about the graffiti on the cliff edges.

'We do but we're a peaceful group. They're the ones who play the stupid games, not us. I think Hoxton is coming to understand that. If you ask me, I think he wants out.'

The smell of dew and stagnant rainwater heralded them to a second clearing. Hidden behind another covering of trees was a cave entrance.

'We call it the Tryst,' said Amstell. 'Do you see?'

Louise was busy thinking about Hoxton and the little coincidences: his turning up on the day she was at the gorge with her family, his receiving the letter, and the way he'd guided her to this commune in the first place. She glanced up at the rocks and made out the loose structure of two lovers entwined in the rock face. 'You were talking about the area's history,' said Louise, peering through the opening into the coldness beyond.

'It's no secret that this place has been used by members of the Wicca religion in the past. We're often associated with them when there isn't any link. There is an uneasy history to this place that has been hard to shake off.'

'Uneasy?' said Louise.

'For a starter the Wicca religion is often misunderstood. When people think of witches they picture pointy hats and broomsticks, but at its heart it is a spiritual movement. Unfortunately, myth and legend prevail, fact and fiction merge. There are rumours of cannibalism and human sacrifice in the area going back hundreds of years, and these are sometimes incorrectly attributed to the Wicca movement.'

Amstell smiled, the sun retreating behind a cloud and sending a shadow over them. 'We're talking centuries ago of course, but some people believe those things linger in the land. For some, the Tryst is a place of significance.'

'Is that why you have so many people staying here?'

'We vet as many as we are able, but you get the curious. However, it's not safe beyond these limits,' he said, stepping over the threshold. 'The rock is very unstable. You go through there, you risk never coming back out.'

Louise didn't know if it was a warning or friendly advice. Either way, Amstell must have known what was going to come next. 'You realise we'll have to search it,' she said.

'That's fine,' said Amstell. 'But I'll need something in writing that indemnifies my organisation if anything happens.'

Chapter Forty-Four

Hoxton puked twice before he left the commune. He awoke in the fetid dark of Amstell's bedroom, the immediate confusion of his surroundings soon replaced by a familiar sense of regret. Search as he might for the memories, he could only hang on to about a third of the previous evening. He recalled a full night's drinking in his room, followed by snippets of driving to the commune and trailing through the woodlands to Amstell's home. He didn't need to acknowledge the nagging feeling in his head to know worse had happened; as if drink-driving wasn't the worst thing he could have done.

Amstell had gone by the time Hoxton left his shack. It was early morning and Hoxton felt the alcohol still in his bloodstream. By the time he reached the car, and saw the scratches and dented panels, more vague memories had returned. He couldn't recall how he'd damaged the car but recalled Amstell mentioning it. He winced as he saw the damage on two other cars. The vehicles were ancient and battered but that was beside the point. He would contact Amstell later and offer payment for the damage, but for now he had to get out of there.

If he'd left seconds later he would have had to stop to let DI Blackwell pass him. He recognised her car as soon as she entered the commune car-park. Thankfully his headlights were switched off and he managed to sneak out, he hoped, undetected.

He pulled up on the dirt track to be sick for a third time. Little beyond acid-like water left his stomach and he was shaking by the time he got behind the wheel again, his head throbbing.

A boy had gone missing last night. That much he did remember. That fact had been the catalyst, as if one was needed, for his drinking. He wasn't as egocentric as some people he knew, but he'd managed to put himself at the centre of this. It had all started that night at the caves, he thought for the hundredth time, dry heaving as the memory of returning to the cave last night popped into his head unbidden. 'Jesus,' he whispered to himself, trying to recall if he'd caused any damage to the place. Maybe that was why DI Blackwell had been at the commune. He knew he'd done something bad last night and maybe it was that. Pictures flashed in his eyes: the moody receptionist at the hotel, the deserted road bisecting the gorge, and that damned imp leering at him from the cave wall.

What in the hell had possessed him to return there last night?

◆ ◆ ◆

As he parked up at the hotel, too sheepish for the time being to set foot in the building, he considered making the same resolution he'd made so many times over the last few years. If this wasn't a strong enough calling card for him to give up drinking, then he was all but damned. The very thought of ever drinking again made him nauseous, but experience told him that could, and would, change later that day.

He took a painful walk along the main road, the strength of his hangover reaching every muscle and sinew in his body, as he stumbled into a newsagent's. The boy's disappearance had made the front page of the national papers. Hoxton picked up one, folded it in two, and handed a ten-pound note to the cashier with a shaking hand.

'Not all bad news though, did you hear,' said the cashier, a portly woman in her late fifties.

'No, how's that?' said Hoxton, summoning his last reserves of strength in speaking.

'The girl. She's back.'

Did he know this already? 'She's back?' asked Hoxton.

'She escaped last night. Must have walked by this very shop earlier this morning.'

'That's great,' said Hoxton, accepting the change. It was wonderful news, but was tainted by the disappearance of the boy, and Hoxton's stuttering memory of the previous evening. He sat on the wall opposite the newsagent's, out of necessity as well as curiosity, and read about the disappearance. The article was rushed and lacked anything beyond the basic information that a nine-month-old boy, unnamed, had gone missing from a farm close to Charterhouse yesterday evening. No mention was made of the missing girl's escape. Hoxton presumed she'd escaped – if the cashier was to be believed – later that night, too late to have made the morning edition. In Hoxton's jumbled mind none of it made sense. He was convinced that he already knew the girl had escaped but couldn't trust his memory.

Fighting dizziness, he hoisted himself off the wall and headed back through the gorge. He stopped at the commercial entrance to Cox's Cave. There was no sign of damage and a lurid memory of staggering along outside the door last night came and went in a flash. Hoxton lowered his eyes at the sight of an empty beer bottle by the entrance. It was more than feasible that it had belonged to him. The thought triggered the memory of being in the cave last night and dropping the bottle of wine. A coppery taste filled his mouth at the recollection, and he looked around before spitting on the ground. More pieces were coming together. He'd gone to the cave because of that first night, because of that bloody sound he'd heard both there and at the commune.

Hoxton shook his head, the movement so painful that he had to sit down against the outside of the cave wall. It was laughable how muddled his thinking had been this morning. Of course that was why he'd made his drunken detour to the commune and Amstell's hovel. He'd wanted answers.

And he was sure now that Amstell had provided him with some.

An elderly couple, walking a decrepit and overweight Labrador, slowed down as they approached him, and for a woeful moment Hoxton thought they were about to give him some money. 'You okay, lad?' said the man, in a northern accent.

'I'm fine, thank you,' said Hoxton.

As they walked away it came to him. He'd confronted Amstell about the sound he'd heard that night in the woods, the man with the erratic breathing. What's more, Amstell had given him a name and it had all made sense.

It made less sense now. In fact it sounded preposterous, but he couldn't sit on the information any longer. Getting to his feet, he pulled out his phone and made another call to DI Blackwell.

Chapter Forty-Five

Farrell checked himself in the vanity mirror before leaving the car. Within MIT he had a reputation for being a stickler about the way he looked. It had been the same in Weston. He took pride in his appearance and didn't care what they said behind his back, or to his face which was more often the case. His dad had told him that first impressions count. He'd worked on the docks for over fifty years and Farrell had never once seen him leave for work unshaven, or without his work overalls being in pristine condition.

Farrell had met Joslyn Merrick on a number of occasions. She had been pivotal in the discovery of Paul's body. Farrell had been in regular contact with her since starting the investigation into Paul's death.

Joslyn greeted him with a firm handshake and a smile. They were parked up on the B road linking the two Cornish seaside towns of Hayle and Portreath. The Atlantic stretched out before them, the blue sea the antithesis to Weston's mud-laden sea.

'Good journey?' said Joslyn.

'It was but probably the wrong time to have left.'

'Great news about the girl. Louise must be delighted, though I guess with the baby going missing . . .'

Joslyn had been the first officer at Paul's murder scene and had found Emily hiding beneath one of the static caravans. She knew first-hand how much finding the missing girl in Cheddar meant to Louise.

'I should be there really.'

'I'm sure Louise can manage without you for a few hours,' said Joslyn, smiling.

'No doubt on that,' said Farrell. But it wasn't Louise he was concerned with. By returning to Cornwall, and following Louise's advice, he was effectively going against Finch's wishes. However oblique the DCI's warnings, he wouldn't approve of Farrell being there and that in part was why he'd approached Joslyn rather than the SIO. He handed Joslyn his iPad and scrolled through the images he'd put together of Bryan Lemanski.

'I realise appearances can be deceiving but he doesn't look like the most welcoming of characters,' said Joslyn.

The old army photo showed Lemanski stripped to the waist, his muscled torso covered in tattoos. His hair had been shaved to the bone. The hardness in his eyes could have been for show, but his record in the army was littered with offences of insubordination and violence, which had culminated in his imprisonment and subsequent dismissal. Whatever Finch's misgivings, Lemanski's proximity to the area where Paul was murdered had to be considered. 'We ready?' said Farrell.

'Always,' said Joslyn.

They drove in Farrell's car. Farrell hadn't wanted to call ahead and risk the man absconding so had asked Joslyn to check that Lemanski was still at home before setting off that morning.

Lemanski lived in what may once have been a holiday home. Overgrown bushes and brambles surrounded the wooden shack at the end of a single-track road. Farrell would have thought it abandoned if it weren't for the man sitting outside on a rusted metal chair smoking a roll-up, a cup of coffee on the ground next to him. 'Help you?' said the man, drawing from his cigarette as his eyes went from Farrell to the uniformed figure of Joslyn.

'Bryan Lemanski?' said Farrell, looking over at an unmoving German Shepherd who was guarding the door to the shack.

'Depends who's asking.'

Farrell opened his warrant card. 'DS Farrell and Sergeant Merrick.'

'Best come in then,' said Lemanski. 'Don't worry, he won't bite,' said Lemanski, glancing over at the dog.

The man was as good as his word, the dog not even lifting his head as Farrell and Joslyn entered the front garden.

'Grab a seat then,' said Lemanski, not moving.

Farrell dragged over two heavy chairs that were leaning against an iron fence, the sound of the metal on the concrete ground causing the dog's ears to flicker.

'Fifteen years old,' said Lemanski. 'Almost unknown for them to reach that age. Poor sod can barely move but I couldn't do without him. So how can I help you, officers?'

Lemanski was no longer the trim man he'd been in the army, but beneath the new layers of fat Farrell sensed the dormant muscle. 'Do you know a man by the name of Paul Blackwell?' asked Farrell.

Lemanski barely reacted. 'I read about him. He was the man murdered over Penzance way? Terrible business.'

'You didn't know him though?' asked Joslyn.

'And why would I know him? I keep myself to myself. He wasn't even local, was he? Thought he was from upcountry.'

Farrell was surprised by the strong lilt of Lemanski's Cornish accent. He hadn't been expecting it from the man, and didn't know why he'd anticipated something else from his photograph. 'You know a man by the name of Nathan Marshall though,' he said.

For the first time since arriving, Farrell felt they had the man's attention. 'Marshall. Haven't heard that name in a long time.'

'From your army days?'

'Yes, from my army days,' said Lemanski, mimicking Farrell.

'You still in contact with him?'

'Not really. Washed my hands of them the day they kicked me out. You know about that I take it?' he said, his glare reserved for Joslyn. 'What's this to do with Marshall?'

Farrell leaned back in the rickety chair, the sound of metal on concrete pricking the dog's ears once more. He'd come a long way to speak to Lemanski, so it seemed necessary to tell him the story about Jodi and Paul's relationship.

Lemanski scratched his ear, his hands dropping to his lip as he flicked the cigarette butt away. 'And this involves me how?'

'We're speaking to Mr Marshall's acquaintances.'

'To what end? You think Marshall killed this guy?'

'We're just trying to get a feel for Mr Marshall's character at this moment.'

Lemanski shook his head. 'A feel for his character,' he said, full of disdain. 'Then why the hell would you want to speak to me? I haven't seen him in years. You must know that or . . .' the man squinted, some form of realisation dawning on him. 'What is this shit?' he said, getting to his feet.

In the corner the dog stirred, its giant head rising to see what all the commotion was about. 'Please sit down, Mr Lemanski.'

'You think I had something to do with this? Unbelievable. What do you think I am? I left the army eight years ago. It fucks with your head. I did some shit I wasn't proud of back then but it's what they train you to do. Then they discard you without a second thought, as if it's your fault you behave like that. I came down here to get away from all that. I help out at the local farm, and in the summer I work the boats in St Ives.'

'That's okay, Mr Lemanski,' said Joslyn, stopping him mid-ramble. 'No one is accusing you of anything.'

The dog lowered its head at the same time Lemanski sat down. If it was an act, it was one hell of a good one, thought Farrell. 'Do you recognise any of these people?' he asked, showing Lemanski the photo of the four men who were suspended along with Marshall on his phone.

'Just Marshall and Goddard.'

'Troy Goddard?'

'Yeah. Look, I'll admit I heard these guys were discharged but I haven't seen Marshall or Goddard since I left the army, and I don't intend to now. I'm sorry I can't help but I don't know anything about the man's murder. If I did, I'd help you.'

'What do you know about Troy Goddard?' asked Farrell.

Lemanski shrugged. 'Look, man, I don't know what you want from me. They aren't very nice guys. I wasn't a very nice guy when I was in the army. If you're asking what they're capable of, then . . .'

'What are they capable of?' asked Joslyn.

'You'd be surprised what people are capable of doing given the right or wrong circumstances.'

'You'd be surprised what would and wouldn't surprise me,' said Joslyn.

'Well that's great, but I have nothing more to say on the matter.'

◆ ◆ ◆

As they were leaving, the dog hauled itself to its feet and accompanied them to the gate. 'Thank you for your time, Mr Lemanski,' said Farrell, bending down to pet the dog and receiving the smallest swoosh of the dog's tail in response. He handed Lemanski his card. 'If you think of anything, please call.'

Lemanski frowned and Farrell thought he was going to say something more. Instead, he gently grabbed the dog by its collar. 'Right you, back in,' he said, shutting the door.

'Ever feel you've been sent on a wild goose chase?' Farrell asked Joslyn as they drove back to Joslyn's car.

'Constantly.'

Farrell parked up next to her car. From the slightly elevated position in the driver's seat, Farrell could see the jagged rocks on the cliff edge. The tide was in and the white foam of the waves crashed into the rocks and curled backwards, evaporating.

'You want me to keep an eye on him?'

'Lemanski? No, I'm sure you have more important things to do.'

'Okay, give my best to Louise. How are things with her?'

The question threw Farrell. He was in Cornwall because of Louise. She'd persuaded him to continue with the investigation when Finch had warned him off. And despite the negative result, he was sure he would do the same again for her. 'She's struggling like the rest of us,' he said.

'It's good of you to help her.'

'Help her?'

'By coming all this way in the middle of an abduction case.'

'It is my case.'

Joslyn gave him a knowing look. 'Let me know if you need me to do anything else,' she said.

Farrell understood then that the officer held Louise in the same level of esteem as he did.

'She wouldn't have asked you to come all this way if it hadn't been potentially relevant,' said Joslyn, leaving the car.

'I know. Thanks again.'

◆ ◆ ◆

He called Louise as he headed back but her phone didn't ring before going straight to answerphone. Both Tracey's and Thomas's phones were also silent, which was either a coincidence or a concern. He was about to call Coulson when Finch's name appeared on his screen.

'Shit,' said Farrell, before answering.

'Where the hell are you, Farrell?' said Finch, as way of greeting.

He considered lying but was sure Finch already knew his location. 'Heading back from Cornwall, sir.'

The line went silent and Farrell pictured his boss on the other end, gripping the receiver tight as rage filled his eyes.

'The Paul Blackwell case?' said Finch, his words muffled as if he was uttering them under his breath.

'Following up a lead.'

'Following up a lead,' said Finch, his anger palpable. 'We have a missing baby and you're following up a lead in Cornwall?'

'I'm investigating a murder case, sir.' Farrell regretted the words the second they left his mouth.

The silence returned. Farrell pictured his boss finding a quiet spot where he could fully vent his anger down the phone.

'Listen, Farrell. I thought we'd cleared this up.'

'Sir . . .'

'Listen,' repeated Finch, raising his voice. 'You need to work out your priorities, Greg. And I don't mean which cases you prioritise. Do you understand, Greg?'

Farrell didn't like the way the man repeated his first name. It was the type of confidence trick they would sometimes use to befriend a suspect. 'Sir.'

'I've told you before that you have a bright future. But you're all potential at the moment. You've made it to the big time, Greg, but all it takes is one call and you're back to Weston. Or worse. You don't need me to tell you that it happens. You've seen it first-hand.'

Farrell didn't answer and Finch hung up.

Chapter Forty-Six

Louise stood on the threshold of the Tryst, waiting for the search team to arrive. Above her, the natural limestone rock formation outlined the loose resemblance of intertwined lovers. After his talk of the Wicca religion and cannibalism, Louise had noted the uncertainty in Amstell's eyes when she'd suggested entering the cave. For now, she was content to wait for the team to arrive but the urge to grab a torch, a hard hat, and to enter the cave on her own grew as the minutes passed.

After her chat with Amstell, Louise had decided to close the commune. She'd called in officers from all the local stations as well as members from MIT. Her team were interviewing the residents in the main hall, no one allowed in or out without her say-so. The news hadn't gone down well with Amstell. He claimed not to have a full register of the commune's occupants and had suggested it changed on a daily basis, but Louise would be content to search every square inch of the land if it gave them a chance of finding Aaron.

She cursed under her breath as Amstell emerged from the trees, followed by Finch. Neither man approached her. They kept their distance as if she were invisible, talking to one another like conspirators. Louise had to fight her paranoia and was pleased when Oldfield and his team arrived, and she was able to divert her thoughts from whatever distracting tactics Finch was employing.

'You're keeping us busy, Lou,' said Oldfield. 'I've left a skeleton crew over in Cheddar. Nothing new to tell you, I'm afraid. So this is the Tryst?'

'You've heard of it.'

'Yeah, not sure how I've never come across it before, though it is on the prohibited list.' He looked up at the formation at the front of the cave and frowned. 'I've seen the photos. Have to say it's a bit of a disappointment up close. Let's take a look inside, shall we.'

Oldfield handed her a hard hat and stepped through the cave entrance, switching on a high-powered torch. Oldfield began shining the light over every inch of the cave walls as if he could read something in the curves and jagged points of rock, at the green slime hanging from the walls.

'You think someone could have been living in here?'

'Possibly. I've seen it before. We've found corpses in such places before as well. I'll lead a team in through there,' said Oldfield, pointing to a small opening in the cave wall. 'It really isn't safe so we should cordon this area off.'

Amstell and Finch were still in deep conversation outside. Louise blinked at the rush of sunlight, Amstell disappearing back into the woodlands with Finch as Oldfield began assembling his team.

'Hey, boss,' said Tracey, emerging from the trees where Finch and Amstell had just departed.

'Is there something going on behind those trees that I'm not aware of?' said Louise, as Tracey approached.

Tracey ran her hand through her black curly hair. 'What's that, boss?

Since Louise's time in MIT, Tracey had been promoted to the same rank as Louise but she still liked to use the greeting for her. 'Never mind. How are Mr and Mrs Bolton?'

Tracey shook her head and Louise caught a whiff of the strong perfume that partially masked the smell of nicotine on her colleague. 'I just can't imagine what they're going through. The mum is fading away fast. It's really worrying. Rachael is with them now, trying to get them to try and sleep but it's near on impossible.'

Louise took some small comfort in Tracey being there. She'd hardly seen her friend since the case began and her presence had a calming effect on her.

'How's my little monster?' asked Tracey, meaning Emily.

Emily loved Tracey. And vice versa. After Louise's forced absence, Tracey had been a regular visitor at Louise's parents' house. She'd taken Emily off their hands when she'd been able, and they all but considered Tracey a member of the family.

'She's well,' said Louise, deciding now wasn't the time to mention the incident with her father. Emily's anger still resonated with her and she couldn't rid herself of the feeling that she was failing her niece.

'Give her my love. I'll need to pop over soon. Parents okay?'

'Yeah, they're fine. We'll have to arrange to meet up for lunch together,' said Louise, even though at that moment it was hard to imagine a time where they could indulge in such frivolities again. 'That reminds me, I need to call someone,' said Louise. She was about to take her phone from her pocket, when Oldfield returned from inside the cave.

'Something you might want to see for yourself, DI Blackwell,' he said.

'Need me to do anything?' asked Tracey.

Louise shook her head and followed Oldfield back inside the cave, her helmet scraping against the low hanging rock as she crawled through the first tunnel. Her hand touched the side of the entrance, the rock cold and slimy to the touch. Oldfield's team had filled the area with portable lamps and with the light hitting the rocks, the area reminded Louise of a smaller version of Cox's Cave.

With the exception of the single mattress in the centre of the cave floor. 'Similar to the one we found in Cheddar,' said Oldfield. 'In fact, it's the same manufacturer. Obviously could be a coincidence but thought you'd want to know.'

'Thanks, Sean,' said Louise, her torch beam revealing the stains and discolouration on the mattress.

'There's more, I'm afraid.'

He led her to two empty buckets in the corner of the cave. The smell, and a cursory glance, was enough for Louise to know what they'd been used for.

'There was also this,' said Oldfield, pointing to a black rubbish bag. 'To be fair, you don't tend to see this level of organisation from the vagrants who normally use such spots. The buckets are empty, if a little soiled, and there is no discarded food which would attract vermin.'

'What's in the bag?'

Oldfield paused. 'Old clothes, mainly, but when I opened the bag I found something new.'

Louise prised open the bag with her gloved hand.

On top was an unopened bag of three white babygrows; all-in-one suits for babies aged nine to twelve months.

◆ ◆ ◆

Louise heard the commotion as she crawled back through the tunnel holding a bag with the babygrows. At first she thought it was members of the commune, protesting at the lockdown, but as she broke through into the daylight she was surprised by the sight of

Richard Hoxton being restrained by one of the uniformed team manning the police cordon.

'DI Blackwell, I've been calling you,' shouted Hoxton.

Louise lifted her hand up. 'Just a minute,' she said, handing the bag to Tracey.

Tracey peered in and saw the babygrow pack on top. 'He isn't in there, is he?' she said, under her breath.

'No, but the abductor has slept there at some point. Will you get these back to headquarters for testing?' Louise said, handing over the bag.

'Friend of yours?' asked Tracey, glancing over at the gesticulating figure of Richard Hoxton.

'In a manner of speaking,' said Louise. She glanced at her phone which had no signal. 'Let him over,' she said, as Tracey left with the bag.

'I've been trying to call you, DI Blackwell,' said Hoxton, running over.

'So I gather. I apologise but I have no reception.'

'That's what I thought. That's why I'm here.'

Dishevelled didn't quite do justice to Hoxton's appearance. He appeared to have slept in the suit and coat he was wearing. His hair was unbrushed and sprouted in random directions, a style matched by his beard. When he managed to look at her, Louise saw his eyes were red and watery. It was hard to believe this was the same man who'd charmed her that day back in Weston, who'd acted so professional and detached at the council meeting in Cheddar.

Louise was sure he'd been drinking but led him away from the crowd to talk. 'How can I help you, Mr Hoxton?'

Twenty seconds in and Louise had to stop the man talking. He wasn't making any sense as he tried to tell her multiple things at once. 'Just slow down, Mr Hoxton. Start from the beginning.'

Hoxton took in a deep breath. A pronounced vein on his neck pulsed, his body vibrating as he tried to control what was either excitement, agitation, or both. He told her about his trip to the commune last night and his reason for being there now. Louise stopped him when he started talking about the breathing noise he'd heard in the caves, and here in the commune.

'Tell me that again, Mr Hoxton.'

'I knew I'd heard it somewhere before. It was a rattling noise. I guess the acoustics of the cave amplified it and made it sound worse than it was, but I also heard it here.'

Louise recalled Madison's description of the monster, how his breathing was distorted as if he was dying. 'You heard it here?'

'Yes, that is why I drove here last night. I wanted to speak to Amstell.'

'I know you spoke to Mr Amstell last night,' said Louise.

Hoxton stood back. 'Good, so he told you then?'

'Told me what?'

'Told you about Ted Padfield. The man who volunteers here. The man with the breathing difficulties.'

Chapter Forty-Seven

Farrell had been parked up outside the Marshall house for thirty minutes. He'd been heading towards Cheddar when Simon Coulson from IT had called with new information on the Paul Blackwell case. It was probably nothing but after deciding to travel to Cornwall, he'd asked Coulson to run a thorough check on Nathan Marshall, and Coulson had uncovered an irregularity in the man's banking. In the period of ten days, Marshall had withdrawn three thousand pounds from different cash machines in Bristol. The last withdrawal had come two days before Paul Blackwell had been murdered.

Although there could be a simple explanation for the withdrawals, the pattern seemed odd to Farrell. Marshall was limited to three hundred pounds per day via cash machines but could have taken the amount out as a lump sum direct from the bank. The matter could be solved simply by asking the question, so why was he still in the car?

The answer for that was also simple: DCI Tim Finch. Farrell suspected that he'd been destined to play the part of intermediary between Finch and Louise ever since the day Finch had recruited him for MIT. Had he been fooling himself all this time? The day he'd been transferred had been the proudest of his career, but had it all been a sham? What if Finch had recruited him solely as a means to mess with Louise?

It was too late to second-guess now. Finch wanted him away from the case, had all but instructed him to step back earlier that day, but he couldn't sit on Coulson's information. He owed it to Louise, but more importantly he had to do it for the sake of the investigation; for his own sense of justice.

Marshall answered the door within a couple of seconds, as if he'd been waiting behind the door for him. Wearing only boxer shorts and T-shirt, Marshall snarled at him. 'What?'

Farrell showed him his warrant card.

'So you're the one responsible?' said Marshall, slurring.

'Responsible?' said Farrell.

'For scaring Jodi off?'

After Louise's visit the previous week, they'd managed to find Jodi a place at a women's shelter in Totterdown. Farrell had seen the purple-black bruise on Jodi's face and knew the man standing before him was responsible. Like so many in her situation, Jodi had declined to formally report her husband, and without her help it was all but impossible to prosecute the man for his actions. 'There was only one person who scared your wife off, and that wasn't me, Mr Marshall,' said Farrell, unable to help himself.

'What the fuck do you want?' said Marshall, stepping towards him.

Farrell didn't back away even though it would make sense to do so. He wouldn't be the first officer to receive a headbutt to the face, but he wasn't about to let Marshall have the satisfaction. 'I'm not here about Jodi.'

Marshall stared at him, his mouth twitching, before eventually taking a step back. 'What then?'

'It's about Paul Blackwell.'

'Oh for fuck's sake. When will you people let it go? I was at the pub all night. Loads of people saw me. You know this shit already.'

'I understand that, Mr Marshall but I've been alerted to a discrepancy. Would you mind if I came in to discuss it?'

'Yes, I would mind if you came in.'

'Have it your way,' said Farrell, listing the period where Marshall had withdrawn the money from the bank machines.

Marshall shrugged. 'Where the hell is the crime in that?'

'No crime, Mr Marshall, but I think you'll agree it's odd behaviour. Three hundred pounds a day for ten days in a row. All from different bank machines? What were you using the money for?'

'Maybe I have a gambling problem?'

'Different bookie every day? Come on, Marshall, you can do better than that. Do you still have that money?'

'None of your business?'

'Where did you spend it?'

'Same answer.'

'I'm not going to stop, you understand that? I'm going to ramp this up until I've found out everything about you. I already know you're a dirty little wife-beater. What else am I going to find out about you?'

It was a risk but Farrell got the response he wanted. Marshall's anger was evident. It distorted his face, his brow furrowing, his eyes narrowed. If he was lucky, the man would attack him and Farrell would have a reason to cuff him and take him away for questioning. 'What's the problem, Marshall, don't like some home truths?'

'Fuck you.'

'Must make you a big man, hitting your wife like that.'

'Fuck you.'

'Where did the money go, Marshall? You're obviously not man enough to do the job yourself. Who did you pay to kill Paul Blackwell?'

'I don't need to take this shit,' said Marshall. He went to shut the door but Farrell stuck his foot in the way. 'I'll be back tomorrow morning, Marshall. And the next day. I'll find out where that money went. You may think you've been careful but you'll have made a mistake. Do yourself a favour and tell me who you paid. You co-operate and it will go a long way to your defence. As you said, you were at the pub that evening. Why should you go away for murder?'

'Murder?' Marshall was screaming now. 'I'm not going away for anything you fucking nonce. Get out of my house.'

The noise was enough to disturb the neighbours. The door next to Marshall's opened up, a woman sticking her head out. 'I have a baby sleeping in here,' she said.

'Sorry, ma'am,' said Farrell, showing her his ID.

As the woman shut the door, he said to Marshall, 'Last chance.'

Marshall stared at him, his eyes looking him up and down. For a second, Farrell thought he was about to speak to him.

Instead he shook his head, and shut the door.

Chapter Forty-Eight

Louise had met Padfield on a couple of occasions. That first day with the sheep, he'd been present on the hill with Sandy Osman and Annette Harling but she couldn't recall reading anything further about either man in her reports. She pictured Padfield now. He'd been quiet, with the kind of shyness that often came over people when faced with authority. She couldn't recall anything else about him aside from his hacking cough and she was worried she hadn't paid him the attention he may have deserved. She drove Hoxton to the address he had for Ted Padfield. Hoxton wanted to drive himself but stopped his protestation once Louise suggested he take a breathalyser test.

'I'm not usually like this,' he said, as she drove him through the woodlands back to Cheddar.

Stale alcohol lingered on Hoxton's breath. Louise wondered if he was fooling himself. Had Paul told himself the same thing during his years of drinking? It was the addict's refrain: the belief that they could stop at any given moment, if they chose to do so. It made her wonder about her choices in men. It was hard to imagine that a few days ago she'd considered going to dinner with the man. Maybe it had something to do with Paul.

At his best, like Hoxton, her brother had been charming and full of life. She'd loved being around Paul at those times, but hated the other side of him when he was either drunk or hungover.

Had she seen something of this in Hoxton? Maybe she was a sucker for sad cases, subconsciously believing she could change them like she'd failed to do with Paul. Not that it mattered. Any attraction she'd had for Hoxton had evaporated. She stopped short of suggesting he seek help – she didn't know him well enough – and at that moment she had other concerns.

Sam Amstell couldn't be located. Finch had told her Amstell was heading for a meeting in Taunton. Louise was suspicious about the coincidental way he'd left the commune once Hoxton had appeared with his news. And now, Amstell's phone wasn't ringing.

'How do you know Ted Padfield?' asked Louise, as she pulled down the main road towards Cheddar.

'I know *of* him more than anything. In fact the reason I paid such attention to him at the commune is because I'd seen him in Cheddar.'

'At the caves?' said Louise, wary about reigniting Hoxton's paranoia about strange sounds and voices in the caves and the woods.

'I know it sounds far-fetched but I know what I heard. That's not where I know Padfield from though. He lives alone in Cheddar but I first saw him at Annette's house.'

'Annette?'

'The councillor.'

'Annette Harling?'

'Yes. They're divorced now but a couple of years back I was having dinner at her place. A business thing, you understand. There were a few others. I was taking a walk outside, smoking I'm afraid, and I heard the noise. There was a room off the courtyard at the back. I thought it was a stable at first but it had been converted. It was the middle of summer and the door was open. I peeked in and saw Padfield on some sort of breathing apparatus. He looked asleep so I didn't approach him. I later found out that he was Annette's ex-husband. She didn't like to talk about it apparently so I didn't think any more of it. And then Amstell told me last night that Padfield was helping out the commune and I put two and two together.'

Louise had seen civilians put two and two together many times in the past, rarely with success. 'And you think you heard him in the caves and the woods?'

'Yes.'

'May I ask, Mr Hoxton, if you were intoxicated on any of these occasions?'

Hoxton sighed. There was shame in his eyes and she didn't question him further. The only reason she'd agreed to speak to Padfield in the first place was the similarity in Hoxton's and Madison's recollections, and as she pulled up outside the address Hoxton had for Padfield, Louise began to question her own judgement.

Louise made Hoxton stay in the car when they reached Padfield's house, a quaint terraced house off the main road outside the village. Green paint came away in Louise's hand as she knocked on the door. No one answered but Padfield's neighbour's front door creaked open, a severe-looking woman in her sixties peering out. 'He's not in,' she said.

Louise displayed her warrant card. 'When was the last time you saw Mr Padfield?' she asked.

'He comes in at all hours but I haven't seen him for a few days. I'd like to though.'

'Why's that?'

'He owes me some bloody rent,' said the woman, her round face cracking into a furious scowl.

'You own this property?'

'That I do.'

Louise peered through the glass of Padfield's front window, her view obstructed by a yellowed net curtain. She made out the shape of a sofa but little else. 'How far is he behind on his rent?'

'A week.'

Louise sighed. 'Is he usually reliable?'

The woman frowned. She touched her forehead. 'Between you and me, I think he's a bit, you know.'

'No, I'm afraid not Mrs . . .'

'Mrs Cartwright. Eleanor Cartwright.'

'Could you elaborate, Mrs Cartwright?'

'I don't like to speak ill of people.'

Louise sucked in a breath as the woman paused, doubting very much the veracity of the woman's last statement.

'I think he has something wrong with him, you know, upstairs. Sometimes he's okay, but then at other times he's miles away. As if he can't concentrate. He's like a child really. And at night . . .' The woman shook her head.

'At night.'

'The noise. My fault really, but our bedrooms back on to each other. He's got something wrong with him for sure. He uses one of them machines to help him breathe. Or to help him not snore, but why would he care about snoring as he's all alone and that?'

Louise took a second look through the windows. 'Would you let me know the second Mr Padfield returns,' she said, handing the woman her card.

'What's he done?'

'Nothing. Please let me know when he's back though.'

'Shall I tell him you were asking for him?' said the woman, revelling in the potential role of co-conspirator.

'If you don't mind, I'd rather you didn't.'

The woman nodded and closed her door.

Louise dropped Hoxton back to his hotel. 'Get some rest. I'll get someone to drop your car off.'

'You think he's involved?' said Hoxton, who looked pale and unnourished.

'Get some rest and please, Mr Hoxton, leave it to us from now on.'

◆ ◆ ◆

The atmosphere at the Pembertons' was a welcome respite. The relief and happiness was palpable. Louise wondered with a smile if Madison would ever escape from the clutches of her parents who both had their arms around her as they sat huddled on the sofa.

'How are you, Madison?' asked Louise.

'I'm fine, thank you,' said the girl. She looked remarkably poised considering the ordeal she'd endured. Sadly, the worst was still probably to come for her. The unfortunate truth was that no one came out of these things unscathed. The family would face a long term of rehabilitation. However she felt at that moment, the trauma of being taken would be something Madison would have to revisit. It would potentially haunt her forever. As for the parents, they would spend the rest of their lives with heightened insecurity about their daughter. They would fear the ringtones on their phones, would be that bit more relieved every time Madison returned home. That Madison had come out of the ordeal physically unharmed was a saving grace they would have to cling on to, and Louise got the impression that they were a strong enough family to get through it.

It pained her to be there but there was another family in turmoil now and she had to think of them. 'Madison, I'd like to show you a photo. Is that okay?' said Louise, holding out her phone.

She was really asking Madison's parents, and the girl turned to her parents for confirmation before taking the phone from Louise.

Hoxton had supplied the photograph. Louise had the team researching Padfield but wanted some feedback from the girl. 'Have you seen this man before?' said Louise, her voice light as if the question was innocuous.

When Madison didn't immediately turn away, Louise thought she may be on to something. The girl's face twisted with concentration as if she was willing something to come from the photo. Madison was nearly six years older than Emily but Louise thought of her niece as Madison's lip began trembling. 'Something about the eyes,' she said, her voice so soft that it was almost inaudible.

'You've seen his eyes before?' said Louise, matching the soft timbre of the girl's voice.

'I don't know,' said Madison, turning to her mother.

'That's okay,' said Claire Pemberton, pulling the girl into her body. 'Is this really necessary?'

'I am sorry to put you through this, Madison. Please, if you could take one more look.'

Madison wrestled herself free of her mother who shot Louise an angry look. 'It may have been him. I saw his eyes when he took me. I thought they looked like this. Wild, you know?'

Louise took the phone back. 'Thank you so much, Madison. You've been so brave and helpful.' She excused herself, heading to the doorway where Tracey was waiting with Thomas.

Thomas ushered her through to the deserted kitchen. 'We've got something of interest,' he said.

Tracey showed her another picture, Padfield standing next to his ex-wife, the councillor Annette Harling. 'We have it confirmed, Mrs Harling used to be Mrs Padfield.'

Louise had been wondering about the councillor ever since Hoxton had mentioned Padfield's marriage. She'd been ever present since that first day following the sheep attack. Did she have a role to play in this?

'There's more,' said Thomas. 'Padfield is originally from Cheddar but moved away when he married Annette. They were living in the midlands for fifteen years. They returned to Cheddar after Padfield was involved in an accident.'

Louise rubbed her forehead. Her chest tightened as she waited for Thomas to explain.

'They lost their child. A three-year-old boy.'

Louise glanced at the ceiling, answers presenting themselves in her head. 'When were they divorced?'

'Three years ago. From what we've gathered so far, they tried to start again in Cheddar but Padfield was seriously injured in the accident,' said Tracey.

'Physically and mentally,' said Thomas.

'Mentally?'

'He suffered severe trauma to the head and was in an enforced coma for six weeks. From what some of the locals have said, Padfield is a completely different person to the one who left Cheddar those years before.'

'We have an address for Annette?'

'Yes, over by Bradley Cross,' said Tracey, by which time Louise was already heading out of the house.

Chapter Forty-Nine

Five minutes into the journey and Louise was heading a convoy of vehicles. Behind her followed Thomas and Tracey; behind them, two patrol cars.

It could be a waste of time but she couldn't care about that now. She needed to speak to Ted Padfield and, with the revelation about their child, Annette's house was as good a place as any to search. She thought about the times she'd met Annette. How confident and poised she'd been. Nothing in the woman's behaviour had hinted at the tragedy of her past. Louise thought of the secrets people carried around with them at all times, and the extent to which those secrets could impinge on their behaviour.

Annette's house was a non-working farmhouse in the village of Bradley Cross, which was only a four-minute drive from the Pemberton house. As Louise entered the small estate, the tiny stones of the driveway flicking up from her tyres, she was taken by two things: the similarity of the building to the Boltons' farmhouse, and the sight of Richard Hoxton standing by the front door in conversation with Annette Harling.

Annette shot her a quizzical look as Louise pulled up outside and opened the car door, the vehicle still running. The confusion increased as three further cars jostled for space behind her.

'What the hell is going on?' asked Annette, as Louise approached.

'We need to talk, Annette. Mr Hoxton, what brings you here?'

Hoxton had changed his clothes and had trimmed his beard, but the hangover was unmistakable in his eyes.

'What is going on?' said Annette again, still bewildered by the swarm of activity.

Louise glared at Hoxton. 'Kev, could you assist Mr Hoxton for the time being,' Louise said to the uniformed officer. 'These are my colleagues DI Pugh, and DS Ireland. May we come in and ask you a few questions, Annette?'

Annette stood on her doorstep, her mouth wide open as if struggling for breath. 'I suppose you better,' she said, after a pause, leading Louise and the other detectives through a small hallway to the kitchen.

'I would offer you tea but I'd like to know what the hell is going on first.'

Louise explained about her conversation first with Hoxton then Madison.

'I wondered what Hoxton was blathering on about,' said Annette, sitting down on one of the wooden chairs. 'Please,' she said, pointing to the empty places.

'So this is about Ted?' Annette lowered her eyes, her sadness apparent. 'You don't really think he has anything to do with this boy's disappearance do you?' she said, as if trying to convince herself.

'This must be very painful to discuss, Annette, but I understand you lost your son?' said Louise, wishing there was an easier way to ask the question.

Annette sucked in a breath, a hardness appearing in her eyes. 'Seven years ago. Ted was driving. A drunk driver ran into them. Our boy was killed instantly as was the driver of the other car.'

'I'm so sorry, Annette. I had no idea,' said Louise, exchanging looks with Thomas and Tracey before continuing. 'What happened to Ted?'

'He died as well.'

Louise waited for further explanation, thinking she partly understood what Annette meant.

'That sounds flippant, I know,' said Annette. 'He came back to us, flesh and bone, but he wasn't the same. In so many ways that was harder. I don't want to say I'd wished he died because I don't. What I wish is that the real Ted had recovered, that the same Ted as before had come back to me. That way I could have . . .' Annette looked up at Louise. 'That way I could have shared my grief with him.'

The hard wood of the chair dug into Louise's back. She didn't want to impinge further on Annette's grief but there were other worried parents out there at the moment. She pictured her own parents, dismayed that the first thought she had was of her mother drinking wine. 'How was he different, Annette?'

'The physical injuries I could take. He broke both legs and damaged his lungs. But that wasn't it. His personality changed. Look, I know what you're thinking; the death of a child would do that to anyone, but it was more than that. He suffered severe head trauma. These types of cases are difficult. His condition isn't bad enough that he can be hospitalised, though I do think it is getting worse. He suffers from delusions, occasional memory slips. He can be kind like he used to be but, I don't know how to explain it other than to say that he's different.'

'Has he ever hurt you?' asked Thomas.

'No,' said Annette, suddenly angry. 'You don't understand. His personality has altered. We moved back to Cheddar as it was a happy place for him in his childhood and for a time he was content again, if not happy. Then he began forgetting things. They played with his medication but nothing really worked. In the end he moved out.'

'Do you still see him?'

'Not since he moved out. I can't bear the change in him any more. He's like a stranger. That accident didn't just take away my boy. It took away my whole family.'

Chapter Fifty

Hoxton had tried to stay at Annette's house but was moved on by the police. Back at his hotel room, he collapsed on his bed. His laptop was on, the light from the screen glaring out, but he couldn't consider work. Walsh had left four messages on his phone that morning, each angrier than the last. Hoxton didn't know if his boss knew about his foray to the commune last night, and his growing involvement in what was happening, and at that moment he didn't care. He only wanted to take personal responsibility over one thing, and that was finding the missing boy.

If only he'd had his wits about him from that first drunken night at the cave, he may have been able to stop all this before it had started.

He glanced at the mini-bar. It had been refilled since last night. Its contents called to him even though he understood there would be no solace to be found in drinking. The alcohol would only make him more paranoid. Rather than make him forget, it would remind him of the fool he'd been.

His fingers hovered over the handle of the fridge as if they had a mind of their own. One wouldn't hurt, he thought, and was about to take out a lager bottle when his phone rang.

Alice Fenney was Jennings' head of legal. It wasn't the type of call he could let ring. Reluctantly, he placed the lager back in the fridge. 'Alice,' he said, preparing for the worst – which he duly received.

By the time Alice hung up twenty minutes later, Jennings' investment had all but been withdrawn. Hoxton understood. Things were too unpredictable. That Jennings had asked Alice to call meant there was little Hoxton could do. Jennings had washed his hands of the situation and no amount of persuasion, or wining and dining, could rectify that.

Walsh would have to be told but Hoxton had other priorities. He called Amstell and told him what he would consider the good news. Amstell couldn't hide his glee but was still wary. 'Why are you telling me this, Richard?'

'I appreciate what you did for me last night. It was good of you, and there's no point trying to hide things.'

'Will you definitely be pulling out of the development?'

'That will be Walsh's decision finally, but Jennings was a major investor so my guess is that's it.'

Hoxton could almost hear Amstell ruminating on the other end of the line. 'How can I help you, Richard?'

Amstell was definitely wasted at the commune. He had an eye and ear for business that would see him soar in industry if he let it. Maybe Hoxton would recommend him for his job when he left Walsh. 'What can you tell me about Ted Padfield?' he said.

◆ ◆ ◆

After his lengthy chat with Amstell, Hoxton made two more calls. For once, his head was clear. He'd listened in disbelief as Amstell had told him the full story about Padfield's accident and the death of his son. It made Hoxton consider how much he was out of touch. He hadn't even known Annette had once been married to Padfield, let alone that they'd had and lost a child.

Hoxton had admired Annette from the beginning. She was professional and diligent. He'd always got the feeling from her that she had the best interests of the village at heart, but she was always willing to listen and wasn't closed to new ideas. It was hard to believe she carried such tragedy around with her.

From what Amstell had told him, she'd separated from Padfield due to the change in his behaviour following the accident. Hoxton hardly knew the man and certainly didn't know the person he'd been. All he knew was that he'd been following him. First at the cave, and then at the commune. To what end, he didn't know. It may have been a coincidence or it may have been a way to undermine the work he'd undertaken in the village.

The next call he made was to a young police constable who worked out of Cheddar. The officer updated him on the current developments on the case. It was then Hoxton realised that his worries might not be as paranoid as he feared.

His last call was to one of Walsh's so-called *special* team, Lincoln Brown. Brown was ex-police. Walsh used him for background checks and Walsh liked to do a lot of checking. Brown would have collected information on all the major players in the development. Hoxton hated dealing with the man but he'd exhausted all other avenues so made the call.

'I need some information,' he said, once the preliminaries were out of the way.

'Who?'

'Annette Padfield.'

'A second,' said Brown, who then proceeded to tell him everything about the woman Hoxton had recently discovered for himself. That the information about Annette's relationship with Padfield, and the death of their child, had only been a call away solidified Hoxton's feelings that he was no longer in the right job. His grip on information was slipping. He understood the source of his failings and maybe once this was all over he could change his life.

'Hang on, there's one more note,' said Brown. 'We believe she is in a relationship with a man by the name of Sandy Osman. Hang on, let me cross-reference. Yes, Sandy Osman. National Trust guy. You know him?'

'Yes. Thanks, Lincoln,' said Hoxton, hanging up.

◆ ◆ ◆

Hoxton would have called DI Blackwell but he'd well and truly destroyed that relationship. Whatever positive impression he felt he'd made on her had been destroyed by his subsequent actions. She'd seen him at his worst. If he called her now with this theory he would be dismissed out of hand, so he decided to act himself.

The conversation he had to have with Sandy Osman was not one he could have over the phone, so he made the journey to Osman's home in Axbridge. Hoxton's lethargy – the hangover coming in waves – was peppered with excitement. It was probably all a waste of his and everyone's time, but the sense that he was, at last, contributing to something was like a jab of adrenaline to his system. He'd been playing over in his head what he would say to Sandy when he arrived and was trying to whittle it down to something that didn't sound, at best, implausible.

When he reached the house and knocked on the door, all that planning vanished.

'Rich, what are you doing here?' said Sandy. When he wasn't out on the hills, Sandy made a point of being immaculately dressed, and didn't disappoint on this occasion. Despite the late hour, he was wearing a full suit, a red tie, fixed in a perfect Windsor, pushed up tight against his throat.

'I have some news. May I come in?'

'Now's not a great time, Rich.'

It was the second time Sandy had called him Rich. The man was old school, and Hoxton couldn't recall him using the abbreviated version of his name before. 'Everything okay?' said Hoxton, the excitement and adrenaline that had fed his system having dissipated, his limbs now loose, his head dizzy.

Sandy tried to signal something with his eyes. It was then Hoxton realised he wasn't cut out for this type of game either, as Sandy was shoved aside and, from behind the door, emerged Ted Padfield.

'Better join the party,' said Padfield, a hunting rifle pointed directly at Hoxton's chest.

Hoxton stepped inside and followed Sandy down the hallway, Padfield's gun rigid against his back.

Chapter Fifty-One

Annette's claim – that Padfield wasn't the same person any more – played through Louise's mind as she drove back to the Bolton farmhouse. She related to the pain in Annette's eyes in more ways than she cared to imagine. As her older brother, Paul had naturally had a special place in her heart and she'd had to experience his transformations on more than one occasion. And while his move from friendly sibling to moody teenager had been difficult to accept and adjust to, it was his change to alcoholic that had destroyed their relationship. It pained her to accept it, but by the time he'd died they were no longer on good terms. The Paul she'd known had changed so irrevocably that he was someone else. Someone she struggled to relate to; a stranger with a familiar face.

It wasn't just Annette's words that had her feeling this way. She'd just finished speaking to DCI Robertson who'd demanded her appearance back in Weston after her visit to the Boltons. He'd refused to elaborate on the reasons but she was sure it was related to Farrell's investigation into her brother's murder.

But she had to put that behind her for the time being. Her focus had to be on finding Aaron and for now that meant trying to locate Ted Padfield.

The muted atmosphere was akin to the Pemberton house before Madison's return. The despair had seeped into the property.

The parents sat in the living area, the curtains shut, the wallpaper and carpets, even the fabric on the armchairs, much darker than Louise remembered. They were still in the first twenty-four hours of the abduction but there was such dismay on the Boltons' faces that it appeared they had given up hope of ever seeing their baby again.

Small talk was wasted breath in such a situation. 'May I?' she asked, sitting opposite the pair, who stared back at her, their expressions as blank as mannequins.

Louise uploaded the images of Ted Padfield and Annette Harling on to her phone and handed them to Liam. 'Do you recognise either of these people?' she asked.

Liam Bolton stared at the images as if looking straight through them. He shook his head without making eye contact with Louise before handing the phone to his wife. Louise didn't want to lead either of them but after Ellie barely registered the images, she asked if Padfield could be the man she'd seen on the hill.

This piqued Ellie's interest. She grabbed the phone with a renewed intensity, staring at the screen as if she could bring the image to life. 'You think this man took my boy?' she asked.

'I'm not saying that, Ellie. But do you recognise him? Have you ever seen them before? Anything you could remember could make all the difference.'

Louise saw the crack of disappointment in Ellie's features. She was trying to remember something that may not have happened and eventually broke down, defeated, as she handed the phone back.

Louise wanted to tell them that Ted Padfield was a significant suspect, that things could change in an instant. Madison had returned, and they could still find Aaron. But they were words she could never utter. She had to stay professionally detached, couldn't offer false hope however well intentioned. All she could do was to tell them what she was doing, and would continue to do: everything in her power to find Aaron.

As she left the pair in the care of the FLO, she hoped that gave them at least a small sense of comfort.

◆ ◆ ◆

Back in Weston, she entered DCI Robertson's office. She spoke before he had the chance to say anything. 'We need to put a wanted mark on Ted Padfield,' she said.

'Good day to you, Louise. Please, take a seat,' said Robertson, not missing a beat.

'I'm serious, Iain. I think he's who we're looking for.'

'Just take a seat, Louise.'

Louise did as instructed though she was restless. 'Every second, Iain.'

'I know,' said Robertson, accentuating the growl of his accent as he did every time he wanted to gain her attention.

'What is it, Iain?'

'A friendly warning,' said Robertson.

'My favourite kind. What about this time?' she asked, already knowing the answer.

'You've been interfering in Farrell's investigation?' It was framed as a question but was more or less a statement.

'His investigation into my brother's murder you mean?'

Robertson puffed out his cheeks. 'Yes, your brother's murder but come on, Louise. You don't need to be told.'

'I haven't done anything untoward, Iain.'

'Don't give me that childish shit, Louise. You know any involvement could jeopardise the case.'

'Finch?'

Robertson lifted his hand up. 'I'm not having this conversation, Louise. I just need you to promise not to get involved.'

Robertson had been good to her since her move to Weston. Louise had brought considerable experience with her and he'd welcomed that, when many others may have felt threatened. He would never come out and say it, but he was on her side in relation to her on-going feud with Finch, and she understood the difficult position he was in. But she couldn't pretend any more. 'If I hadn't got involved, Iain, then the case would be shelved. I uncovered a lead no one else was prepared to investigate.'

'I don't want to hear this, Louise. I want to hear you're not going to be involved, and that anything you've done has been minimal.'

'I'm not involved at the moment,' said Louise, noting the hint of a grin forming on Robertson's face as she raised her eyebrows.

'To be continued,' said Robertson. 'Tell me about Ted Padfield,' he said, Louise relieved that, for now, he wasn't pushing things further.

◆ ◆ ◆

Farrell called her as she was driving back to the commune. Padfield had been put on the nationwide wanted list, every officer in the local area having been alerted to his details on their mobile data terminals. 'I shouldn't be speaking to you,' said Louise.

'Nor me, you,' said Farrell. 'But what are we going to do?' He told her about the trip to Cornwall and his meeting with Bryan Lemanski. 'Joslyn sends her regards.'

Louise smiled, surprised how her mood was lifted by the words. 'I need to phone her,' she said. 'So what next?'

Farrell hesitated. 'I want to apologise. I should have pushed the Marshall angle harder.'

'You think there's something to it?'

Farrell told her about his encounter with Marshall and his money withdrawals.

'I'm glad we've got Jodi out of that situation,' said Louise.

'Couldn't have timed it better. Tracing the money is going to be difficult. I'll track down the CCTV images but with it being cash . . .'

'You think he used that money for . . .'

Farrell came to her rescue, interrupting before she had a chance to say the words. 'I certainly wouldn't put it past Marshall. He has that inflated type of ego, probably views his wife as his property. I was thinking . . .' Farrell paused again.

'Don't keep me in suspense,' said Louise.

'I know this is going to be a difficult one but perhaps I could speak to Emily again.'

Louise went quiet. She'd been thinking along the same lines ever since showing the photographs of Ted Padfield to Madison. She'd allowed Emily to be questioned at the beginning and they'd even shown her some photographs of the Mannings family but it had proved too traumatic for her niece. Every time Paul's death was mentioned, Emily retreated further into herself. And with her recent behaviour, Louise was worried about how detrimental it could become for her.

'I could show her the pictures I have for Marshall and his chums. See if it helps her recall anything,' said Farrell.

Louise wasn't sure she wanted Emily to recall that night. She was desperate to find Paul's killer, but had to weigh that against the damage it could do to Emily. She thought about the three thousand pounds Marshall had withdrawn from his account. Could Paul's life really be that cheap? 'Let me think about it. In the meantime, can you send those photos to me?'

'Finch wouldn't be too pleased with that.'

'What Finch doesn't know can't harm him. Thanks, Greg. I really do appreciate all your work on this.'

'No problem, boss.'

◆ ◆ ◆

She tried calling Amstell again as she drove to the commune, and fought the conspiratory thoughts of him being somewhere with Finch. Now was a time for logic and pure thought, not wild speculation.

Despite which, she kept returning to the three thousand pounds. Chances were high that there was a logical explanation for Marshall withdrawing the money but it was hard not to see the sum as a gross estimation of her brother's life. Worse, however, was her fixation on the amount rather than its purpose. That her whole family could be destroyed, and her niece's future put at risk, for such a trivial amount was so difficult to comprehend. It was distracting and again she had to remind herself that, for now, Emily was safe and sound. Her full attention had to be focused on finding Aaron.

It was dark by the time she reached the commune. Some of the restrictions had been lifted, the population allowed to leave once they'd been questioned.

She updated the team on Ted Padfield, giving them the unpleasant information that everyone from the commune would have to be re-questioned. As well as being on the wanted list, pictures of Padfield and Aaron were with both local and national press agencies. From what she'd been told of Padfield, it seemed unlikely that he had the resources to escape from the area unchecked. And even if he did, it would take a mammoth amount of resourcefulness for him to keep the child undetected.

Unfortunately, that didn't mean the child was safe. The abductor had proven to be unpredictable and violent. If Padfield had taken the child, there was no telling what he would do.

She tried Amstell again as she stood outside the Tryst, where Oldfield and his team were continuing their search. Floodlights lit the area, illuminating the outline of the two lovers on the cave wall. Louise was beginning to understand the history of the area, of the caves and the hills. Like so many desolate areas, the place held secrets she would never learn; secrets that were probably best left untold. Peering through the entrance, into the abyss of the tunnel and caves, made her feel small and she wondered what Madison had felt during her confinement, and what would happen to Aaron if he didn't escape his.

She stayed on site long into the night as the questioning continued. Repetition was necessary but at times the words stopped making sense. Most of the residents knew of Ted Padfield, and had seen him at the site. They gave much the same feedback. He was a bit of an oddball, kept himself to himself. Everyone had heard his erratic breathing but no one had ever heard a baby.

Louise wished now that she hadn't let Hoxton go. Although she believed he meant well, his behaviour had an erratic side. She considered calling him, wondering if he was in contact with the elusive Sam Amstell, but for now it was one extra complication she didn't need.

With the teams thinning out for the night, she sat in her car and waited. It was too late to call her parents, and not for the first time in recent memory, she felt neglectful. Her phone listed five unanswered calls to Sam Amstell but none to her family. What did that say about her?

She tried to clear her mind, to work through the case from day one, but her tiredness made it impossible. Her thoughts and recollections merged as her eyes lowered. She daydreamed about the cliff walk and Madison's imprisonment, the dead sheep, Finch and Amstell in cahoots in some bar somewhere, Paul dead in the caravan, the fire on the old pier.

The piercing wail of her phone jostled her back awake. She pressed the answer button expecting to hear Richard Hoxton slurring down the line, but all she heard was static.

'Hello,' she said, turning up the volume on the phone. As she strained to hear, she caught the jumbled sounds of people talking. No doubt Hoxton was in some late night dive drinking his concerns away and had pocket-called her. But still she listened, her attention only diverted when a car entered the commune area.

She left the car, the phone still pinned to her ear. She was cloaked in darkness, the lights from the car her only guideline through the fog that had descended over the compound. Walking towards the rumble of an engine, she froze as the car's headlights winked off and, for a second, she was alone in the dark with the twin sounds of the static in her ear and the car's engine her only companions.

A light popped on in the car as the driver switched off the engine and left the vehicle. Louise was upon him before he had time to take a breath. 'Mr Amstell,' she said, holding the phone away from her ear for more light.

The man surprised her with a sound that went from high pitched wail to angered slur. 'You scared the hell out of me,' said Amstell. 'Jesus, what are you trying to do?'

At this stage Louise couldn't care less how much she'd spooked the man. She wanted answers, and she was annoyed at him for ignoring her all day. 'Tell me everything you know about Ted Padfield.'

'I need to piss,' said Amstell.

'Have you been drinking, Mr Amstell?' asked Louise, wondering if she was the only person in the area not succumbing to the lure of alcohol.

'No.'

'Shall we check that officially?'

'Come inside. I'll tell you whatever it is you wish to know.'

'Here will be fine,' said Louise, trying not to shiver. 'Why didn't you tell me about Ted Padfield's ex-wife?'

Amstell's car door was still open and light spilled out, illuminating his hesitation. 'What, Annette? I don't know. Didn't think it was relevant.'

'You didn't think it was relevant that Padfield had a relationship with a councillor. That they'd lost a child?' It was conceivable that Amstell hadn't seen any relevance in Padfield's past but Louise felt as if the oversight was intentional and she had to wonder if he was protecting Padfield somehow.

'Now that you say it like that.'

'It's all working out well for you. I understand that Stephen Walsh is pulling out his investment.'

'I've just been out celebrating,' said Amstell, realising too late that he was incriminating himself.

'So you have been drinking. Not with Ted Padfield I presume?'

'No, of course not. What the hell are you suggesting?'

'You tell me, Mr Amstell. I have a feeling you may have been withholding important information from me. Rest assured, if I can prove that, you will face the full consequences.'

Amstell grimaced, the gesture made sinister by the poor light of his car interior.

'Do you know where Ted Padfield is, Mr Amstell?'

'Of course not. Have you tried Annette's house? I know she helps him out now and again. With his medication and whatnot.'

'She hasn't seen him recently. Where else?' said Louise, keen to keep the man talking while she could.

Amstell pursed his lips. 'Look, I don't want anything to do with all this. But . . .'

'But?'

'You hear rumours, don't you?'

'Do you, Mr Amstell? And what rumours have you heard?'

'Annette and Sandy Osman.'

'What about them?' said Louise, placing the name Osman to the man from the National Trust she'd met on the cliff trail the day after the sheep had been slaughtered.

'Between me and you, I heard they were having an affair. Maybe if Padfield found out . . .'

Louise stepped towards Amstell, the man instinctively stepping back and coming close to falling back into the car. She recalled seeing the way Osman and Annette had been together, and worried that a lack of focus had made her miss the significance of their relationship. She hadn't known how serious this case was. It had just been a couple of dead sheep. And now . . . 'This better not be a joke.'

'It's a poorly kept secret if you ask me,' said Amstell, trying to be nonchalant.

Louise thought about the time she'd seen the two councillors together. Now Amstell had said it, the possibility of an affair didn't sound that unreasonable. 'Do you have an address for him?'

Amstell smiled as if he'd won something, retrieving the address on his phone.

'Get some sleep, Mr Amstell. If I catch you drinking in charge of a vehicle again I won't be so lenient.'

Chapter Fifty-Two

Louise checked in with Tracey at the Bolton farm, as she drove to the address Amstell had given her.

'You need any backup?' asked Tracey.

It was 1.30 a.m. and she was only attending the house on the back of idle gossip. 'I'll be fine. If you haven't heard from me in an hour, expect the worst,' she said, a joke line she sometimes shared with Tracey lifted from some long-forgotten TV drama.

'Look after yourself, boss.'

Louise was becoming used to these late night drives through empty roads. It was too dark to appreciate the beauty of the gorge as she drove through the deserted village, but she sensed the looming presence of the cliffs on either side of her as she drove out towards Sandy Osman's farm.

Despite its beauty, she wouldn't miss the place when this was all over. The remoteness of the area – the caves and hills beyond – made her uncomfortable. She'd only begun to get a glimpse at the secrets the area held, and feared that too many things would be left unresolved.

As she pulled up the single track to Osman's farmhouse, she was reminded of a similar journey she'd made with Finch another lifetime ago when they'd been chasing the serial killer Max Walton. Just like on that night, there were no lights on in the main building but, whereas the Walton farm had long been abandoned, the sight of three cars parked outside the entrance suggested people within.

Louise had been armed that night with Walton, special dispensation given due to the nature of their task. History demonstrated the mistakes of that evening and although she felt no immediate danger as she left the car, she was glad of the baton and the pepper spray she wore on her activity belt; the feeling intensifying when she noted that one of the cars in the driveway belonged to Richard Hoxton.

She texted the number plate details of both of the other cars to Tracey, who replied immediately with a suggestion for backup. Louise would have been more reluctant to agree if she hadn't seen Hoxton's car but there were enough discrepancies to suggest that backup was necessary. She was about to reply when a movement from the side of the house caught her eye. She glanced down at her screen, at the half-finished message, and was about to hit send when Ted Padfield emerged from the shadows holding a hunting rifle.

◆ ◆ ◆

Hoxton lowered his eyes as the policewoman was led into the barn. This was his fault. He should have gone directly to DI Blackwell about Annette and Osman; would have done so if he hadn't already embarrassed himself on so many occasions. He couldn't look as Padfield shoved the gun into the woman's back and proceeded to force her to sit on one of the free-standing chairs next to Annette and Sandy Osman.

If only he hadn't run that night in the caves, everything that happened could have been prevented. Whatever Padfield's motivations were, it was clear he needed help. If Hoxton had kept his nerve that night, instead of giving in to alcohol-fuelled panic, then maybe he could have helped the man. He swore to himself at that moment that if he ever got out of this situation he would give up drinking for good; he'd promised himself so many times before, but he thought maybe this time he could do it.

He glanced at Louise, trying to express his guilt as best he could in a simple facial gesture. She offered him a nod. She appeared to be remarkably calm as she turned her attention to Padfield. 'Ted. May I call you Ted?' she asked. 'Ted, we can sort this out between us. You've got yourself into a terrible situation but we can resolve it.'

Padfield, on the other hand, was anything but composed. Hoxton didn't know where he'd obtained the hunting rifle but it looked, much like Padfield, as if it had seen better days. Padfield swung it by his side and Hoxton caught Louise glancing at the movement of the rifle in the air, as if waiting for a moment to reach out and snatch it.

As if reading Hoxton's thoughts, Padfield took a step back and held the gun aloft.

The barn was silent save for Padfield's laboured breathing as he pointed the gun at each of them in turn.

◆ ◆ ◆

He remembered . . .

He didn't remember why he was here. Something that had seemed so clear in his mind only minutes before was as vague and cloudy as low hanging fog. Annette was the only person he wanted to see and she was staring at him as if he was a monster. The man tied next to her was awash with a hatred and rage he couldn't understand.

Annette's face softened. 'Where's the baby, Ted?'

He smiled. The baby. 'Jack's safe,' he said.

A cloud came over Annette's face then. She glanced at the policewoman who was sprung like a coil. 'That's not Jack, Ted. Jack died. Remember?'

He rubbed his eyes. 'Jack is back at my house, sleeping,' he said, but even as he said it, it sounded wrong.

'Oh Jesus, Ted, what have you done?' said Annette, bursting into tears.

◆ ◆ ◆

Louise watched the gun as close as she watched Padfield. It was the only thing stopping her attacking the man. He clearly wasn't in control of the situation and hadn't tied her to the chair.

She closed her eyes when he called the baby by his dead son's name, his ex-wife fighting a losing battle to make the man see sense.

'Is the baby safe?' asked Louise, after Annette began crying.

Padfield snapped his head left to look at her, as if he'd forgotten she was there. 'Of course he's safe.'

'He's at your house?'

'I said that, didn't I? What do you want from me?'

'It would be nice if we could check on him, don't you think? Can I go and do that, Ted? We shouldn't really leave a baby alone for this amount of time, should we?'

'You don't need to do that,' said Padfield. 'Annette and I are going now.'

'What do you mean, Ted?' said Annette, her face distorted with tears.

'Don't you understand? Jack is back. We can start again.'

Louise watched as Padfield lowered the gun from his shoulder. The wooden overlays on the handle looked worn and chipped, the shaft rusted. If it was functioning, it only had the two chambers so Padfield would only be able to get off two shots before reloading. If he lowered his hand away from the trigger, she was sure she could reach him before he could fire.

'Ted, this is madness,' said Annette, diverting his attention.

'I did this for us, Netty.'

As Louise turned to look at the woman, Padfield swung the gun in her direction once more. 'Easy,' said Louise. 'Maybe you should go with him now, Annette. Make sure the baby is safe.'

Annette was close to shock. Her eyes were wide, panicked, but she accepted Louise's guidance. 'Untie me, Ted,' she said.

'We can go? Start again?' asked Ted, with a childish innocence that was hard to witness.

Louise continued watching Annette, nodding her head half an inch.

'Yes, Ted. We can start again,' said Annette.

Louise was on the man the second he lowered the gun and moved towards his ex-wife. A speck of the pepper spray caught her in blowback as she ran forwards, the can outstretched. Padfield turned to face her and caught a blast of the spray in his eyes. He roared and began to stagger but managed to keep hold of the gun.

'Put the gun down now, Mr Padfield. You don't want to hurt anyone,' Louise said, her throat burning from the droplets of spray in the air.

Padfield still couldn't see. He started to aim the shotgun at random targets. If he did manage to fire off a round, it could go anywhere. It must have taken all his will to stay upright. His eyes were streaming and the pain must have been unimaginable. 'Last chance,' said Louise. 'If I spray you again it could do you some serious damage.'

Tears streamed from the man, the whites of his eyes now a sinister-looking red. 'Now,' she said, the spray poised.

Padfield wobbled on the spot. Louise was about to hit him with a second blast that would have risked blinding him when he lowered the gun, his left hand instinctively rubbing at his eyes.

The man was still a threat to everyone in the room, and now wasn't a time for orthodoxy. Louise kicked Padfield straight between the legs, the man falling as if she'd emptied the gun directly into his head.

In all the commotion, Louise had barely registered the sounds of vehicles arriving at the farmhouse. As she took the gun from Padfield, Tracey emerged, flanked by Thomas and two uniformed officers who cuffed Padfield.

Louise stood, fighting the urge to wipe her eyes where the haze of pepper spray had reached her. 'The baby,' she said, running for the door before her fellow officers could question what she was doing.

◆ ◆ ◆

Louise blinked her eyes as she started the car, blasting a horn at a startled colleague who had blocked the driveway. She kept her hand on the horn, as the driver reversed the police vehicle back down the track until he'd left enough space for her to get by.

She let go of the horn, the sound still reverberating in her ears, and sped down the driveway on to the lane. Adrenaline flooded her system and she eased off the accelerator as she took a corner sharper than intended.

It was difficult to remain calm but it wouldn't help anyone if she crashed before reaching Padfield's house. She thought about Ellie and Liam Bolton, and how much it would mean to them to see their son again; she pictured Madison reunited with her family, reminding herself that it was possible, that Aaron could be safe.

But most of all she thought about Emily, as if it was her niece she was racing to save.

She left the engine running as she skidded to a halt outside Padfield's house. She would never be able to forgive herself if the baby had been there earlier that day when she'd stood on this very spot. She did what she should have done then, smashing the lock with her second solid kick of the day. The door gave little resistance, Louise's instincts driving her upstairs, her ears attuned for sound. Padfield had said he'd left the baby sleeping and Louise had never wished for someone's words to be literal more than she did at that moment.

Her increased heartbeat was making her dizzy and she stopped at the threshold of what must have been Padfield's bedroom and stared over at the sight of a baby's crib next to the bed.

Louise closed her eyes, trying to rid herself of every other distraction. She wanted to hear the sound of the child breathing but all she heard was the sound of blood pumping through her body.

Outside, flashing blue lights filtered through the bedroom window throwing flashing shadows against the wall.

Louise stepped forward, her muscles tensed as if she was walking against an invisible force. Behind, she heard the hurried steps of officers rushing up the staircase but time had lost all meaning.

At last, she reached the crib and looked in.

What she saw stayed with her forever.

Chapter Fifty-Three

Louise still thought about that moment a week later. The incomparable relief she'd felt at the sight of Aaron Bolton asleep in his white babygrow, oblivious to all the fuss surrounding him. Louise couldn't recall ever seeing a more peaceful sight and she'd found herself returning to that night whenever things threatened to overwhelm her.

The memory of Ellie and Liam taking the baby from the paramedic always threatened to move her to tears. The sheer joy she'd witnessed in the parents' eyes one of the precious moments of reward she received for doing her job.

Interviewing Ted Padfield had proved to be difficult. After being taken into custody, he'd been assessed and immediately hospitalised. He'd remained in a secure ward at Weston General as he'd been reintroduced to the medication he'd stopped taking, and only now had Louise been given permission to question him.

The hospital's interview room had the feel of a prison cell. Padfield, sitting behind a desk fixed to the floor, was wearing a hospital gown. It was Louise's first real chance to get a look at him. She'd visited the hospital every day since finding Aaron but Padfield had always been prone in his hospital bed. He was much calmer than the night at the farmhouse and she wondered how far his medication was subduing him.

Louise recognised the man sitting next to Padfield as his clinical psychiatrist, Dr Said Darzi. 'I think we can only do five minutes today, DI Blackwell,' he said.

Louise would usually be irked at the delay but her most pressing concern – the safety of the missing child – had been resolved, and although there were many matters to be determined, she would wait for another opportunity if necessary.

'Hello, Ted. Do you recognise me?' she asked.

Padfield was motionless, his face fixed in an expressionless gaze. Louise was surprised when the skin around his lips cracked and he spoke. 'You're the policewoman?' he said.

'That's right. DI Blackwell. You can call me Louise if you like?'

'Louise,' said Padfield, tentatively. He glanced at the doctor as if for moral support before continuing. 'I'm sorry for what I did,' he said.

'That's good to know, Ted. There are still a few things we're trying to piece together. Maybe you could help us with that?'

'I'll do the best I can.'

◆ ◆ ◆

He remembered . . .

Everything seemed clearer now. The present, at least. The past was a distant, imagined place. He tried as best as he was able to explain to the policewoman but he didn't really understand himself. He would never be able to fully articulate the rage and frustration, the confusion and time lapses. All he knew was that for a time, Jack had existed again and that had been enough.

◆ ◆ ◆

It all started when Padfield had discovered Annette's affair with Osman. Padfield had stopped taking his medication and began making frequent trips to the cliff walk. With the help of his doctor he explained the time lapses he'd experienced, a long-standing side effect of the trauma, both physical and mental, he'd received the day Jack had died.

Louise had encountered numerous defendants who'd claimed insanity, or restricted capacity, as a defence. Sometimes it was justified, other times a ruse. It wasn't her concern if Padfield was playing a part now. She'd done her job, the majority of it. The children had been returned, the culprit caught. Whatever society and the system did with that information wasn't within her remit. Yes, she wanted justice. Padfield had caused unknown damage to the families of Madison and Aaron, and in particular Louise feared for the girl. Madison was old enough to understand what had happened and would have to contend with it for the rest of her life. Padfield had to pay for his crimes, but whether that was done in prison or an institution felt like a moot point at that moment.

Padfield went on to explain his growing paranoia. The anger at not finding Jack that had caused him to kill the sheep and then attack the man. The mistaken identity that had led him to take Madison, believing her to be a boy, and eventually the delusion that Aaron was his lost child, Jack.

Louise had obtained more information from the man in the five minutes than she expected. It was possible to feel sorry for him. Through no fault of his own, his life had been shattered. He'd lost his child, and effectively his true personality. But she couldn't afford to think along those lines.

'Do you know Richard Hoxton?' she asked.

Padfield nodded. 'He's part of that development company.'

'He was, that's correct,' said Louise. Hoxton had resigned the day after Padfield's arrest, the development plans for Cheddar subsequently shelved by Stephen Walsh's company. 'He claims that he heard you on numerous occasions, following him.'

Padfield continued nodding. 'It was part of my role.'

'Your role?' said Louise, recalling her own feeling of being followed on the cliff walk.

'What does it matter now?' said Padfield, his face still eerily expressionless.

'The commune?'

Padfield was still nodding as if his muscles had become stuck in the movement. 'The commune gave me a purpose, when . . .' He faltered, his chin stuck in place on his chest.

'That's okay, Ted. We can do this another time,' said Dr Darzi.

Padfield lifted his head as if he'd been switched back on. 'No, I can tell her now. My whole life has been in the land. I know I'm confused now, not the man I was, but this land was mine from when I was a boy. I spent whole summers on the cliffs, in the woods, in the hills. You could do that back then. As I got older I began climbing, potholing. There is something magic out there that I forgot about when . . . when Jack died. And I managed to get something of that back with the commune.'

'And Hoxton?'

'He threatened all that. They've already done their best to ruin the village. That you have to pay to walk up on to the cliff walk,' he said, shaking his head, his face showing the first signs of animation since Louise had entered the room. 'But what Hoxton's firm was threatening was so much worse. The land isn't ours to do with as we see fit. All they cared about was the money. They would have destroyed the land, the environment, the history, and then pissed off to let us pick up the pieces.'

'So the commune hired you to scare off Hoxton?'

'No, nothing like that. Everyone did their bit. I wasn't the only one but when I saw them all in the bar that night I knew they were up to no good. I followed them into Cox's Cave – where they broke in I might add – and tried my best to freak them out. I guess it did the job,' said Padfield, as the colour drained from his face and he slumped back in his chair.

Louise went to ask another question but Dr Darzi stood up. 'I think that's enough for today, Inspector,' he said.

Chapter Fifty-Four

The smell of disinfectant she'd encountered the last time she'd been to the pub hit Louise as she entered The Mariner. Farrell was already waiting for her. 'I got you a coffee,' he said, as he took a seat at the end of the deserted bar.

'How does this place make any money?' she said, sitting next to him.

It had been Farrell's suggestion to meet here again. 'Are you sure you want to go through with this?' he asked.

Louise had discussed the issue with her parents. It had been a tough decision but they'd reached it together; although the condition that came with it had been more than Louise had expected. She took her first, and final, sip of the lukewarm coffee. 'We're ready,' she said. 'Does Finch know?'

Farrell shifted, his hand running through his slick groomed hair. 'He's not happy but he has no logical reason to object. But if nothing comes of this, I think this line of investigation will be exhausted.'

Finch was a problem Louise had to solve, but that was for another time. She would never forget the glee with which he'd all but threatened Emily back at the Bolton farm and she was grateful that Farrell had shown enough courage to stand up to the man, whatever the cost of that might eventually prove to be.

'I understand, Greg. I appreciate what you've done. Shall we go? I don't think I can take any more artisan coffee today.'

Farrell grimaced. 'I wondered what that was,' he said.

Her parents were waiting for her at the house. Louise shot them both a quizzical look as she walked Farrell to the lounge. Both were dressed as if they were planning to go out for a fancy meal. 'You remember Greg, don't you, Emily?'

Emily was sat on the floor leaning against the sofa, her knees pulled to her chest as she watched the television. 'Hello Greg,' she said, not looking away from the screen.

'I'll make some coffee,' said Louise's mother. 'She'll be here soon.'

The child psychologist, Dr Morris, was due any minute. With the psychologist's help, Louise had spoken to Emily about the possibility of looking at the photographs and she'd agreed. But already Louise could see the tension in her niece and worried again about whether she was making the right decision.

'She's in the safest place she can be,' said Louise's mother, noting her concern. 'We'll stop it as soon as she becomes agitated.'

Emily appeared to relax as soon as Dr Morris arrived. The psychologist was calm and measured and Louise felt herself relaxing as she sat on the floor with Emily and chatted to her like they were best friends.

'Your aunty is going to show you some pictures. You remember talking about that, don't you?' said Dr Morris, as Louise and Farrell joined the pair on the carpet.

To the side, Louise's parents stood, arms folded. Louise signalled for them to sit, their tension palpable as Farrell placed his iPad in front of Emily.

Louise realised she was holding her breath as a picture of Nathan Marshall appeared on the screen and Emily shook her head. 'You've never seen this man before, Emily?' she asked.

Emily shook her head again and Farrell scrolled to a picture of Jodi Marshall.

'That was Daddy's friend,' said Emily.

The revelation was too much for Louise's mother, who suppressed a yelp while reaching for a bottle of wine on the sideboard.

'Do you know her name, Emily?' said Louise.

Emily shook her head. 'We didn't, you know, meet. I saw her with Daddy and he told me she was his friend. I remember her hair.'

Louise nodded as Farrell scrolled to the next image of Marshall's former colleague Troy Goddard. Emily sucked in a breath but shook her head. She had the same response with images of Bryan Lemanski from Cornwall, and the rest of Marshall's former colleagues.

'Do you have anything else?' Louise asked Farrell.

'I have the group photograph.'

Louise shrugged and Farrell scrolled to the last image.

'You can zoom in on the people if you wish. Do you know how to do that?' said Farrell.

Louise laughed as Emily squinted her eyes and glared at Farrell as if he was stupid.

The laughter stopped abruptly as Emily zoomed in on the image and began to scream.

Chapter Fifty-Five

The image on the screen had been a tattoo, a skull and crossbones Louise recalled seeing on the forearm of Troy Goddard from her one meeting with the man. As her mother had consoled Emily, Louise had zoomed back out on the image to reveal Goddard's smiling face.

That had been enough for Louise and she'd driven with Farrell to question the man again. 'Let me lead,' said Louise, as they knocked on Goddard's door.

Louise had to control herself as Goddard opened the door and sneered at them. 'I told you I'm not speaking to you lot any more,' he said.

She considered hauling the man in for questioning but they had nothing beyond Emily's reaction to the photograph and bringing him in now would be a mistake. 'We have a few more questions we need to ask you, Mr Goddard. May we come in?'

Despite his bravado, Louise sensed a twinge of doubt in the man as he glanced from her to Farrell and back again. 'I'm fine talking here,' he said.

Louise decided to call the man's bluff. 'If you're happy to tell everyone in your street why you were in Cornwall on the night Paul Blackwell was murdered then by all means we can discuss the situation outside.'

Farrell didn't blink as Goddard glared at him for confirmation. 'I wasn't in Cornwall and you know it,' said Goddard.

'Let's go inside and you can prove it.'

Goddard's living room was a sweatbox. Clothes were scattered over a black leather sofa, an empty pizza box on the floor. An oversized television screen took up one of the room's walls. On it was a paused video game.

'*Call of Duty*,' said Farrell. 'Reliving your past?'

'Fuck you both.'

'Take a seat, Mr Goddard,' said Louise, unmoved by the man's aggression.

'Or what?'

'Or we'll arrest you and take your fingerprints, DNA and blood. See what we come up with,' said Louise, sitting uninvited.

'I don't know why you keep looking at me,' said Farrell, who remained standing, blocking the exit of the living room door.

Goddard sighed and sat. He was on edge and Louise decided not to hold back. 'You have been identified as being at the murder scene of Paul Blackwell.'

'Bullshit.'

'Care to show me your right forearm,' said Louise.

Goddard instinctively covered up the tattoo on his arm. Smiling, he uncovered it once more. 'Hundreds of people must have this tattoo. If not thousands.'

'Maybe. Maybe not. But you were there weren't you?'

'Of course not.'

'Think very carefully. You tell us everything now and that will be taken into consideration. My guess is you were coerced into it.'

'Am I under arrest?'

'You will be. I'd like to find out what happened before I take you in. Find out why you thought three thousand pounds was enough to take my brother's life.'

It was a risk but Louise wanted to gauge the man's reaction and she received all the information she needed as his whole face slackened. Farrell sensed it too. He was alert, ready for Goddard to make a move.

'Come clean now. Tell us what we need to know before we run our tests. I can't promise anything but it will help you in the long run.'

'That motherfucker,' said Goddard, collapsing back on to the sofa.

Initially Louise thought he was talking about Paul but realised he meant Nathan Marshall.

'I should never have listened to him. He said he was an easy target. I was supposed to hurt him, teach him a lesson.'

Heat rose in Louise. 'Hurt him? You're talking about Paul.'

Goddard glanced at the floor. 'Look, I'm sorry. He was a tough bastard.'

'Oh Jesus,' said Louise, looking away.

'What do you mean you were only meant to scare him?' said Farrell, edging closer to Louise as if readying to either protect or restrain her.

'Marshall wanted me to give him a beating. Make sure he didn't come back.'

'What the hell happened?' said Farrell.

Goddard bit his lip. 'I lost it. Couldn't help it.'

He went to pull up his shirt and Louise sprung from her chair. 'What the hell are you doing?' she said, her extendable baton out in front of her.

'You'll see,' said Goddard, lifting his T-shirt to reveal a line of scar tissue. 'It was his knife. He came at me like a madman and managed to get this one in. I was lucky but . . .'

'But what?'

'I'm trained, he wasn't. I took the knife from him. Fight or flight.'

'You stabbed him seventeen times,' said Farrell.

'Fight or flight.'

Louise raised the baton and brought it down, only for Farrell to step forward and deflect the impact as he cuffed Goddard and read him his rights.

'You saw my niece there?' said Louise, her hand still gripping the baton.

Goddard thrust out his chin. Lacking any sign of remorse. 'I saw her hiding. There was nothing I could do. She shouldn't have been there.'

Louise nodded. Her fingers tingled as she dropped the baton. 'That's one thing you're right about,' she said, clenching her fingers into a fist and punching Goddard straight in the face.

Epilogue

For once, Louise was able to walk the steps of Jacob's Ladder without fear of what she would find at the summit. She still had twenty minutes until she was due to meet the Pemberton family and she took her time, savouring the array of trees and plants that lined the walkway, the ripples of sunlight filtering through the green coverings.

Tourism had returned to the village and a pair of squabbling siblings rushed by her, sprinting up the steps as if they were level ground, followed by out-of-breath parents who offered gasping smiles as way of apology. With the threat of Ted Padfield eviscerated, the village was getting on with life as if nothing had happened. All except for the two families who'd been most affected.

It had been a few weeks since Louise had seen Ellie and Liam Bolton but she understood they were going through a separation. She wasn't overly surprised. Such incidents either brought people closer together or tore them apart, and she'd seen the accusing way the Boltons had looked at each other the night their child had gone missing. Liam had blamed his wife for allowing him to be taken when she'd been in the house, and Ellie had blamed him for not having the window fixed.

Thankfully, the family she saw idling by the entry to the lookout tower were faring better. Madison instinctively inched closer to her mother as Louise approached, but she beamed as Louise said hello to her.

'Thank you for coming,' said Claire Pemberton.

'My pleasure,' said Louise.

Claire and her husband had called her last night asking to meet. Madison had decided she wanted to return to the cliff walk on the proviso that Louise went with them. Louise had grown close to the girl over the weeks of the trial. Among other things, they'd discussed books and Madison had lent her a number of titles from her shelves. 'Are you ready?' she said to Madison, who surprised her by grabbing her hand and heading towards the walk.

The recent weeks of good weather had dried the ground and made the ascent a bit easier. 'You okay?' asked Louise, as they stopped by a wooden bench.

Madison smiled and turned. 'It always makes me think of a spaceship,' she said, pointing to the rippling circle of water in the distance.

'I know what you mean,' said Louise. The artificial reservoir looked otherworldly and she could picture a UFO exploding from its depths.

Claire stopped her as Neil walked ahead with his daughter. 'Thanks again for doing this. I feel we're starting to get a handle on things again. Hopefully this walk is a good idea.'

'How is she sleeping?'

'Much better. Still reading those scary books but, if anything, I think they help her.'

Louise agreed. Madison had shown great resilience during the trial. As her mother suggested, the books she read were a way of facing her fears and that was why they were here today. There would still be more stages but Madison had insisted that she wouldn't let Padfield take the walk from her.

Ahead of them, Madison had stopped with her dad. 'You need to be strong now,' said Louise to Claire, as they joined them.

Madison stood at the top of the cliff. Below, the ground sloped seventy metres to a sheer drop. In between was the entrance where Madison had escaped from her captivity. Louise glanced over to the girl who looked composed as she gazed out to the scorched ground and the rocky cliff face on the other side of the gorge.

Padfield currently resided in a secure psychiatric unit having been sentenced for the unlawful kidnapping of Madison and Aaron Bolton. Louise wanted to tell Madison that Padfield could no longer harm her, but the girl didn't need that assurance. The only thing that would truly help her would be wiping out history. But she was a strong girl with a loving family and Louise was confident she would survive.

Louise bent down so she was eye level with Madison. 'I need to go now but you know where I am when you need me,' she said.

Madison nodded, a smile forming then fading. 'Can I keep sending you book recommendations?'

'I'd have it no other way.'

◆ ◆ ◆

Richard Hoxton was waiting in the coffee shop on the main road. He'd been asking to meet her for the last few weeks and she'd finally relented today.

'Rather fitting that we should meet here,' said Hoxton, as he returned from the counter with two cups of coffee.

'I hear you've moved?' said Louise.

The easy charm she'd initially associated with the man had returned. He'd lost weight, had his hair and beard trimmed. 'Literally and metaphorically,' he said, with a smile. 'I'm back in Bristol and have said goodbye to the corporate world.'

Stephen Walsh had pulled his development before it had reached the final planning meeting. The abductions had spooked some of his investors and all momentum had been lost.

'What will you do with yourself now?' asked Louise.

'I'm looking at a few things but I'm in no rush. I'd like to set up a little something for myself. I'm sure something will present itself.'

Louise sipped her coffee and studied the man. For all his outward show of confidence, there was an insecurity to him. It had demonstrated itself during the case in his drinking, and she sensed his hesitation now.

'Thank you for coming to see me. I've been thinking a lot recently and I wanted to apologise to you,' said Hoxton.

'What for?'

'As you probably ascertained, my head wasn't always straight. If I'd been a little clearer in my thinking then I may have been able to point you in Padfield's direction much sooner. I could have stopped everything that happened, or at least something of it.'

'I appreciate the apology, Mr Hoxton, but you're talking about that night in the cave when you first heard him following you?'

During his interrogations and examination in court, Padfield admitted that he'd been part of a plan to scare off the investors in the village though he denied sending any note to Hoxton, the tests on the letter having proved fruitless. He'd mentioned Sam Amstell on more than one occasion but despite Louise's best efforts they'd yet to come up with enough evidence to mount a prosecution against Amstell or any of the other members of the commune.

'Yes, if I'd just put two and two together . . .'

'You said your head hadn't really been straight that night?'

They both knew they were talking about Hoxton's drinking. 'No, I guess not.'

'So if your head had been straight, I doubt very much you would have led a bunch of drunk businessmen into the caves at night?'

'I see your point, Inspector. Still . . .'

'If you need forgiveness, you have it,' said Louise with a smile. 'In many ways, we may never have found Padfield in time if it wasn't for you.'

'It doesn't feel that way.'

'Time for you to move on now, Mr Hoxton. Thank you for the coffee,' said Louise.

She was about to leave when Hoxton spoke. 'I've stopped drinking,' he said.

'That is good to know. I'm pleased for you.'

'Three months now.'

Louise smiled again. She couldn't help herself. There was an innocent charm to the man. She was drawn to him despite what had occurred.

'Talking of threes . . . I thought maybe now would be a good time to ask you for dinner again. Third time lucky?' said Hoxton.

Louise had feared such a question was coming. She liked the man and in other circumstances would have considered the invitation. But too much had happened between them. She'd seen him at his worst and didn't think she'd be able to get past that.

'You know what happened with my brother?' she said.

'I do, yes. I'm glad to see you caught the killer.'

Both Goddard and Marshall were behind bars now but that wasn't what Louise meant. 'Paul had his addiction problems. It's not something I can risk bringing into the family again.'

Hoxton nodded. 'I understand. I wish you well, Inspector,' he said, holding out his hand.

'And I you,' said Louise.

◆ ◆ ◆

Louise made one final stop before returning to Weston. The last few months had been difficult on Emily but she was definitely showing signs of returning to her former self and Louise had agreed with her parents that she deserved something special; though if she was being candid, Louise would have to admit the gift was in part for her.

Troy Goddard had repeated his confession at the station, and his blood and DNA had been discovered at Paul's murder scene, so Emily hadn't needed to testify. Goddard had naturally turned on Marshall who had also been prosecuted as an accomplice to murder. And although nothing would bring Paul back, there was some small comfort for the family in knowing those responsible would be making a long-term stay in prison.

During the court case, Louise had agreed with her parents that things needed to change for Emily, and two weeks ago they'd all moved into a split-level house in Sand Bay. Emily still technically lived with her grandparents. Louise had the upper floor of the house, with its own separate entrance, but they shared the garden and Louise now saw Emily and her parents every day.

She was still coming to terms with effectively living with her parents again but she was willing to do anything to protect Emily. Her niece was starting a new school in Weston in the autumn and Louise understood the move was preparing her for the day when she would take over her niece's guardianship.

They were now waiting for Louise outside as she pulled up the drive. Emily couldn't contain herself. She was jumping up and down and was being restrained by her grandparents as Louise parked and switched off the engine.

'Did you get her, Aunty Louise?' said Emily, breaking free of her grandad's grip and sprinting to the car.

'I sure did,' said Louise. 'Come meet your baby sister.'

Emily's eyes were wide as Louise slowly opened the caged area of the hatchback. Her niece glanced at her, open-mouthed, the look so reminiscent of the happy-go-lucky girl she'd been before that Louise had to stifle a cry.

In the car, the Labrador puppy pawed against the door of its travel cage. 'Are you ready?' said Louise, opening the door.

The puppy eased through the opening and, as Emily placed her hand on its head, its tail began wagging.

'Does she have a name?' asked Emily.

Louise placed her arm around her niece. 'If you don't mind, I was hoping we could call her Molly,' she said.

'Hello, Molly, come and meet your grandparents,' said Emily, as Louise placed the dog on the ground.

Louise locked the car. The top floor of the house had sea views and she heard the incoming tide and the squawking gulls that accompanied it. By the front door, Molly was in a frenzy, running from Emily to Louise's parents and back again. The moment was touched with melancholy by Paul's absence but for the first time in a long time, Louise felt positive about the future.

Molly jumped up on her as she joined the rest of the family. Emily grabbed her by the waist and said, 'Thank you, Aunty Louise. Thank you so much.'

ACKNOWLEDGMENTS

In part, the inspiration for this book came from a windswept walk along the cliff path in Cheddar Gorge with my family. I'd like to thank them – Joe, Carla, Alison, Freya and Hamish – for accompanying me on that tiring and treacherous journey!

I'd like to thank the people of Cheddar and Weston-super-Mare. Despite the events in the books, I hope I do justice to this wonderful area of my birth. The feedback for the series from the people who live in Weston has been fantastic and it's been so lovely to hear your thoughts on the books.

Thanks as always to: Jack Butler and Russel McLean for their editorial support – the books wouldn't be the same without them; Joanna Swainson and all the team at Hardman & Swainson for their continued support; and everyone at Amazon Publishing for giving the books the best opportunity to reach a wide audience.

ABOUT THE AUTHOR

Photo © 2019 Lisa Visser

Following his law degree, where he developed an interest in criminal law, Matt Brolly completed his Masters in Creative Writing at Glasgow University.

The Gorge is the third novel in the Detective Louise Blackwell crime series. The first two, *The Crossing* and *The Descent*, were published in 2020. He is also the bestselling author of the DCI Lambert crime novels, *Dead Eyed*, *Dead Lucky*, *Dead Embers*, *Dead Time* and *Dead Water*, the Lynch and Rose thriller, *The Controller*, and the acclaimed near-future crime novel, *Zero*.

Matt writes children's books as M. J. Brolly. His first children's book is *The Sleeping Bug*.

Matt lives in London with his wife and their two young children. You can find out more about him at www.mattbrolly.co.uk or by following him on Twitter: @MattBrollyUK.

Printed in Great Britain
by Amazon